CONVERGENCE

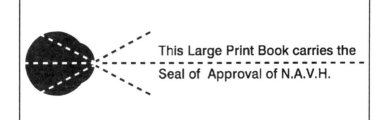

This Large Print Book carries the
Seal of Approval of N.A.V.H.

CONVERGENCE

GINNY L. YTTRUP

THORNDIKE PRESS
A part of Gale, a Cengage Company

Farmington Hills, Mich • San Francisco • New York • Waterville, Maine
Meriden, Conn • Mason, Ohio • Chicago

LIBRARY OF CONGRESS CIP DATA ON FILE.
CATALOGUING IN PUBLICATION FOR THIS BOOK
IS AVAILABLE FROM THE LIBRARY OF CONGRESS

ISBN-13: 978-1-4328-6344-9 (hardcover alk. paper)

Published in 2019 by arrangement with Barbour Publishing, Inc.

Printed in the United States of America
1 2 3 4 5 6 7 23 22 21 20 19

I don't know your name. I never had the chance to meet you, but I will never forget you. Your life was taken too soon, at the hands of a man who stalked you and ultimately killed you. Your death that early morning of May 17, 2017, shattered the peace of our quiet neighborhood and broke our hearts for your sons, left to face life without you. I pray for your sons each time I pass the place that was your home, the place where you were robbed of your life. May God bless your precious boys.

God gave us a spirit not of fear but of power and love and self-control.

2 TIMOTHY 1:7 ESV

If weather portends outcome, as poets suggest, she'll enjoy a perfect day.

A cool breeze caresses her face as the sun warms the tarmac beneath her feet. A mirage waves just above the runway in the distance, and the acrid scent of tar melds with the signature scents of spring, freshly cut grass and honeysuckle. She closes her eyes, lifts her face to the sun, and breathes deep. The aroma wafts then dissipates. When she opens her eyes, the azure expanse, watercolor clear, beckons.

But just beyond her view, charcoal-colored clouds coalesce on the horizon.

Anticipation, like the wings of hummingbirds, flutters within her. She adjusts the harness on her shoulders and thighs, then shields her eyes and looks at the sky again. This time a shiver trembles through her despite the warmth rising from the asphalt. Anticipation or fear? She wraps her arms around herself.

Behind her, unnoticed, a man stands in front of one of the hangars. Deep lines etch his clean-shaven face, the ink of his beard a shadow under his pale skin. He hides his eyes behind sunglasses while nursing wounds so deep they hemorrhage hatred. He takes a drag from the stub of a cigarette, exhales a ribbon of smoke, then drops the butt and grinds it under his foot. He stills, and watches her.

Another man, young, lanky, a chute packed on his back, breaks from a group of pros — professional skydivers, she was told — and saunters her way until he stands next to her. "Ready to ride the currents?"

She is familiar with currents, having spent almost as much time riding the white rapids of rivers as she's spent on land. She knows rivers and respects their power. But air currents? The shake of her head is almost imperceptible. "Absolutely." She attempts a smile as she bends the truth.

He studies her face for a moment, and then the fair skin around his eyes crinkles and he laughs. He turns and heads back to the group, tossing advice over his shoulder as he goes. "Stay loose and enjoy the ride. There's nothing like it."

She wipes damp palms on the jumpsuit

10

she wears then glances at the group he rejoined. Divers practicing for an upcoming competition. Though she'll ride up with them, the pros will jump from a lower altitude. She opted to do a tandem jump for her first experience. Attached to an instructor, they'll jump from nearly twelve thousand feet. During the free fall, they'll drop at a rate of nearly 120 miles per hour. She rehearses what she learned during the brief instruction she received.

An engine throttles in the distance, and soon sunlight glints off the silver wings of a small plane taxiing toward them. The plane rattles as it approaches. Loose nuts and bolts, she imagines. The sound unsettling.

"Betty!" one of the pros yells.

"Come to Daddy!" shouts another. Laughter and catcalls welcome the plane, *Betty Boop,* with her pouting red lips painted on its tail.

A man walks out the door of the office nearby and heads her way. He sticks out his hand when he reaches her. "I'm Mike. You're jumping with me. This marks my thousandth jump, so let's make it memorable. Deal?" His thick white hair lifts then falls with the breeze.

She wipes her hand again then takes his and shakes it. Her voice is lost to her now, so she only nods.

"Once those bozos jump" — he gestures to the others — "I'll connect you to my harness, you in front of me, then we'll go to the door. When I say 'go,' we jump. If you don't jump, I will, and you're going with me. Better if you take the lead." He chuckles. "Ready?"

She nods.

"Good. Remember what you learned — arms stretched out, wrists straight, palms flat." He demonstrates. "Got it?" Before she responds, he strides toward the plane that's pulled up in front of the group. She follows behind him.

As she waits to board, she takes the young man's advice and works to loosen up. She shakes her arms and hands, from shoulders to fingertips, then does a shimmy as though she can shake off the spiders of fear skittering up her spine. But then that's the point, isn't it? To shake off fear, once and for all. That's what she's come to do. To prove to herself that the phantom known as Fear no longer holds her in its grip.

She straightens, squares her shoulders, and takes a deep breath as she climbs aboard the plane. There no seats, the other divers are piled close to one another on the floor. Mike points to an open space near him. She lowers herself, sits, pulls her knees to her chest, and then looks out the oval window next to her.

That's when she sees him.

Her breath catches. She leans in, cups her hands on the glass to cut the glare, and peers out.

It can't be. . . . Mouth dry, she tries to swallow. She looks away.

Her heart batters her chest and her pulse roars in her ears, nearly drowning out the clamor of the plane's propeller. It isn't him. *You're imagining things,* she tells herself. She inhales then exhales. She takes another look then stares at the man near the hangar. He pulls something from his shirt pocket, sticks it in his mouth. A cigarette? She watches as he lights it. It isn't him. He doesn't smoke. Anyway, it's impossible. She knows where he is, and it isn't here.

He's seen her staring at him through the window of the plane. He takes a drag, flicks ash to the ground, and smiles. But his eyes behind the sunglasses are cold. Hard.

She steadies herself as the plane shoots down the runway then lifts. As memories flash, perspiration trickles down her back. She inhales again, deeper this time. It wasn't him. *Let it go,* she admonishes, then shakes her head.

Fear will not win. Not this time. Not ever again.

Within what feels to her like mere moments, the group of professional skydivers have all jumped, and she stands, back pressed against Mike, hooked to his harness. They brace themselves against the pummeling force of wind as they wait near the gaping opening in the side of the plane. She pulls goggles from the top of her head down over her eyes.

There's no room in her mind now for thoughts of the man on the ground, or of the man who haunts her memories. There's no room for thoughts of any kind. Terror, as she well knows, is all-consuming. Her breaths are shallow, her pulse races.

"Step to the edge," Mike yells. When she doesn't move, he yells again, this time his breath hot against her ear. She hesitates then steps forward, him stepping in sync with her. There's nothing to see but the vast expanse.

"Go!" Mike shouts.

Heart hammering her rib cage, she leans forward, eyes squeezed shut, and falls more than jumps into nothingness, arms stretched wide. She anticipates the sensation of falling — stomach lifting to throat — but it isn't evident as she'd expected. Nor is the

14

velocity at which she knows they're falling. She dares to open her eyes, only aware of the force of air pushing her cheeks back to her ears, which makes her laugh.

The free fall is like nothing she's experienced. She laughs again, the sound carried heavenward on the drafts, she imagines. Too soon she's jerked, hard, the harness cutting into her thighs, and pulled upward with what seems like exceeding force. She hadn't expected the force.

But then they're floating. Soaring. "Oh," she whispers. She wants to take it all in, remember every exhilarating moment. These currents she could ride forever. Tension is replaced by peace, pervasive peace.

Quietude. Silence. Wonder.

"That was a hard pull." Mike's shouted words behind her threaten to break the spell, but she's enchanted and pays little attention. She assumes the pull — the parachute opening and catching air — was harder than usual but fine. They're fine. She doesn't understand. Doesn't know what's to come. How could she?

As they float, her eyes are trained on the ground below. The earth is a patchwork of tones. She sees the river, a thread, stitched across the quilt of colors. She searches for familiar landmarks as her sense of confidence soars. She's done it. Faced fear, terror even, and —

Suddenly they're plummeting.

Tumbling.

Head first. Arms and legs akimbo.

Land and sky spin as they interchange. Her lungs deflate. Pressure. The currents, tumultuous, pull her under and then spit her out. She can't breathe. Why can't she breathe? She gasps. She's drowning. Help! Someone, help! But no . . . There's no water. Instead, she's above, where there's nothing. Just . . .

Nothing.

Nothing to reach for. Nothing to grab. Nothing to save her.

A scream sounds in her mind. Rings in her ears. Scathes her throat.

Her scream?

Awareness hits. She's going to die. It's her only thought. There are no thoughts of those she loves. Those who love her. Memories don't flash. No, just the one thought. The only thought she has time for.

She is going to die.

Then . . .

Everything goes black.

On the ground he waits and watches as he's done so many times before — patience his vice. He counts off as each of the pros lands. Finally, he sees it. A rainbow of color fluttering against the deep blue sky. A single parachute drifting. Flailing. Falling.

No one attached.

His heart pangs, a brief reminder of what she once meant to him. But no more.

She ruined all that.

This is goodbye.

He drops another cigarette butt, grinds it under the toe of his boot, and then turns and walks away. His laughter, like the cackle of a crow, carries on the breeze.

Perfect.

A perfect day.

■ ■ ■ ■

PART ONE

■ ■ ■ ■

You drown not by falling into a river but
by staying submerged in it.
PAULO COELHO

CHAPTER ONE

Denilyn
January 9, 2017

I inhale, filling my lungs with cold air. I exhale, counting as I do. *One, two, three, four.* I inhale again, the air thick, damp. My chest rises as my lungs expand then fall as I exhale. *One, two, three, four.*

Rain beats a disjointed rhythm on the windshield and roof of the parked car. My hands rest on the steering wheel at the ten and twelve o'clock positions — the leather polished to a sheen with wear, firm and cold under my palms.

The interior of the SUV is icy, but warmth still radiates through me following a hard morning workout and a hot shower, yet goose bumps prickle my arms anyway.

"I'm in my car, in my driveway," I whisper. "It's Monday, January 9th, 2017, first day of the spring semester. I am going to work. Max has water. The house is secured. The alarm set." I inhale. "My family is safe." I exhale. Then I glance at the digital numerals on the dash — 6:24 a.m. The numbers glow, casting a blue sheen in the dark interior of the SUV.

I intentionally inhale and exhale one more breath. The engine purrs. I back away from the garage and turn the car toward the gate at the front of the property. Gravel crunches under my wheels as I follow the narrow drive lit by landscape lanterns placed two feet apart along both sides of the drive. When I pull up in front of the smooth redwood-paneled gate nearly hidden in the red-wood-paneled wall surrounding the property, I repeat my mantra. "It's Monday, January 9th,"

The gate yawns open.

"2017."

My wipers screech across the windshield, smearing spatters of rain, making the road ahead nearly indistinguishable. I tighten my grip on the steering wheel and slow. When was the last time I replaced the wipers? Before the drought — five, six years maybe? Could it really have been that long?

Like a child hiding in the folds of her mother's skirt, the morning sun shrinks behind dark, billowing clouds, seeming to have forgotten its own power.

I focus on the terrain sheathed in hues of gray. As I maneuver the SUV through the turns in the road, light from my headlamps bounces off the embankment where rivulets of water and mud cascade onto the roadway. Somewhere below, the river roils and rushes, I imagine. But I don't dare look.

California's drought, daunting and devastating, has finally come to an end. Or, at the least, we're offered a reprieve. The snowpack, well above average with several more months of potential snow in store, will yield water throughout California's summer months. Plenty of water. Which translates into, among other things, raging rivers. White water. I can almost hear the owners of local rafting companies sighing with relief.

Water is good for the economy. It's good for the psyche too.

When I finally pull into the faculty parking lot of Pacific Covenant University, situated cliffside along the northern fork of the upper American River, my neck and shoulders ache. I park and then grab the insulated mug in my cup holder and swallow the last of my coffee. I tuck the mug into the outside pocket of my briefcase. It's definitely a two-, maybe three-mug morning.

I reach for the door handle then hesitate. Sheets of water curtain the windows. Raindrops ricochet off the car's roof. Locks on the doors keep the world at bay. Reluctantly, I pull the handle and push the door open, get out, and spring the umbrella. I duck under its cover, a poor substitute for the protective cocoon of the car.

Keys in hand, I sling my briefcase over my shoulder, tuck my hair into the collar of my coat, then slosh my way through the parking lot and follow one of the pathways through the verdant, tree-studded campus to the wide steps leading up to the psychology building. The brick building is the oldest on the campus, the original structure when PCU acquired the site.

I run up the steps and, once undercover, shake the umbrella until water puddles at my feet. I enter the building and make my way up the stairs to the second floor then down the quiet, dimly lit hallway. The scent of chalk dust, ground into every corner and crevice of the building, tickles my nose. Chalkboards were replaced with whiteboards more than a decade ago, so the lingering scent is more likely association than actuality. But the building, having been closed over the winter break, is indeed musty. I stop in front of one of the offices that line the hall and fumble with my keys until I find the right one.

"Hey, Deni."

I jump, and my keys jangle as they drop to the floor. I turn from the door toward the voice, heart thumping against the cage of my chest. "Willow . . ."

"Sorry, I didn't mean to scare you."

"No, it's just . . . I didn't see you. Hi." I bend to retrieve my keys, hands trembling. "Did you enjoy your break?" I slip my hands into the pockets of my coat.

Willow, a sophomore whose slender, graceful frame lives up to her name, shrugs. "It was okay. Family drama. The usual holiday stuff."

"Ah . . . Makes dorm life look good, huh?"

"Totally."

"Were you waiting to see me?"

"No. Dr. Alister." She gestures to the office next to mine. "I'm meeting with him. I'm his TA this semester."

I point down the hallway. "Dr. Alister's office is —"

The door of the office next to mine swings open, and Ryan Alister steps into the hallway. "Thought I heard voices out here. Willow" — he glances at his watch — "you're prompt. Thank you." He turns to me, his smile warm.

"You moved?"

Ryan looks back at his office then to me. "Over the break, remember?"

"Oh . . . Right." Did we talk about the move? I don't remember. We must have — Ryan wouldn't take that type of liberty. "You're lucky to have Willow this semester, Dr. Alister. She's an excellent student. She'll make a great assistant."

He raises one eyebrow and looks back to Willow. "A recommendation from the esteemed Dr. Denilyn Rossi, department chair? Impressive."

As Willow's milky complexion blooms, Ryan looks at me and winks.

"It was good to see you, Willow." I pull my keys from my pocket as Willow follows Ryan into his office. Caught in a snare of confusion, I stare at the linoleum as I try to bring up the details of Ryan's move, but they're lost to me. Throat tight, I swallow. I'm slipping. Forgetting things. Letting the stress get to me.

Stress? It's more than that. My mind is betraying me, and it stings like the betrayal of a trusted friend.

I turn back to my office. The murmur of Ryan's and Willow's voices drift out Ryan's open door. I'm grateful for the company in the still nearly empty building — actually,

I'm grateful the empty office is occupied again. It was vacated midsemester when Dr. McPhee took early retirement due to ongoing medical issues. That I *do* remember. I find the key on my ring again and unlock and open my office door.

Before entering, I reach around the doorjamb and flip on the light switch. I stand in the doorway and take stock. Everything appears as I left it. Desktop empty except for my computer monitor and inbox. Beside the window that frames my desk, diplomas and designations hang. Shelves line another wall, stocked with books and a few decorative items, mostly mementos from students. Nothing personal.

I hold the office door ajar, take a few steps inside, and then lean in and peek around the edge of the desk. I lean back, exhaling as I do. Nothing amiss.

I leave the door open and hang the umbrella, along with my coat, on the rack in the office. I pull a nubby cardigan off the rack and drape it across the back of my desk chair, then tuck my briefcase under the desk. Once seated, I power on the computer and wait as it loads. I knead a knot in my shoulder.

The calendar app beckons, but I open my email instead. A perusal of the contents reveals faculty updates, what look like a few emails from students — the number of which will grow exponentially as the semester progresses — and junk. Nothing unusual.

The time posted in the upper right-hand corner of the monitor indicates I have less than an hour until my first class. I shift my gaze to the calendar icon at the bottom of the screen, but again I ignore it and begin working through the emails, deleting and responding.

But the calendar pesters.

No, I tell myself. But finally I give in. I open the app, click ahead to the first of the month branded on my mind, and begin counting back to today's date. The number of remaining days isn't a surprise. With each setting of the sun, I mentally tick off another day. Though, I admit, the date is a guesstimate, at best.

I worked hard to put the time frame out of my mind and focus elsewhere during the break. To stay present. Live the moments. I recognize the fixation I'm developing isn't helpful. Isn't healthy.

With the calendar still open, I click back to email and type a quick note to my therapist to confirm my appointment for later this week. I haven't seen her in almost a month.

I press SEND, close the email server, then swivel my chair away from the monitor. My gaze lands on the bookshelves and the spines of my published works — my doctoral dissertation and the book that followed. I turn back to the desk, reach into my inbox, and pull out the file containing the publishing contract and emails from my agent I'd printed before the holidays. The contract is another thing I worked hard to forget over the break.

My publisher has suggested another book. My first, *Beating the Bullies: Turning Shame into Gain* was based on research I completed for my dissertation.

But so much has changed since that first book. *Because* of that first book. What I hoped would offer others encouragement and empowerment robbed me of almost everything I held dear, including my marriage. Had I known what the book would lead to, would I still have written it?

No.

Perhaps that's a selfish answer, but it is the only answer I have.

The book hit the *New York Times* bestseller list the week it released and stayed there for more than a year, catapulting me onto the public stage. The stage where I crumbled and my marriage disintegrated.

No.

I never finished the second and third contracted books. I broke the contract. My agent assured me at the time that I'd likely never receive another offer from any publisher.

But now, nearly eight years later, they've sought me out and offered another contract. A young actor, one of Hollywood's hottest, was arrested recently after he was tied to the death of a young woman he'd dated. Following their breakup, he ridiculed her repeatedly, publicly, and without mercy. His vicious verbal attacks are well documented in both the media and online.

Allegedly, he bullied her to death. She committed suicide.

Based on the publicity the case is receiving, the topic of bullying is center stage again, as it should be. In a fast turnaround, my publisher is repackaging and rereleasing my first book, and they're revisiting the second and third books I was originally contracted to write.

I open my desk drawer and reach for the pen I keep in a tray at the front of the drawer — a silver Cross pen engraved with my name — a gift from my dad when I received my PhD. He'd taken me to lunch and given it to me. He used to do that — take me to lunch. Just the two of us. But that was the last time. Just before he died.

The pen is one of the only personal items I keep in the office. I want to make a few notes as I go through the contract again. But when my hand doesn't land on the pen, I scoot back from the desk and search the drawer. I open another drawer then another.

The pen isn't there.

I reach for my briefcase, then dig through the contents. But it isn't there either. Why would it be? I never take it home. It's always in my desk drawer.

Or . . . did I take it home?

I get up, leaving the file on my desk, and turn to the window. Rain beats on the glass and slides down the panes. The light inside makes it difficult to see out through the window, so dark is the day. Instead, an obscured image of the interior of the office and of myself, front and center, reflect on the glass. My eyes, light green against the dim backdrop, stand out.

"Open your eyes, Denilyn. Open your pretty eyes."

Memories unspool and images play on the glass, accompanied by the soundtrack I can't tune out. At least not permanently. Trembling, I take a step back and turn away from the window before the haunting images project on the pane again.

I wrap my arms around myself, inhale deeply, and then exhale. "One, two, three, four," I whisper. I take another grounding breath, working to stay present. "I'm in my office. Those are my books on the shelf. The framed quote was a gift from Jen before she graduated." I glance at the monitor on my desk. "It's 7:48 a.m. on Monday. I'm safe. I'm okay."

I am safe. But okay? I'm no longer sure.

When I dare to turn back to the window, I squint to see through the reflection. Oak trees, their branches sharp and spindled, stand against a brooding sky. I swallow the lump in my throat and swipe at the edges of my eyes where tears brim.

The lights in the office flicker as the soundtrack murmurs in my mind again, stilled only by the low growl of thunder in the distance.

I turn away from the window and reach for the sweater hanging on the back of my desk chair. Longing to hide within its folds, I pull it close and shrink behind its thick weave.

I walk into the classroom and set my mug of fresh coffee on a table at the front of the room. I pull my laptop from my bag and connect it to the projection system. Once that's done, I scan the faces of the few students who've arrived early. As others filter in, I survey each face. It takes another ten minutes for the seats to fill. I'm grateful for the time to gather myself.

At the top of the hour, I get up from a stool where I've perched myself. "Good morning. This is Introduction to Psychology, and I'm Denilyn Rossi. If that's not the information on your schedule, now's your chance to, like Elvis, leave the building."

Eyebrows rise. Others offer blank stares.

" 'Blue Suede Shoes'? 'Blue Christmas'? C'mon, I'm not that old. He died before I was born, but *everyone* still knows Elvis, right?" The tension in my shoulders eases.

A student standing with a dozen or so others at the top of the room, behind the rows of theater seats, raises his hand.

"Great! A fellow fan." I point, and a hundred or so heads turn toward him.

"Um, no. I . . . I just have a question. Dr. Rossi, will you be —"

"Deni." The heads turn back toward me.

"Wha . . . What?"

"Call me Deni. We're all adults here. First-name basis. Call me doctor, and I'll think you're referring to my OB/GYN."

Nervous laughter from the gallery punctuates my comment. Ah, freshman. I love them. They're the reason I still teach Intro to Psych. I smile at the young man whose hand is still in the air. "And your name is . . . ?"

He slowly lowers his hand. "Jason."

"Go ahead, Jason. You had a question?"

"Um, yeah . . . Will you be taking adds?"

"The class is full. Overflowing, actually. But check with me again after we go over the syllabus. We'll see how many of those with seats I scare off. Sound good?"

Eyes wide, he nods again, and another nervous titter goes through the class.

"For all of you interested in adding, check with me after class today. I'll put your name on a list, and if you're willing to hang out and do the work for the first couple of weeks, based on the usual drop rate, there's a good chance you'll earn yourself a seat."

About half the students who are standing at the back of the classroom turn and walk out, which I'd expected.

"Now, speaking of the syllabus —" I flip on the projector and then go to click on the file on the desktop of my laptop where I keep a copy of the syllabus and PowerPoint presentations I use with my lessons. But the file isn't there. "Excuse me a minute . . ." I search the desktop again, but I still don't see the file — the file that's been on my desktop for years. I click on the search icon and type in the name of the file, but nothing comes up anywhere.

It makes no sense. What could have happened? Did I inadvertently delete the file? It contained years of lesson plans and presentations. I shake my head and look at the students again. "I'm sorry. Technical difficulties."

Who else has had access to my laptop? I had it at home with me over the break. But no one would have deleted the file.

Flustered, I run my hand through my hair, my fingers grazing the ridge of scar tissue on my head. Then it occurs to me that I can log on to the school system and access the syllabus. Within moments it fills the screen at the front of the room.

"Okay . . . you'll find the syllabus online, if you haven't already done so."

I walk the students through the syllabus and my requirements for the class on autopilot, all the while another conversation is taking place in my mind. *How could I have lost the file? Could I really have deleted it? What is wrong with me — with my mind?*

After two classes, lunch with a few staff

members, a meeting with PCU's president, and another class, it's late afternoon by the time I return to my office. The file with the publishing contract sits on my desk where I left it, demanding a decision.

I finger the file, flip it open, and drop into my chair.

"How'd it go today?" Ryan stands in the doorway of my office, his dark jeans, crisp oxford, and wool blazer impeccable, as always.

I close the file. "Great. The classroom is still one of my favorite places. How about you? Good group of students?"

"I spotted a few slackers, but all in all, it promises to be a good semester."

"I'm glad Willow's TA-ing for you. She really is a great gal. Bright too."

"Yeah, I can tell." He leans against the doorframe. "So, how are you, really?"

I read the concern in his expression.

When I don't respond, he takes a step inside my office. "How are you today, January 9th?"

"Fine. Thank you." My tone is more curt than I intend. I appreciate his concern, but I don't want the reminder of what the date signifies. Nor have I ever wanted the memories to tarnish my work environment. My job at PCU came later — a fresh start. I hoped I could separate the past from my present. Although lately, I have to admit, the memories have encroached. It isn't that some of the faculty don't know what happened. It was well covered in the media before I accepted the position here, a position offered because of Ryan's recommendation. But I don't care to revisit the details with the faculty, and I didn't expect anyone to remember the specific date. Although, had I given it more consideration, I would have anticipated Ryan's sensitivity. We have a history I don't share with the other faculty.

"Deni?"

"I'm sorry. What?"

"I said, I'm here if you need anything. I'm happy to walk you out lat —"

"No." I look down at the open file on my desk, then glance back to him. "I said I'm fine. I just have a few things to get through, and then I'll head home."

He stares at me for a moment and something flickers in his eyes, but I can't read the emotion. Then he turns and walks away.

I rest my head in my hands and close my eyes. I was short with him. His offer was considerate. I get up and pace the office, landing in front of the window again. *Focus, Denilyn.*

If I sign the contract, the books could bring further awareness to the general population, especially adolescents, young adults, and their parents, as did the first book. Reach a new audience, even.

A bolt of lightning flashes, dividing the sky, then crackles. A rumble of thunder almost immediately follows, shaking the glass in the pane.

"Who am I kidding?" I whisper.

The words, frigid, seem to bounce off the window and back at me. A shiver snakes up my spine. The same issue I've considered over and over taunts again. My publisher has big plans. They've discussed book tours, appearances on TV's most popular talk shows, another TED talk.

Just like last time.

I've intentionally stayed out of the lime-light since the first book. I turned down job offers from prestigious universities, speaking engagements, and interviews until the offers finally dwindled. I'm content with my life and work now. PCU offers all I need. Well, almost. But it does suit my primary need.

Anonymity.

Although, as the contract attests, I'm still not as anonymous as I'd like. I reach for the mouse on my keyboard tray, click, and open my calendar app again, then scroll through the months and look at the date I have marked.

I finally let the truth I worked so hard to evade over the winter break sink in. I've deluded myself. Denied that others still remember my work. And me.

But willingly put myself on public display again? There's no decision to make. The stakes are too high. The risk too great.

And not just for me.

I close the file on the contract.

CHAPTER TWO

Denilyn
October 2009

The first time I noticed him was at Kepler's Books in Menlo Park during a signing on the first leg of the three-week book tour my publisher had arranged. Two days later I flew out of SFO and landed in New York, where the blitz of publicity really began. But Kepler's is where I remembered seeing him that first time.

Head down, signing my name for what felt like the hundredth time that afternoon, the sense of someone watching me intruded. I lifted my head and handed the book back to the woman who'd waited as I signed.

"Thank you for coming." I worked to maintain eye contact with her until she turned to walk away.

Before the next person in line stepped forward, I glanced at the faces of those waiting in line. At least thirty or forty people were visible from where I sat, but then the line wound out of my view. Many of those not engaged in conversation with someone were at least looking my way, if not directly at me.

A whole line of someones are watching you. So what? My internal moderator offered the obvious perspective. The next young woman in line — I guessed she was nineteen or twenty — appeared to have attended the signing alone. I recalled her sitting by herself in the audience as I'd spoken earlier. She stepped forward and handed me her book.

"Hi there. Am I signing this to you?"

She nodded, and her fair, pocked complexion blushed. As she pushed thick-lensed glasses into place on the bridge of her nose, I wondered if she hadn't lived, maybe was living, the isolated life of someone shunned by her peers. Was she like the individuals detailed in many of the case studies I'd written? One of the many teenagers or young adults I'd interviewed who endured life enshrouded by the shame the bullies in their worlds assigned to them?

I reached out my hand. "I'm Deni. Thanks so much for coming, and" — I motioned to the crowd behind her — "for waiting. That line is longer than I'd expected."

She shook my hand. "It wasn't too bad."

"I hope you'll enjoy the book."

"Thanks, I did. I mean, I've already read it." She dropped her gaze to the floor. "It . . . helped." She looked back to me from beneath a fringe of long bangs.

"Thank you. It means a lot to hear that. What's your name?"

She smiled, then looked away again. "Aubrey."

"Aubrey?" I waited until she looked back at me. "A beautiful name for a beautiful young woman."

Her shy smile revealed lovely teeth, likely straightened by years of orthodontia, and her blue eyes sparkled behind her glasses.

"Spell your name for me so I'm sure I get it right." I opened the cover of the book and lifted my pen as she spelled her name. But as I put the tip of the pen to the page, the hairs on the back on my neck stood at attention as the sense that someone was watching me assailed me again. I paused, looked up, and let my gaze rove through the line of people and around the front half of the store once more. This time I spotted a man standing off to one side, a few feet down one of the aisles of books. He looked about my age and wore a rumpled army-style jacket. He was just visible behind an endcap of bestsellers. My book, identifiable by its lime-green spine, dangled at his side. He watched me, his gaze unshifting, even as I made eye contact with him.

There was something about him that tugged at a memory. Did I know him? Had I met him somewhere? If so, I couldn't place him, but there was something vaguely familiar about him.

Especially his eyes.

It's his eyes I remembered, like two bits of coal. So dark, I suspected if I were close enough, differentiating between the iris and pupil would prove impossible.

As he watched me, the intensity of his stare seared like an open flame held to my skin. I jerked back against my seat — a reflexive move to get away lest I get burned. My grip on the pen I held loosened, and it dropped onto the open book. Flustered, I looked from him to the book, the title page now marred by a scribble of ink.

"Oh . . . I'm sorry."

I looked back to where he'd stood, but he was gone.

Again, I apologized to the young woman, then glanced over my shoulder. "Paige, hand me a fresh book." The assistant from my publishing house pulled a book from a box behind the table.

"Thanks." I took the book and returned my attention to Aubrey. I held up my hand, opened and closed it a few times, the thin platinum and diamond wedding band I wore catching the light and winking. "Writer's cramp."

I picked up the pen. "Let me try that again." After I'd signed her book, when she turned to leave, I pivoted slowly, taking in the few customers milling about behind me and on either side of the store. When I finally looked through the line of faces again, it seemed the man had vanished.

It wasn't until much later — ninety minutes or more, maybe — after I'd pushed the thought of him aside, that he reappeared. He stood outside, one hand cupped on the glass of one of the large windows, a book in his other hand. He held the book clutched to his chest as though it were an object of great value, something treasured. He peered into the store, staring at me.

Was it my book he still held?

I pulled away from his gaze. "Paige," I whispered. She was straightening a stack of books on the end of the table. When she looked up, I turned back and gestured to the window, but again, he was gone.

Paige looked from the window to me. "What?"

Mouth dry, I reached for my water bottle, unscrewed the cap, and took a sip.

"Deni? What's wrong?"

"I just . . . Never mind."

Had I signed his book before I noticed him watching me? If so, could I retrieve his name from the hundreds I'd heard that afternoon? It seemed unlikely. Although I tried to make eye contact with each reader and listened as they said their name, I didn't recall him. Anyway, why was he different than any of the others looking at me? I was making something out of nothing. He probably just hadn't wanted to wait in line for me to sign his book. Maybe he'd left and then come back to see if the line had dwindled.

What did it matter? I successfully put him out of my mind. In fact, I didn't even think to mention him to Keith when I called home that night.

I didn't think of him again.

Until the next time.

CHAPTER THREE

Adelia

May 5, 2017

Knowledge equals protection.

I held that belief the way some women hold their keys positioned between their fingers when walking alone through a dark parking lot. Or the way some hold the grip of a handgun, placing their faith in its force.

Knowledge became my higher power. Pursuit of knowledge my religion.

A woman must know how to protect herself.

But intellectual knowledge and experiential knowledge are the difference between life and death — the chasm between the two unknowable, too vast to understand. Circumstances aren't ours to control. It is only faith, belief in what cannot be fully known or understood, that truly saves.

That realization was hard-won and ultimately determined my course.

The twisting two-lane highway is flanked by orange and lemon orchards on either side, with wheat-colored foothills rising above the lush green trees. The landscape belies the dry, hot wind laced with grit that roars through the interior of the open Jeep, exfoliating my bare arms, face, and head as my foot weighs on the accelerator. The sun overhead punishes. Just days ago it rained — a cold, pounding storm. It seems we skipped spring.

The rock outcroppings rising from the rolling hills stand like personal monuments, affirming my course. I lift one hand from the steering wheel and run it over my bare scalp.

There is no room for doubt.

When I fly by a road sign marked with a gas pump icon, I steal a glance at the gas gauge on the dash. I know I have enough fuel remaining to make it to my destination, but when I reach the small station in Lemon Cove, just fifteen minutes or so outside Three Rivers, I stop anyway. The station looks like something from a time warp. Vintage 1950 at least. I slow and pull off the highway and into the station. As I make my way to the single pump, disintegrating asphalt crunches under my tires, and when the Jeep drops into and out of a gaping pothole, muddy water splashes. The runoff has made its way down to the foothills.

The Jeep parked in front of the pump, I get out and stretch, my muscles stiff from sitting for so long.

After topping off my tank, I pull away from the pump and park along the side of the station near the restroom. I grab my backpack off the backseat and hop out. When I realize I need a key for the rest-room, I head back around to the front of the station and go inside. Behind a counter cluttered with packets of gum, mints, ciga-rette lighters, maps, and postcards, a man about the same vintage as the station looks up from the newspaper he's reading and eyes me, his expression wary.

"Restroom key?"

He studies me, his gaze shifting to the ink on my scalp.

I lower my eyes and stare at the cement floor worn to a sheen.

He grunts. "Here."

I look back up and take the key that's at-tached to an old dented black and gold California license plate. "Thanks."

When I walk into the restroom, I'm as-saulted by the sharp scents of deodorizer and what it's meant to mask. But I'm grate-ful for the privacy and the lock on the door.

I hang my backpack on a hook, then lay the key and license plate on the edge of the sink. I turn on the faucet and bend to splash my face and head with cool water. I rinse the grit from my face and scalp. Eyes closed, I pull paper towels from the dispenser and dry off.

I dare a peek into the cracked mirror hanging over the sink. The image reflected startles me, as it always does — it is incongruent with who I am, or at least who I perceive myself to be. Even my eyes, the portals to my memories, are unfamiliar. Fire smolders in their depths.

The sun has darkened my olive-toned skin, despite sunscreen. I turn a bit so I can see the side of my head in the mirror. I trail my fingers over the intricate tattoo inked there and let it remind me of why I'm here.

I turn away from the mirror and don't look back. I throw the paper towel into the trash, then dig through my backpack, pull out a tube of sunscreen, reapply it, and toss it back into the pack. I check the time on my phone. This is my last stop before Three Rivers. Am I ready? Yes. I've done everything necessary, except for one thing. It's the reason I stopped here.

I reach into the backpack again and pull out my wallet, which is light in my hand.

The black leather is smooth, worn. I open the wallet to the driver's license in the first plastic pocket. I stare at it a moment.

Adelia Lynn Sanchez

DOB: 06/03/78

I flip through the rest of the plastic flaps where I've kept just the essentials. When I reach the last flap, it's there. One photo. I've kept it as long as possible. But now . . .

I trace the small smiling face in the photo with one finger, almost feeling the silk of his skin through the plastic sheath. The scent of his shampoo — baby shampoo, even at seven years old — mingled with grass, sweat, and his own scent, all boy, seems to rise from the picture. I swallow the ache in my throat. A shock of dark hair covers his tanned forehead. How many times have I pushed that hair out of his eyes?

Will I see him again? I have to see him again. Hold him again. There is no other option. I won't entertain other options.

I wedge my fingers under the plastic and pull the photo out of the pocket. When I do, something else comes with it and drops to the floor. I stoop and pick up a business card that must have been tucked behind the photo.

Denilyn Rossi, PsyD

Clinical Psychologist

Chair, Department of Psychology, Pacific Covenant University

I flip the card over and read the contact information as I shake my head. I have no need for her here. I should have bought one of the lighters on the counter inside the station so I could torch the card. Instead, I set my wallet and the photo on top of the rest-room key and tear the business card in half, then tear it again. I rip the card until my anger is spent and just bits of paper remain. Then I gather them up, dump them into the toilet bowl, and flush.

I turn back to the sink, pick up the picture and memorize, again, each contour of his face. I close my eyes and press the photo to my chest. "I'm sorry," I whisper. "I'm doing this for you. It's all for you. One day, I pray you'll understand." My voice is thick. His face in the photo wavers as tears fill my eyes, then spill. I choke back a sob as I pull toilet paper from the roll to wipe my eyes and nose.

These are the last tears I'll shed. I can't afford to indulge my emotions. I can't allow them to douse the fire within.

It's time for a singular focus.

I tear the photo to shreds. I can't have him linked to me in any way. Not here. Not now. I hold the pieces over the toilet bowl and drop them one by one. They flutter, land in the water, and float, his image scattered and distorted. I take a deep breath, reach for the handle, and flush again.

This time my life, my heart, swirls and disappears.

CHAPTER FOUR

Denilyn
January 9, 2017

I pull on my coat, grab my briefcase, and close and lock my office door — the mirrored image of my morning routine. But before leaving, I have something to take care of. I tap on Ryan's partially closed office door, then lean around it. "Have a minute?"

"Sure. Come in." He turns from his computer monitor and motions to a chair across from his desk.

"No thanks. I have to run. I just want to apologize. You know, for earlier . . . I'm sorry I was —"

He holds up one hand. "No need. I knew today might pose some challenges. Just here to help if you need anything."

"It was a long time ago, right?"

He shrugs.

"Anyway, I am sorry I was short with you. Have time for lunch later this week? We can catch up."

"Sounds good. Let me know what works."

I take a step inside his office. "Wow, it looks great in here."

He turns toward the window. "Can't beat the view, right?"

"It's beautiful, especially in spring when the oaks are green and the buckeyes blossom." I point back toward the hallway. "I have to go. Don't work too late. You can't get it all done in one day."

"I'll get out of here soon."

A few students linger in the hallway, waiting for meetings with professors, still trying to add classes or change their schedules in some way. Things don't really settle until midmonth, sometimes later. A few of the faces are familiar.

It's good to be back, isn't it? To have a schedule and work to occupy my mind. I think of Willow as I make my way to the stairs. What drama did she endure over the break? I've spent enough time with her to suspect her home life has left scars.

As I reach the exit to leave the building, a gust of wind pushes an unlatched door open and it clatters back against the frame then slams shut. The bang reverberates in the quiet hall, and my heart rate accelerates as though a shot were fired. I stop, put my hand on my chest, and watch as the door blows open again. The rain has subsided for the moment, but the storm still brews.

When my heart rate slows, I pull an elastic band from my coat pocket, gather my hair into a ponytail, and secure it. I exit the building and lean into the wind as I cross the campus and head to the faculty building where most of the faculty offices and the faculty mailboxes are housed. Under the canopy of oak trees, leaves that survived fall now twirl around my feet and dance across the pathway and grass.

I pick up my pace, anxious to check my mailbox before the building is locked for the night. I enter the brick building and make my way to the mailboxes. When I reach the boxes, I pull a stack of envelopes and papers out of my box.

Before I drop the mail into my briefcase to go through later, I shuffle through the items. When I come to a plain white envelope, heavy in my hand, I set it aside, curious. I put the rest of the items into my briefcase, pick up the envelope, and turn to go. As I walk back down the hallway to leave the building, I turn the envelope over, slide my finger under the sealed flap, and look inside.

I stop in the hallway, reach into the envelope, and pull out a silver Cross pen. I roll it over and read my name engraved on the side.

How did it . . . ?

I turn and head back to the mailboxes, intent on finding out who put the pen there. But my steps slow as I go. I stop before I reach the boxes and look at the envelope again. No name on the front. I open it again and look inside — no note with the pen. Students and faculty alike have access to the boxes. Anyone could have put the pen there. The logical explanation, I know, is that someone found the pen, saw my name on it, and dropped it in my box.

"You look perplexed."

I look up from the envelope. "Jon . . ." His french-blue shirt matches his eyes, and his sandy-blond hair looks windblown, not unlike I imagine mine looks. "It's good to see you." I glance at the envelope again. "Perplexed?" I look back to him. "Good assessment. I'd lost a pen — a favorite pen. It just turned up in my mailbox."

"Nice. Someone found it?"

"Evidently. There was no note or anything. Just the pen in an envelope." I pull my briefcase off my shoulder and drop the envelope with the pen inside one of the

56

pockets."

"Happy New Year, Deni. How were your holidays?"

"Peaceful. Good. How about yours? How'd the kids do?" Jon lost his wife to cancer four years ago. They had three children under ten years old when she died.

"Not bad. We've established new traditions, and it seems to get a little easier each year. Although, the holidays are always a reminder."

"I can imagine. Well, actually, I probably can't."

Jon points down the hallway. "Heading out?"

"Yes."

"I'll walk with you if that's okay."

"Of course."

We turn and head toward the front of the building, walking side by side.

"I've missed you, Deni."

I glance at him as we walk, unsure of how to respond. A pang of guilt, or maybe regret, nudges me.

"Sorry, just being honest. I will respect the boundaries you've set."

"Thank you. I appreciate that. And honestly, I've missed you too. I'm just . . ."

He slows and puts a hand on my shoulder. "Hey, it's okay. I know. I don't respect just your boundaries — I respect you. I can't say I understand, exactly, because I haven't been through what you've been through. But I trust that when, or *if* the time is ever right, you'll let me know. In the meantime, I'm satisfied with friendship. I'd like to maintain our friendship."

I stop, turn toward him, and look up into his eyes. "I'd like that too. Really. I appreciate you. More than you know."

"Careful, you don't want to lead on the romantic English professor." He chuckles.

"I may want to, but I won't." I take a step back. "I'm sorry," I whisper.

When we step into the biting wind and part ways, it isn't the conversation with Jon that I dwell on. Instead, it's the pen.

Who found it? If that is indeed what happened. And again, I know it's the only logical explanation. But . . . The pen is always in my desk drawer — or *was* always there. I never took it with me anywhere. I'm sure of that.

At least I think I'm sure.

When I reach the edge of the parking lot, I slow my pace then stop.

I reach into my pocket for my keys, but as I do, the sensation of someone watching me creeps up behind me. My breath catches and my back tingles. Every instinct screams at me to flee, to run. Instead, I plant myself. "No one's there," I whisper. "No one."

My senses, hypervigilant, are often misguided. I take a few steps into the parking lot as I work, and fail, to ignore the sensation. I stop again, and this time I spin around. I survey the path behind me, the area around me. The only people out in this weather have heads ducked and are either jogging across campus to another building or making a quick retreat to their cars.

I turn back to the parking lot and continue my own brisk retreat. But the sense that someone is monitoring my every move persists. When I reach my SUV, I take another quick look around the parking lot then click my key fob, open the door, toss my briefcase across the console onto the passenger seat, and jump inside.

By the time I reach to lock the doors, my breaths are coming in rapid bursts, and my hands, despite the cold, are damp. My heart pummels my chest, and I swallow back tears. I try to take a deep breath, but my windpipe feels constricted and I'm certain air isn't reaching my lungs. I gasp. "I'm . . . here." I inhale, my breath still shallow. Then exhale. "One, two . . . I'm . . . safe." I lean my forehead on the steering wheel and continue the intentional breathing, trying to keep myself grounded in the moment. Instead, panic accosts me until I'm sure I'll pass out. "One . . ." I gasp again, and this time my lungs inflate just a bit. I inhale again, and more air reaches my lungs. "One, two . . . three."

When the panic finally subsides, I lift my head. "What . . . is wrong with me?" The question seems to echo in the car. But no answer comes. One isn't really needed anyway. I know exactly what is wrong with me. I'm experiencing symptoms of post-traumatic stress disorder triggered by . . . what? Today's date? My return to work — leaving the safe haven I've created at home? I'm not sure.

But the panic feels real. Is real. What's wrong with me is the issue I can't seem to change. Can't fix. I can't roll back the clock and prevent what happened to me. Nor, it seems, can I move forward and forget.

But why? I've worked so hard. Spent so much time in therapy focused on working through the trauma. Why have the symptoms reappeared?

I have all the psychological training the educational system offers, yet I feel powerless to help myself.

■ ■ ■ ■

As I wind my way along the river, the wind buffets my car. This evening I'm grateful for the miles between PCU and home. It isn't a long drive, only twenty minutes or so depending on the weather, but it's enough time to gather myself, to weave my frayed emotions back into something resembling normalcy — whatever that is.

As the adrenaline that coursed through me wanes, my limbs grow heavy, and just gripping the steering wheel seems to take more energy than I have. I blink several times as I work to focus on the road.

When my phone rings through the car speakers, I glance at the monitor on my dash to see who's calling. I have neither the physical or emotional energy to expend on conversation. But when I see it's Jaylan, I press the button on my steering wheel to answer. "Hi there."

"Driving home?"

Everyone needs someone who knows not only their schedule but the perfect time to check in. Jaylan is one of those people in my life. We met during grad school, the same time I met Ryan. There were four of us who bonded — we were the Fearless

Four in those days — the days before we settled into real life with all its responsibilities and messiness. I've maintained my connections with Jaylan and Ryan. Jay is my closest friend, or "sister" as she would say. When I was still practicing, Jay and I shared a suite of offices.

"I left a few minutes ago."

"How'd it go today?" The warmth of Jay's voice fills the interior of the car.

"Good. It was good. Great to be back in the classroom. So, yes, really good."

"Who you trying to convince? Me or yourself?"

I hear the smile in her voice.

"Myself. Definitely."

"That bad, huh?"

I hesitate. "No. It *was* good to be back in the classroom. But the rest of it? I don't know, Jay." I bite my lower lip and change the course of the conversation. "Tell me about you. You're in between clients?"

"You're not getting off that easy, lady. But yes, I'm in between clients. I'm seeing someone new at six, and then I'll take off. The evening hours seem longer this time of year, you know?"

The headlights of an oncoming car glare, and I avert my gaze to the white line delineating the side of the road on my right until it passes. "I do know. How's Gabe? Work?"

"He's okay. Tough week to be a cop. But you know him — he wouldn't do anything else."

"I know." A story took over the news broadcasts two nights ago — a Placer County sheriff's deputy shot and killed during an investigation. I was standing in the kitchen when I heard the report coming from the TV in the den. I held my breath as I waited to hear the officer's name. *Not Gabe. Please, not Gabe.* It wasn't Gabe, but it was someone else's husband, a child's father, a mother's son, and I know their lives are forever changed, marred by tragedy. "I'm sorry, Jay. I heard the news. It was so senseless."

"Always is. Okay, enough of that. Give me the best and the worst. Dump 'em on me."

"That's not fair. It's your turn —"

"I don't have time to do fair. Talk to me."

I concede because it's easiest. Or maybe because I need to talk. "Best? That's easy, the classroom. I'm not sure why, but I'm at ease there. It feels safe."

"You feel a sense of control?"

"I don't know. It could be that. Or maybe it's as simple as safety in numbers. Or, more likely that I'm focused on others rather than on myself. But also, I still have purpose there. It's one of the few places where I still know who I am."

"The worst?" Her tone has softened and is laced with compassion. It's the tone I imagine her using with clients when she's not, as she'd put it, kicking their butts. If you truly want to change, want to grow, Jaylyn's who you want to see.

"Okay, the worst was leaving the campus. I thought . . . someone was watching me. Following me. And I lost it." I hesitate. How many times have I said things like that to Jay? To my therapist? My mother? "But it was just my imagination."

"Maybe someone was looking your way. Lots of people on that campus. Doesn't mean their intent was malicious. Maybe your sense was accurate but your response was exaggerated."

"Maybe. Ryan offered to walk out with me, but I told him no. I should have taken him up on his offer."

She's silent for a moment. "Why'd he offer to walk you out?"

Her question isn't what I expected, though it shouldn't surprise me. "Because —"

"Never mind. Listen, you are the only one who expects you to act like the Rock of Gibraltar. What you went through?" I can picture her shaking her head, her short dark curls bouncing as she does. "No, ma'am."

"I know. But Jay . . . why can't I get over it? Early this morning I had a nightmare. When I woke it was as though it had all just happened. I've had to fight to stay present all day. The memories . . ." I swallow. "Is it just the date? The anniversary?"

"Could be that, or something else. A trigger of some sort, but you know that. Maybe your meds need adjusting. You seein' Heather soon?"

"I have an appointment later this week."

"Good. She's golden. You'll work through it with her. In the meantime, go easy on yourself. Give yourself a dose of the same grace you dish out to others. And if you need me, you know where to find me. Got it?"

"Got it. Hey, I'm going to lose you in a minute. I'm heading into the canyon."

"Your mama gonna be there when you get home?"

"Yes. What a godsend she is."

"You got that right. Okay, sister, you good for now?"

"I'm good. Thanks, Jay."

"No need to thank me. I didn't do nothin'."

As Jay and I are exchanging goodbyes, the road drops into the canyon and static

65

crackles through the car's speakers, followed by silence. Although the section of road without cell service is just over a mile in length, I'm always relieved when the dark, twisting road rises out of the canyon and service is restored.

Although it was eight years ago today that I was attacked, every detail of that horrendous night is indelibly marked on my mind. It's said that time heals all wounds, but time hasn't dulled either the memory of that night nor the wounds I sustained — at least not the emotional wounds — let alone heal them.

So on a dark, stormy night, traveling a road alone without cell service, even for just one mile, produces anxiety that's become all too familiar.

I glance in my rearview mirror and see headlights coming up behind me. A truck, maybe? The lights seem higher than if it were a car. I look back at the road ahead until lights flash in my rearview mirror. I glance back, and this time the truck is closer. Too close, in fact.

Why did the driver flash his lights? I check my speedometer — I'm going the speed limit. I look ahead for a place to pull over so the driver can pass me, but there's only a narrow shoulder on this section of the road.

Before I can decide what to do, the lights flash again, and the truck pulls out, crosses the double yellow lines, passes me, and then flies up the road ahead.

What's the rush?

It was nothing. Just an impatient driver.

Right?

I take a deep breath. "One, two, three, four . . ."

CHAPTER FIVE

Denilyn
November 2009

Although I'd succeeded at putting him out of my mind, the next time I saw him, I recognized him immediately, as did my sympathetic nervous system, but I wouldn't process that until much later.

Keith and I, paper coffee cups in hand, had just left the café of our large church following a Saturday evening service. I pulled the collar of my coat up around my neck, the hot cup of coffee warming my hand. Crisp fall leaves cartwheeled across the brick courtyard, and when a gust of wind blew through, it whipped my hair into my face. With hair covering my eyes, I laughed and held out my cup to Keith. "I can't see."

He took the cup, and I swept the hair from my face then turned toward the building nearest us to look at my reflection in one of the tinted windows. It was dusk, and the white lights hanging across the courtyard had just come on, their reflection twinkled in the window, and the orange and purple burst of reflected sunset cast an alluring glow. I could just see myself against the backdrop. I smoothed my hair back into place and tucked it into the collar of my coat. I checked my reflection once more, and just as I was going to turn back to Keith, my breath caught.

The man standing behind me wasn't my husband.

I stared at the reflection, and even as dim as it was, the inky, unkempt hair, pale complexion, and dark eyes were unmistakable. I untucked my hair from my collar, pulled it back again, and then tucked it back in. I'd hoped if I stalled he'd leave. When he didn't, I slowly turned to face him.

He wore the same khaki-green jacket, although this time he wore a wrinkled plaid shirt and knit tie, which hung askew under the coat. His hands were stuffed into the pockets of his jeans.

"Who are you?" My voice was hoarse, so I cleared my throat, and spoke again. My tone firm this time. "Who are you?"

His eyes were almost black, and again there was something familiar about him.

"You know my name."

As he spoke, I looked over his shoulder to search for Keith. He stood several yards away, a cup of coffee in each hand, talking to someone.

When I looked back at the face of the man in front of me, he was staring at me. I glanced Keith's way again, but this time the guy's gaze followed mine. He was staring at Keith when I turned back. When he looked at me again, his expression had changed. Hardened.

I swallowed as I tried to make sense of what he'd said. Did I know him? Know his name? I was sure I didn't. I worked to keep my tone even, "I'm sorry. You'll have to remind me."

When he didn't respond, I continued. "Your name? I'm sorry, I don't . . ." This time when I glanced over his shoulder, Keith was coming toward us.

When he reached us, he looked from me to the man it seemed I was having a conversation with. He reached out his hand. "Hey, I'm Keith."

The guy lifted his chin, nodded at Keith, and then turned and walked briskly away, head down.

"Who was that?" Keith handed me my cup of coffee.

I took the cup from him, but I stood rooted, my pulse thrumming in my ears and my breaths coming in quick succession. I was also perspiring, despite the chill of the breeze.

"Deni?"

I took a deep breath, trying to calm myself — to stem the adrenaline coursing through me.

When Keith put his hand on my shoulder, I jumped.

"Whoa. You okay?"

"I just . . . I don't know. Sorry."

"What'd that guy say to you?"

He'd said nothing to garner the response I was having. "Nothing. Let's go."

I turned and strode toward the parking lot. Keith followed me, and when he caught up with me, he put his free arm around my shoulder and took a sip of his coffee. "Good java."

I nodded, but I wasn't present. I couldn't absorb what Keith said as he continued talking.

As we crossed the courtyard where hundreds of people milled about, I spotted the guy again. He'd reached the giant heritage oak between the courtyard and the parking lot. He leaned against the trunk, his frame silhouetted against the setting sun, but I knew it was him. As we got closer, just a few feet away, it was evident he was watching me. When our eyes met, his posture seemed to relax. He stuck his hands back into his pockets, but they fidgeted there. Then he looked down and dug the toe of one of his booted feet into the dirt. Eyes down, he appeared focused on whatever he was trying to unearth.

I nudged Keith and pointed. "You don't know him?"

Keith lifted his coffee cup in the guy's direction "That guy you were talking to?"

"Yes."

"Nope. How do you know him?"

I slowed, and Keith turned and looked at me. At the same time, the guy lifted his eyes from the ground and stared at me again.

"I don't know him."

He glanced back to the guy and then looked at me, eyebrows raised. "What's the deal?"

I picked up my pace, and Keith kept in step with me. When we reached the parking lot, I stopped and faced him. "That guy was at the book signing in Menlo Park."

"So?"

I searched Keith's eyes. "Doesn't that seem odd to you?"

"No, why? You have events posted on your

website. Anyone interested can see what you have going on and attend, right?"

"Yes, but . . ."

Keith shrugged. "You have a fan at church, and he went to your signing. Why is that a problem?"

"All the way to the Bay Area?"

"Whatever floats his boat. Welcome to the world of celebrity, babe. People follow you now." He put his arm around me again. "C'mon."

We walked the rest of the way to the car in silence. But I couldn't let it go. When we got into the car, Keith set his cup in the holder in the middle console, then looked at me. "You're really bugged by that guy?"

"Something's just off. He said I know him — know his name. But I don't. I know I don't." My heart was still racing and my palms were damp. "And the way he stared at me the day of the signing. And here. It didn't feel right."

"You're the type of woman men stare at. You just live in here" — he tapped my forehead — "too much to notice." Then he planted a kiss on my lips. "Don't worry about it." He straightened, started the car, put it in gear, and backed out of the parking spot.

It seemed obvious that, at least in his

mind, there was nothing to worry about.

While I'd always appreciated the independence our marriage afforded me — our mutual respect for one another — sometimes Keith's lack of concern or his cavalier attitude bothered me. "I feel like you're dismissing what I'm feeling."

Keith glanced at me. "Really? I was going for reassuring."

I bit my bottom lip.

He glanced at me. "Okay, what are you feeling?"

"I . . . I don't know. Something about the guy just freaked me out. But" — I turned and looked out the passenger window, then turned back — "you're right. There's probably nothing to it."

By the time we pulled into our garage, I'd convinced myself that Keith was right — there was no need to worry about the man I'd encountered at the signing and then again at church. Although I'd also given talks and done signings at local bookstores, it wasn't that far-fetched that someone from our area might attend the signing in the Bay Area — it was only a couple hours' drive. Maybe my book had touched something in him. Helped him in some way. That's what I'd hoped for as I wrote it. Maybe he felt I understood something about him that others hadn't.

Or maybe it was just a coincidence. Wasn't that possible? He was in the Bay Area, at the store, and happened to see me — recognized me from church. Maybe he'd bought my book after noticing me.

There were myriad possibilities.

I desperately wanted to believe my husband was right, that there was nothing to worry about, so I ignored my instinct. But not just my instinct, also everything I knew about the way the limbic and nervous systems work. Before my mind had time to process the encounter, my amygdala, that part of the limbic system closely tied to fear, had sounded the "fight or flight" alarm and my body had responded, releasing a rush of adrenaline that resulted in a rapid heartbeat, quickened breathing, and sweating, along with other less noticeable symptoms.

Essentially, my body perceived a threat before my mind processed the situation. But I wouldn't consider any of that until much later.

Instead, I ignored my reaction.

Although the release of the book and its ascent to the *New York Times* bestseller list, where it appeared it was going to stay for a while, was exciting, there was also some stress involved as I attempted to balance my therapy practice and teaching with travel, interviews, speaking, and book signings. And our first year of marriage.

It was a lot. I was tired, I reasoned. I over-reacted.

But now, looking back on that day, I know I made a critical error, the first of many.

I didn't trust myself.

I didn't trust what both my mind and body knew to be true.

CHAPTER SIX

Adelia
May 5, 2017

As I near Three Rivers Village, my past, my present, and my future, like the forks of the Kaweah, converge. The last time I was here, I'd just graduated with my MS in psychology. We'd come to spend our last summer together, friends drawn to one another by our mutual fascination with the mind — the way it functions and the behaviors it affects.

Soon we'd each enter the next phase of our lives, which meant putting in the necessary hours to receive our licenses, further education in the pursuit of doctorates, or both. Marriage was on the horizon too for more than one of us.

That final summer marked our third spent in the artist's enclave of Three Rivers Village — the gateway to Sequoia National Park, as it was known. But art wasn't what lured us to the tiny town nestled in the southern Sierra foothills. We shared another common bond — our love for the river.

The Kaweah's drainage — a drop of almost 2.5 miles from headwaters to Terminus Reservoir — make it one of the steepest in the United States, offering some of the most challenging class IV and V rapids in Central and Southern California. With names like Chutes, Osterizer, Bumper, Powerhouse, and Suicide Falls, the rapids draw thrill seekers and experienced paddlers alike. And it drew us, summer after summer.

The Kaweah called our names.

I have no intention of allowing my mind to linger on memories of our collective past. Instead, I will let my mind wander within boundaries I've set, but only for a time.

The past is why I'm here. It fuels the fire within. It will also determine my future. But I don't dare look back for long lest I lose myself to the fantasy we created. Instead, I will let the past push me forward.

"The past is either a shadow that haunts us or a force that propels us." The words stop me short.

But thinking of Denilyn exceeds the boundary I've set.

Landmarks on either side of the two lanes

of Highway 198 lead me back in time, including the small farm where Jaylan spent her summers, her dark skin covered by long-sleeved chambray shirts and jeans as she helped with chores, tended animals, and wrangled an overgrown garden until it produced a bounty. She lived on the farm in a small guest cottage, saving her earnings rather than spending them on rent like the rest of us did.

Jaylan worked harder than all of us put together.

As I enter Three Rivers, I pass Ride the Kaweah, where Ryan and I worked as guides leading trips down the rapids. It was exhilarating work, if one could even call it work. For us, digging oars into the water and navigating the rapids was a shared passion. Pure play.

Play? That was true for me. But for Ryan it was something more.

We each interacted with the river in our own way — took what we needed from it. Ryan's need was mastery. That need drove him to Three Rivers each summer. He used his keen intelligence to learn the topography of each straightaway, twist, and chute of the Kaweah. The constantly changing levels of the river, based on the heat of the week and the snowmelt it produced, were the undulating rhythm he lived by. His ability to read the river, his deft use of a paddle, and the apt instruction he offered customers achieved, if not mastery of the river, the respect of the company's owner.

Jaylan sought the natural beauty — the power and solace the river offered. The way the cold, clear water slipped over the rocks and boulders of the river's bed, and the deep swirling pools where trout hid under the ledges of rocks spoke to her. The graphic design etched in the banks by runnels and rivulets was the art that evoked her passion. In both the roar of the rapids and the burble of the creeks and streams that fed the Kaweah, Jaylan heard the voice of her Creator.

Ryan and Jaylan were opposites from the beginning. Like oil and water. Ryan brought out a side of Jaylan rarely seen. During our master's programs, they debated schools of thought, theories, and treatment modalities. During the summer, if they had nothing better to argue about, they'd debate what time the sun was expected to rise the next morning. Whatever the topic, they assumed opposite views and sparred. When they were called on it, they said it was all in fun. But there was an edge to their relationship, one that I'm only now beginning to understand.

Back then I needed the opportunity to shift gears, to break away from the intense study and work I pursued. The river afforded me that opportunity. But now the idea of powering through the rapids evokes feelings I refuse to entertain. Now it isn't the river that's wooed me to the village. The call comes from another source.

It's a call I can't — I won't — refuse.

Whereas Three Rivers may have offered me an escape in the past, now as I enter the canyon wedged between steep mountains, canopied by overhanging sycamore, willow, and oak trees, I feel trapped — as though the mountains and trees are closing in, suffocating. Even the river, flowing freely, is rife with obstacles — boulders protruding from the water, dead tree branches caught in eddies, chutes that will soon be too narrow for rafts to pass through.

If I leave here this time — when I leave here — I will never return. It's a vow I make to myself and one I intend to keep.

I am here to close a chapter, finally.

As I pass through the village, the coffee shop where we'd often meet before our days began and the café where we'd sit on the deck as the day came to a close still stand. I slow as I tick off familiar sights and take in new businesses. I follow 198 beyond Three

Rivers, cross the Pumpkin Hallow Bridge, then pull into a parking place in front of the Gateway Restaurant. The house is back in the direction I've just come from. I could have cut off the highway several miles back, but the memories served a purpose.

Knowing cell service is spotty in this area, I printed directions to the house. I lean over, open the glove compartment, and pull out the directions and read through them. Then I pull out of the spot and backtrack, not allowing the memories to accompany me this time.

I turn off the highway onto a narrow drive almost hidden by the overgrowth. I follow the driveway for almost a quarter mile before it widens in front of what I assume is the house. All but the peak of the roof is hidden behind a wall of scrub oak and manzanita. A large sycamore tree provides an umbrella of shade.

Satisfied, I park the Jeep in front. Later I'll pull it into the garage, out of sight should anyone make their way down the drive. That was one of the provisions I checked for when looking for the rental, either a driveway around back or a garage where I could park the Jeep. This property has the garage, along with two more essential provisions.

I secure the emergency break, turn off the ignition, lean back in the seat, and exhale. It seems I've held my breath for weeks. Months maybe. Or has it been years? It doesn't matter. I'm here now.

And I've made the right choice.

The only choice.

CHAPTER SEVEN

Denilyn
January 12, 2017

During my office hours, my door is always open, even when I'm meeting with a student. It's a policy I adopted when I began teaching and one I established for the faculty under me when I came to PCU. So when I look up from the lesson plan I'm going over and see Willow standing a few feet outside my door, eyes cast down, I observe her for a moment, then make a decision.

"Willow?"

She looks up as though she's surprised I've noticed her. But I suspect that's what she was hoping for. She takes a few steps forward but hesitates at the door.

"If you have a few minutes, come in and catch me up. I miss not having you in a class this semester."

She shrugs the backpack off her shoulders

and sets it inside my office, then comes and stands on the other side of my desk.

"Pull a chair over." I motion to the corner of my office. "Have a seat if you'd like. How's your week going?"

She pulls a chair over and then drops into it. Her shoulders droop and her eyes are ringed with dark circles. "Okay, I guess."

"Did you get the classes you need?"

"Yeah." She tucks a piece of her long, straight blond hair behind one ear.

"Full load?"

"More than full." Her slim frame, all limbs it seems, looks lost in the large chair.

"Ah, does it feel like more than you can handle?

"I don't know. Not really, I guess. It's just . . . other stuff."

"What else is going on?"

She shrugs and looks away. Her demeanor tells me she's troubled, so I don't say anything more. Instead, I give her a little time and space. When she looks back at me, her large blue eyes reveal a storm within, not unlike the one that's raged outside this week.

"Deni, can I ask you something?"

"Sure."

"You know last year in Intro to Psych?"

I nod.

"You said something about how the past either follows us or . . ." Her brow furrows. "What was it? Do you remember?"

I recite the statement I've often made. "The past is either a shadow that haunts us or" — it's my turn to look away — "a force that propels us."

When I look back to Willow, she seems to search my face, looking for what, I'm not sure.

"How do you let it become a force that propels you?"

I lean forward and rest my arms on my desk. "Willow, do you also remember I said I believe it's our choice? We can either choose to let the past haunt us or choose to let it propel us. I also said it isn't black and white. We may desire to let go of the past, even choose to do so, but sometimes it requires very hard work to facilitate the healing of wounds we've sustained. Actually, I'm still learning just how gray that choice can feel."

I lean back. "We let it propel us forward by working toward healing, by learning from our experiences and taking that knowledge and, hopefully, wisdom garnered, into the future. We use the experience to grow. We let it strengthen us."

She seems to consider what I've said

before she continues. "Did what you went through" — she drops her gaze to her lap, then glances back up at me — "you know, before . . . Does that, like, haunt you? Do you still think about it a lot? Or did it make you stronger?"

Since coming to PCU, only a handful of students have asked me about the well-publicized events that took place. Whether that kind of news wasn't on their radar, or now, because it happened so long ago, it has rarely come up. To quell speculation for those who had seen the media coverage of my case — parents of students and faculty members, mostly — before starting at PCU, I changed my last name. I reverted to my maiden name, Rossi. It was time anyway. The divorce was final, and I needed a fresh start, in many ways.

"So, you've heard about that?"

"Sort of. Some people were talking about it last semester, so I googled you. It didn't come up right away —"

"Because my last name is different now."

She nods. It's clear that revealing that she dug up the information embarrasses her. But that tells me just how important this conversation is to her, though I don't yet know why. "It's okay, Willow. As much as I'd like to think people no longer remember what happened, or talk about it, I know that's wishful thinking on my part. The stories are just a few clicks away; I know that." I pick up a paper clip from my desk and unbend its curves. "I've worked hard with a therapist to put the trauma of that experience behind me, but I'm not there yet. I still struggle." I take a deep breath. "That's hard for me to admit. It both frustrates and embarrasses me. It seems like, because of my degrees and the work I do, I should be further along in the process. But when I let my mind dwell on thoughts like that, shame creeps in, and that can derail me if I let it. I guess what I'm learning is that we can't always control how we'll respond to something, or how we'll heal. I do believe healing is possible, and I'll continue working toward that end."

"I'm sorry you had to go through that."

"Thank you." I drop the paper clip into the trash can under my desk. "Now, may I ask you something?"

She hesitates. "Um, okay."

"Is there something you're working to deal with?"

She looks down at her lap and mumbles. "I mean, maybe. Sort of."

Within moments, red blotches flush her face and neck, and she'll no longer look at me. "I'm sorry for whatever it is you've gone through."

She shrugs. "It's not that big a deal."

I'm silent a moment as I consider what she's said. Then I lean forward. "Willow?" My tone is gentle, and I wait, hoping she'll look at me. It takes a moment, but finally she meets my gaze again. "Sometimes at night, when I wake from a nightmare that's made me feel like the whole thing happened all over again, or during the day, when I have a flashback of what happened, I let that voice in my mind tell me that it wasn't a big deal. That I just need to get over it. And I'll wonder what is wrong with me. Why can't I move on? Why am I making such a big deal out of something that happened so long ago? When I find myself asking those kinds of questions, I know I'm listening to the voice of shame."

"What do you do then?"

I consider the answer I want to give her versus the truth. I offer her both. "Sometimes I tune out that voice. Recognize it for what it is and do something good for myself, like remind myself that what I went through was traumatic and it's okay to still struggle, or I'll talk to a friend or my therapist, someone who can help me see the truth of my circumstances and someone who will remind me that the voice I'm listening to isn't God's voice." I hesitate a moment, then continue. "But other times, more often than I'd like, I believe that voice. Because, honestly, a lot of times it's easier to believe the voice of shame than it is to believe I'm okay, that I'll heal, that God loves me. Oftentimes that voice affirms what I *feel* inside. But my feelings don't always line up with the truth. Does that make sense?"

She nods as tears streak her face. She wipes them away, and I reach for a box of tissues and hand it to her.

"When I listen to that voice, when I let it affirm negative feelings I struggle with about myself, then I make choices that aren't helpful. They aren't emotionally healthy. And then" — I sigh — "things get kind of ugly. Know what I mean?"

She smiles briefly, despite her tears. "Yeah, I know."

"I thought you might. May I share one other thing I've learned?"

She nods again.

"It isn't helpful to compare whatever it is we've gone through to what others may have experienced. If whatever happened hurt me or hurt you, then it may take some time for us to heal. We're all uniquely created, and we'll all deal with things differently. And that's okay."

She sniffs and wipes her eyes with a tissue.

"Anything you want to share or talk about?"

She shrugs.

"Have you talked to anyone about it?"

"Not really."

"What about a counselor? Would you be willing to talk with a therapist?"

She darts a glance at me then looks away again. When she finally looks back, there are tears in her eyes again. "Aren't you a therapist?"

"I am, but I'm not practicing now, but even if I were, because of our relationship here, at school, I couldn't work with you. That's considered a dual relationship and goes against the ethical codes counselors are required to adhere to in order to protect their clients. We can talk some as friends, but the therapy relationship is different than friendship. I'm happy to refer you to someone."

"Doesn't therapy cost a lot?"

"Yes, it can be expensive, but there are services for those who can't afford a fee. There are also many excellent therapists who take insurance. Are you covered under your parents' plan?"

"Yeah, but I don't . . . I can't . . ." She shakes her head.

"It's okay, Willow. If you decide you'd like me to refer you to someone, let me know, and we'll talk about what would work best for you."

"Okay. I'll think about it. Thanks though. I mean, for telling me some of what, you know, you go through."

"Anytime."

As Willow leaves, I know I mean what I've said. If what I've gone through, am still going through, can help her in any way, I will share it with her.

Even when it's difficult.

I leave the building, briefcase in hand, and stand at the top of the steps. The rain that's spit and spattered much of the day has stopped for the moment, replaced by a cold northern wind. I pull my raincoat tight and fasten the top buttons, and then I make my way down the stairs and head for the parking lot. I follow one of the pathways that cuts across a large expanse of lawn dotted with trees where, in the fall and spring, students are sprawled on the grass, hanging out with friends, studying, or dozing in the sun. This evening the lawn area is saturated and deserted. Bare branches whip in the wind, and the same gray hues, the only palette we've seen this week, enshrouds the campus as dusk falls.

As I walk, I consider my conversation with Willow, and my heart aches for whatever it is she's endured. Or is enduring. It does no good to speculate on what she's suffered, the possibilities are endless, but my sense that she's sustained wounds was accurate — I saw further evidence of that today. As I near the parking lot, I notice a hawk gliding above the other side of the lot where the asphalt meets the natural landscape. Then it makes a steep descent to the river. The bird, wings stretched, lifts and falls with the wind, trusting, it seems, the currents to carry it.

I slow my pace and watch for a moment, then whisper a silent plea. "Help Willow to trust You to carry her." As I watch the bird, it isn't lost on me that while I pray for Willow and believe God will not only hear my prayer but also answer it for her, I no longer hold that same faith for myself. Loneliness tugs at my soul. A longing for the intimacy I once experienced in my relationship with God.

Help me to trust. . . .

As I begin to form the silent prayer for myself, images ambush me and the soundtrack plays in my mind, snuffing the flicker of hope that had sparked.

How do you let it become a force that propels you? Willow's question comes back to me.

The truth?

I haven't let what happened propel me forward.

I can't seem to do so.

CHAPTER EIGHT

Denilyn
November 2009

I crossed the hallway in the suite of offices Jaylan and I shared and grabbed a new box of tissues off a shelf in the room we used to store supplies, make coffee, and occasionally microwave our lunch or dinner. I took the tissues back to my office and sat it on the end table next to the loveseat. How many of these boxes had clients gone through this week?

I turned off the Tiffany-style lamp that cast the office in a warm, maybe even safe, glow. At least that's the effect I hoped for. Then I went to the red oak, mission-style desk and locked the drawer that housed client files. I hit the switch that turned off the overhead lights as I left the office and stepped into the hallway.

"Long day?" Jaylan looked at me over her

shoulder as she pulled her office door closed.

"Very long. How about you?"

Her purse dangled from her shoulder as she cradled files in her arms. "Same. I'm not telling you nothin' you don't know, but people can be horrible to one another. Some wounds? I don't know." She shook her head. "God can do anything, but . . ."

"But He doesn't always heal, at least not in the time frame we'd like to see."

"You've got that right."

"I don't know how you do this every day, Jay." I'd already cut my client work in half and was focusing the extra hours on promoting my first book and outlining the second book. "I can't bear that many burdens. You know?"

"Yeah, I know. We each got our capacity, right?"

"Right. I nodded toward her armload. "You're taking work home?"

"I gotta transfer my notes to the files while things are still fresh. But I'm not staying here to do it. I'm goin' home, making dinner with my husband. Then while he watches the game, I'll take care of these." She dipped her chin toward the files.

We stopped in the office waiting area, where I set the alarm, and then we walked out together.

Fall had given way to winter sometime during the week. We walked into the already dark evening, pricks of starlight dotting the sky, the night air chill. The trees in the parking lot were bare, branches exposed, and the small patch of lawn in front of our office that was lush and green just weeks before, had faded. It seemed death surrounded us. Or at least the dormancy that accompanies winter. I shivered and wrapped my arms around myself.

Although I anticipated the evening ahead, dinner with Keith at Bandara, one of our favorite restaurants, I carried the weight of my clients' agonies in my soul. Some days we celebrated victories, but there were few celebrations today. At least I assumed that was what encumbered me. I tried to shake off the mood. Keith and I had agreed we were due for an evening out, and I'd looked forward to the time together. I didn't want to spoil it. We were less than a year into our marriage, and time alone together was already becoming too rare amid the busyness of building our careers.

"I'll see you day after tomorrow." The alarm on Jaylan's car beeped as she unlocked the doors.

I waved. "Have a good evening." I climbed

into my car and then reached into my purse for my phone. I kept it on silent during my sessions and often forgot to turn the ringer back on. If Keith was running late, as was often the case, I didn't want to miss his call or text. I dug through the purse but couldn't find the phone. Then I recalled I'd plugged it in to charge it — I'd left it in my office.

I got back out of my car just as Jaylan was pulling out of the parking lot. I let myself back into the office, turned off the alarm, and as I was crossing the waiting area, a small package sitting on our reception desk, where clients signed in when they arrived, caught my eye.

I stopped, picked up the package, and saw that it was addressed to me. I carried it into my office and set it on my desk as I un-plugged my phone. Just as I was about to turn on the volume, the phone vibrated in my hand. A text from Keith saying he was running a few minutes late. I'd called that one.

With some time to spare, I sat down at the desk, reached into the top drawer for my letter opener, and then picked up the package. It was wrapped in brown shipping paper and hand addressed. I didn't recog-nize the handwriting when I glanced at the box. I slipped the opener under the packing tape, slit it, and pulled the wrap off the box. I crumpled the paper and tossed it into the trash can beneath my desk. Then I lifted the lid and found another, much smaller box inside, this one wrapped in gold foil gift paper.

Before opening the gift, I rifled through the packing material in the box to make sure I hadn't missed a card. But I didn't find one. Perhaps one was enclosed with the gift.

I pulled the wrapping paper off to reveal a black velvet jewelry box. I opened the hinged lid. "Oh . . ." I picked up a thick gold linked bracelet. From one of the links hung a single gold charm — the letter *D*. As I unhooked the clasp, I noticed it was imprinted with *14k.* I draped the bracelet over my wrist and could see it would be a perfect fit.

Puzzled, I set the bracelet back in its box then backed away from the desk and reached underneath for the trash can. I pulled the crumpled paper out of the can and looked at it again, more closely this time. There was no return address. And although the paper bore a stamp with the postage amount, as though someone had taken it to the post office to mail it, there was no postmark.

Had someone intended to mail the gift

then decided to deliver it instead? Or had the post office just missed postmarking the box?

Again, I checked the handwriting. I couldn't place it. It certainly wasn't Keith's usual hurried scrawl, but if I had to guess, I'd say a male wrote it. I tossed the wrapping back into the trash.

A client, perhaps? I mentally ran through the list of clients I'd seen during the day, but I couldn't imagine any of them leaving a gift like this. I picked up the jewelry box, closed the lid, and then turned it over, hoping to find the name of a jewelry or department store printed on the bottom, but there was nothing there.

Nothing identified either the sender or where the bracelet had been purchased.

I picked up my phone and scrolled through my contacts until I came to Jay's name.

She answered after the first ring. "Hey, you miss me already?"

Her confidence made me smile in spite of the unease settling over me. "I have a question for you. I had to run back into the office after you left. There was a package on the reception desk addressed to me. Do you know where it came from?"

"A package? Nah. No idea."

"You're sure? I thought maybe someone dropped it off."

"If so, they just left it. Like you, I went from one client to the next today. I've been tellin' you we need to hire a receptionist."

"Maybe you're right. It's odd. There was no card or note, so I don't who it's from. It's a nice gift, and it looks expensive too."

"Secret admirer?"

I heard the smile in Jay's voice, but I didn't — couldn't — respond.

"You there? Or did I lose you?"

"No . . ." I pushed the jewelry box away from me. "I'm here. Listen, thanks. I'd better run — I'm meeting Keith for dinner."

I hung up the phone and stared at the box on my desk. Weary, I closed my eyes. *Secret admirer?* With a start, I opened my eyes, but the vision of a man's face, eyes like bits of coal, was seared on my mind.

I backed away from the desk again, reached back into the trash can, and pulled out the brown paper the shipping box was wrapped in. I stared at my name and memorized the handwriting. Then I folded the paper into quarters. I reached for my keys, unlocked the file drawer in my desk, and tucked the wrapping behind the file folders.

I put the black velvet box in my purse.

Then I prayed Jay was wrong.

I scooted into the booth, took the menu from the waiter, and breathed deep. The fragrant scent of the wood-fire rotisserie and the low, warm lighting of the restaurant eased some of the tension I'd carried in with me. I opened the menu and perused the offerings.

"Hey . . ." Keith leaned down and gave me a quick kiss. "Been here long?" He scooted in across from me and loosened his tie.

"No, I just arrived."

We filled each other in on our days and then ordered an appetizer. When the waiter had gone again, I reached for my purse. "Hey, you didn't happen to send me a gift today. A bracelet?"

He raised his eyebrows. "Uh, that depends. Do you like it?" He chuckled.

"Keith, I'm serious."

"Okay, no, I didn't. Why?"

I pulled out the jewelry box, opened it, and handed it to him.

"Wow, swanky. Who's it from?"

"I don't know. It turned up at the office today. No card or return address. It appears someone dropped it off. Jaylan doesn't know either."

"Huh."

I took the box back from Keith and look at the bracelet. "I used to have a bracelet almost like this. My dad gave it to me when I turned sixteen." I looked across the table at Keith. "He always did that — took me to lunch and gave me a gift. Something special he'd picked out for me." I smiled at the memory. "He'd do the same for my mom."

"What happened to it? I've never seen it."

I swallowed the ache in my throat that always accompanied memories of my dad. My grief at losing him was still fresh. "I'm not sure. I lost it during one of the summers I spent in Three Rivers. It's probably at the bottom of the Kaweah. The clasp must have come undone or broken." I fingered the charm bracelet in the box I hold. "It was also gold and had a single charm, the letter *D,* like this one. The style is a little different, but overall, it's very similar."

"Have you checked with your mom?"

"Not yet. But why would she drop it off at the office without saying anything? Anyway, the address was handwritten, and it wasn't her handwriting."

He shrugged. "Well, whoever it's from, you might as well enjoy it." He picked up the menu. "What are you having?"

"Um . . ." I looked at the menu again, but all I could think about was the bracelet and Jaylan's comment. "Keith . . ."

He looked at me over the menu.

"You don't think . . ."

"What?"

I set the menu down. "It's just something Jaylan said. She was teasing, but she said maybe I have a secret admirer." I shrugged. "Do you think?"

"Sure, why not?"

"Wouldn't that bother you?"

"Should it?"

"No, I just . . . I mean, you don't think that guy . . . the one from the book signing . . ."

"What guy? The guy from church?"

I nodded.

"You think the bracelet's from him?" He chuckled as he shook his head.

Just hearing Keith say it out loud made me realize how ridiculous the thought was. Of course it wasn't from him. I hadn't seen him again since that evening at church more than a month ago.

"I don't mean any disrespect, but the guy didn't look like he had much money. He looked kind of down on his luck. That" — he pointed toward my purse — "doesn't look cheap. Anyway, you don't even know him."

"You're right. I know. It was an absurd thought."

I glanced at the menu again, then closed it and set it on the table. "I'm having the filet. I feel like splurging. You with me?"

Keith smiled and reached across the table for my hand. "Always, babe."

Later that night as I lay in bed, the dark room offering few distractions and Keith's rhythmic snore accompanying my thoughts, I replayed our conversation in the restaurant and let myself feel what I'd denied in the moment. The emotion, though unfamiliar, was clear: anger.

I was angry.

Though I had an intellectual knowledge of anger, of course, it was an emotion I'd rarely experienced. I'd had little cause. I grew up in a loving home with parents who rarely displayed anger toward one another and never toward me, their only child. Discipline, yes. Anger, no. But the emotion festering within was exactly that.

I was angry with Keith for dismissing my . . . What was it? Fear? Or was it something more? Questioning whether the bracelet could have come from the man I'd seen twice now, the one unknown to me but who approached me at church and claimed I knew his name, sounded far-fetched to Keith, and even to my own ears when he'd repeated my question.

Ridiculous? Yes. Unless you're familiar with some of the delusions that drive people.

Without knowing it, Keith may have affirmed my sense at church that Sunday evening when he welcomed me to the world of celebrity and reminded me that people follow me now. I know he didn't mean they literally follow me, but . . .

I rolled over, turning my back to Keith, and stared into the ink of night.

Why was Keith dismissing my feelings? It wasn't intentional, I was certain. As he'd said that Sunday evening, he was attempting to reassure me. Perhaps, he'd done the same tonight.

God knew, I wanted reassurance. I wanted to feel safe.

But I also wanted respect. I needed Keith to respect both what I was feeling and the knowledge that supported those feelings.

Was I angry with Keith? Yes. But again, anger was new to me. Of course Keith and I had disagreements from time to time, but we worked through those issues.

Maybe I just needed to try harder to make

him understand what I was feeling.

Or maybe I was just making a big deal out of nothing. That was it, wasn't it? I was imagining things. Allowing the stress of this new life — marriage, success, celebrity — to get to me. It was all unfamiliar. My mind was looking for something wrong, when in fact, everything was right.

Like adding water to dilute an alcoholic beverage, the train of thought diluted my feelings and their impact. The anger I'd identified slowly dissipated and was replaced by a sense of, if not peace, at least calm.

And relief.

I turned back over and slid closer to Keith and wrapped my arm around him.

Eyelids weighted, my breathing slowed, and soon I felt myself drifting into what I was certain would be a deep, restorative sleep.

CHAPTER NINE

Adelia
May 5, 2017

With my backpack slung over one shoulder and my duffel bag dangling from my hand, I enter the house and drop the duffel and backpack in the entry hall. I brought just the necessary clothing — jeans, hiking boots, shorts, T-shirts, a swimming suit, and a few other items. I won't need much, even if I end up here longer than I hope. If all goes according to plan, I'll be long gone in five weeks, by mid-June. Maybe sooner.

I wander through the house to get my bearings, accompanied by the rumble of the river running behind the house. Riverfront property was one of the other essential items on my checklist when looking for a rental. After checking out the two bedrooms and kitchen, I wander into the small living room next to the kitchen and open the sliding glass door. I step onto the large deck that overlooks the middle fork of the Kaweah.

The river below rages, and I'm ravaged by its roar — assaulted by the memories the deafening sound draws from my depths, where I thought they were safely locked away. I turn and walk back into the house, shutting the door on the river.

I wander until I find the small laundry room, and finally the family room, where a leather sectional sits in front of a massive brick fireplace that covers almost the entire back wall. A large-screen TV placed at an angle in the corner faces the sectional, and the floor beneath the sofa is covered in a soft shag area rug. None of those items really interest me. The items I'd seen online that ticked the final box on my list are off to one side of the large room — a universal weight machine, a rack with free weights atop a dense rubber mat, and an exercise bike.

I go and perch on the bench of the universal machine, lean against the backrest, and reach for the bar above my head. I pull it down to chest level then loosen my grip and let the pulley system take it back up. I let go of the bar, get up, and go to the back of the machine, where I move the pin to increase the weight load.

I do a few stretches then sit back down and do reps until my shoulders burn.

By the time I've unpacked, unloaded my ice chest, and put away the groceries I've brought, it's late afternoon and the sun has already dropped behind the mountains. I have one more thing to do. I go back to the entry hall and dig through the backpack. I pull a phone out of one of the pockets, along with the charger. I tap the six-digit code into the phone — the code known only to me. Then I make the call I agreed to make before I left. I wait as the line rings. As soon as it's answered, I speak the words he's waited to hear. "I'm here."

I tap the icon on the phone's screen for the organizer app I use, log in with my password, and then scroll through the list of instructions, the timeline we've created, and additional notations. When I've read through everything, I close the app, make sure the phone is locked again, and then plug it in to charge in an outlet near the bar.

That done, I stand in the kitchen for several minutes, staring out the window. The house, even with the constant drone of the river, is still. Perhaps it's time to confront what's beyond the window. I cross the kitchen to the slider off the nook and step onto the deck. In the diffused light of late afternoon, I take in my surroundings and notice what I didn't take time to see when I arrived. From the deck, looking upriver, Moro Rock, that domed granite monolith, and snowcapped Alta Peak loom above, the sentries of Sequoia National Park.

I make my way to the deck's railing where the river roils just beyond the deck, frothing and angry.

Kaweah, the name given the river by the original people, the Yokuts, means "cry of the crow." The symbolism of the crow, that of death, meant nothing to me during the first summers we spent here. But that last summer changed that — it changed everything.

And now truth has unraveled the lies so tightly woven into our pasts.

Planted on the deck, I look out at the swirling water. "I won't die here — I won't let you have me!" I shout my vow, but my voice, even to my own ears, is lost to the tumult.

Has the river heard me and taken my oath as a dare? I would expect nothing less.

Something upstream flutters, a bird maybe, and draws my attention away from the water. But it's only Moro Rock I see.

Understanding comes as I stare at the dome. Moro will be *my* sentry while I'm here — a constant reminder of my Rock.

I am not alone.

There is One who goes before me and with me.

And my rage, the anger that matches that of the surging Kaweah below, is His anger. Righteous in all its fury. It is this anger that will drive me forward. That will push me beyond my own limits, leaving me fully dependent, despite the strength I've fought to build.

A breeze catches the mist from the crashing water beyond the deck, and I lift my face and let it cool my burning skin, and soul, allowing it to subdue my rage. But only for the moment.

Again, I take what I need from the river.

As we all did.

And as I will do again.

One final time.

CHAPTER TEN

Denilyn
January 12, 2017

As I head west on I-80, the sun breaks through the dark gray ceiling as it dips westward, making the distant cityscape glisten. A sea of red taillights separates me from the center of downtown Sacramento, also dubbed River City, at least forty-five minutes away at this rate. As I stop and start my way down the long, straight interstate to the valley floor, my mind floods like the swollen creeks and rivers have done this week. My tempest is within, raining unanswered questions and doubt.

I'm grateful for the counseling appointment I scheduled weeks ago. Although, I glance at the clock on my dash, I need to figure out a way to make my appointments with Heather at a different time of day. Rush hour traffic does nothing to assuage my nerves. More often than not, I'm a bundle of knots by the time I arrive at her office.

But it isn't just the traffic that knots my nerves this evening. My conversation with Willow highlighted what I already knew to be true. I am not moving forward the way I'd hoped. In fact, this week it feels as though I've taken ten steps back at least.

Why?

That's the prevailing unanswered question.

I circle the block, watching for a parking space to open near Heather's office housed in a brightly painted, two-story Victorian home converted to office space, as many of the downtown homes have been over the years. When a car pulls away from the curb right in front of the Victorian, I exhale my relief. I'm already a few minutes late.

I rush up the steps to the front door, enter the foyer, and then cross the living room turned waiting room. Just as I take a seat, Heather rounds the corner. "Deni, hello. Come in."

We chat about the holidays as we make our way down one of the hallways to her office, where I take my usual place in one corner of the overstuffed olive-green down sofa. I sink into the soft cushions and then reach for one of the throw pillows and pull it onto my lap.

Heather takes her seat across from me and smiles. "I know I've said this before, but with your dark hair, warm complexion, and green eyes — it looks like that sofa was made for you."

"I should buy it from you."

"What are you willing to pay?"

As we laugh, my shoulders relax. My appreciation for Heather has grown over the years I've seen her. When I knew I needed to begin processing with a therapist myself, I had a hard time finding someone in the community I hadn't either gone to school with, taught with, or worked with in one capacity or another. I knew I needed someone who specialized in trauma recovery. It was Jaylan who finally recommended Heather. Although she hadn't met her, she'd heard of her work through Gabe. Heather works with officers struggling with trauma encountered on the job and the accompanying PTSD symptoms.

When Heather picks up a pen and the yellow legal pad from the table next to her chair, I know she's ready to dive into our session.

"What are we talking about today?"

I sigh as reality brushes the smile from my face. "I'm . . . struggling."

Heather's expression grows serious. "In what way?"

"Nightmares, flashbacks . . . All the PTSD symptoms have started again. I'm not sure what triggered them."

"Monday was the anniversary, right? Was that the trigger?"

"Maybe, but I've done okay previous years." I shrug. "That, combined with the upcoming date, maybe? I'm not sure. This week has been the worst I've experienced since right after the attack, but . . . I think the symptoms began, subtly, a while back." I twist the fringe of the pillow on my lap. "About the date . . . I'm fixated on the calendar. It's becoming an issue."

"Have you received notification? Do you know the exact date yet?"

I shake my head. "No. I'm guessing. But it's coming. He's eligible for parole June 1st." This isn't news to Heather; we've discussed it many times. "But it's more than the anniversary, or his release. I can't pinpoint it. Maybe it's just . . . me." I swallow. "I can't escape my own mind. There's nowhere to go, to get away, to . . . make it all stop."

"Is it any wonder why alcoholism is prevalent among those who suffer with PTSD?"

I nod. "Alcohol is an escape, of sorts, but

it leads to more issues. I know that. Maybe for some it feels like the lesser of two evils."

"Yes, I'm sure that's true."

I shake my head. "I can't, I won't, go that route. It's more than just the nightmares and flashbacks though. I feel like something's wrong with me. I'm forgetting things, losing things . . . On Monday I had a panic attack. I was sure someone was watching me. But there wasn't anyone. It . . . it was just me, my imagination." I shift on the sofa, wrap my arms around the pillow, and pull it tight against my chest. "I'm beginning to understand how clients felt — the ones who said they were going crazy." I swallow the lump forming in my throat. "What's wrong with me?" I whisper.

Heather leans forward. "What would you tell those clients?" Her tone is gentle. "The ones who felt crazy?"

"I know, I've thought of that. I'd tell them to pay attention to what they're feeling. To talk through those feelings, work through them with someone. But . . ."

"But what?"

"I've done all that. I'm still doing it. I'm working to stay present, grounded. I'm breathing, counting, focusing on what's in front of me — anything to keep my mind from . . . going back. I'm exercising to stay

connected to my body. I've processed everything with you. With close friends. So . . .
why? Why do I still feel so . . . lost?"

"Tell me about what triggered the panic
attack. You said you felt like someone was
watching you?"

"Like I said, it was just my imagination."

"Are you sure? You know the biological
studies that support that *seventh sense.*
Most of us have experienced it at one time
or another. You feel it, then turn around,
and a child behind you in line at the grocery
store is staring at you."

"Yes, I'm familiar with the research. But
there wasn't anyone. It was a blustery day,
and when I looked around, no one was
there. Like everything else, there was nothing to substantiate my feelings."

"*Everything* else?"

I sigh. "You know what I mean."

Heather nods. "I do. You mentioned forgetting things and losing things. Talk to me
about that."

I wave her suggestion away. "They're
meaningless too. Just silly things."

Heather is silent for a moment. Then she
leans back in her seat, makes a note on her
pad, and looks back to me. "Do you remember what you told me about the first year of

your marriage — the issue you struggled with?"

"What does that have to do with anything?"

"Maybe nothing. How about humoring me, doctor?" She smiles.

"Fine. Yes, I remember."

"What was your primary struggle at that point?"

I think back until the memories, clear as if they'd just occurred, come back to me. "Well, initially I was upset that Keith was discounting what I felt — wasn't trusting what I knew both intellectually and instinctually. At least what I thought I knew once I stopped denying my feelings."

"What are your knowledge and instinct telling you now?"

I stare at Heather as I consider what she's asked. Then I set the pillow aside and lean forward. "But what I'm feeling, or . . . sensing, doesn't . . . fit."

"Why not?"

"Because . . ." I stop, heart pounding. "He — that man — is in prison. He can't get to me."

Heather's gaze is intent as she puts one hand over her heart and the other on her forehead. "Pay attention to what you know and what you feel, Deni. Pay attention."

I know exactly what she's saying — what she means. I need to trust myself now the same way I wanted Keith to trust me then. Somewhere along the way I've begun doubting myself. But trusting the knowledge I've garnered through years of education, work, and personal experience, and trusting my instincts means . . .

Tears prick my eyes.

The implications are too much.

It's all just too much. I double over.

"Breathe, Deni, breathe."

As I leave my appointment and get into my car, I pull my phone out of my purse to turn the ringer back on and notice I have two messages from a number I don't recognize. I cradle the phone between my ear and shoulder to listen to the messages as I buckle my seat belt. The first message is nothing but a hang-up. The second message is the same.

Just a wrong number, I assure myself.

I toss the phone back into my purse and start the SUV. Just before I pull out of the parking spot, the phone rings through the SUV's speakers and the same number appears on my screen on the dash. After several rings, hands trembling, I answer the call.

"Hello." I put the car back into PARK. "Hello?"

Though it sounds like someone is on the line, no one responds. I still and listen more closely until I'm sure of what I'm hearing through the speakers. Someone breathing.

"Who is this?" I whisper. My hands begin to tremble. "Who are you?" I've raised my voice and can hear the fear in my tone. I take a deep breath to steady myself. "What do you want?"

When there's still no response, I end the call, and then, as quickly as my shaking fingers will move, I pull my phone back out of my purse and block the number.

I stare out the front windshield until I stop trembling. I take a few deep, intentional breaths. It was just a wrong number. I'm overreacting.

Pay attention, Deni. Heather's words come back to me, along with my own unanswered question: *Why?*

Why have the PTSD symptoms returned?

Why do I feel like I'm losing my mind, myself, again?

I look at my hands, now gripping the steering wheel, knuckles white. My heartbeat still more rapid than it should be.

Do I really believe those calls were mistakes? Wouldn't the caller have known upon receiving my voice mail the first time that he or she had called the wrong number?

Mouth dry, I reach for the insulated tumbler in my cup holder and take a sip of water, then force myself to take a few more sips. I set the cup back into the holder, my movements slow, intentional, as I give my mind time to accept what it seems my body already knows.

As much as I want to believe the calls were made in error, it seems unlikely. And the pen my father gave me? While it's possible I inadvertently carried it out of my office, it's also unlikely. Like puzzle pieces, I turn over each event in my mind that's felt odd or crazy-making during the last several days, trying to make it fit into a picture I can see. The missing file from my computer's desktop, the pen showing up in my mailbox, a vehicle that followed me too close for comfort, and now a few calls.

A couple of other odd incidents come to mind.

Although I can't yet see the whole picture, pieces are falling into place. What I do see — and more importantly, perhaps, what I *feel* — is all too familiar.

Hauntingly familiar.

The only question that matters now is this: will I afford myself the respect I wanted from Keith?

I can't allow myself to slip into denial again. The last time I did that, the consequences were devastating. In so many ways.

I close my eyes.

I can't do this again. Any of it. I can't. Neither can I deny what I feel, nor can I face the . . . truth.

Truth. Is that what it is? *Oh Lord . . . Not again. Please. I can't go through this again.*

CHAPTER ELEVEN

Denilyn
November 2009

One week after the charm bracelet appeared, I sat at my desk, laptop open, working on my second book after a client had canceled her appointment at the last minute. I was grateful for the time to focus on the manuscript and, hopefully, make some progress. Between promoting the first book, seeing clients, and taking care of a home and spending time with Keith, which I hadn't done enough of recently, I'd had little time to write.

The sound of voices from behind the closed door of Jaylan's office and strains of the instrumental music we played in the waiting room drifted into my office. Outside the valley was draped in dense, cold fog, which hugged my windows and obscured the view beyond. My office was cast in the warm glow from my lamp, and I sipped a cup of steaming coffee as I lost myself in the words I wrote.

Later I'd have a vague recollection of hearing the outer door to the offices open and close, but I hadn't allowed it to disrupt my focus. Thirty minutes or so later, Jaylan's office door opened and she walked her client out. I stopped writing, checked the time, and stretched. I had another hour before my next client. Time to grab lunch and, maybe, finish the draft of the first chapter.

"Hey, I found another package for you sittin' on the reception desk." Jaylan came into my office and handed me a box. "Ever find out who sent that bracelet?"

"No. I don't know and I don't care. If I have a secret pal or admirer who wants to send me gifts, I'll take them." That was the attitude I'd adopted sometime between last week and today. It felt good not to worry about it. I glanced at the box. It was wrapped in the same brown paper, and the handwriting appeared to be the same as well.

"Okay, but if this is another anonymous gift from the same person, then that borders on weird." She raised her hands. "Just my opinion."

I rolled my eyes at Jay, unwilling to allow

her unsolicited opinion to douse my good mood.

"Don't leave me hangin'. Open it. I got work to do."

I picked up the box, tore the paper from its exterior, and opened the mailing box. Inside I discovered a small black velvet bag. I held it up for Jay to see. "More jewelry."

I opened the drawstring bag, peered inside, and then dumped the contents — a gold charm — onto my palm.

Jaylan leaned over my desk to see it. "What is it?"

I held out my hand. "The letter *I* for *Isabelle,* I assume." I smiled. "The bracelet is from someone who knows my middle name." There was comfort in that realization. "That narrows the list of suspects, I'd say."

"Nice." Jaylan raised one eyebrow. "Of course, anyone could find that information online."

"That's reassuring, Jay. Thanks."

"Anytime, sister." She laughed. "But I'm tellin' you, it is a little weird." She threw the quip over her shoulder as she left my office.

I stared at the charm a moment, and uncertainty rippled through me. No. I wouldn't let myself overthink the gifts. I dropped the charm back into the bag and then put the bag in my desk drawer. Maybe I'd take the bracelet to a jeweler and have the charm attached and wear the bracelet — might as well enjoy it. I crumpled the paper and tossed it, along with the mailing box, into the trash.

I decided I wouldn't bother telling Keith about the gift this time. He was right — as a public figure, people were following me. My social media numbers and the emails flooding my inbox had attested to that since the book hit the bestseller lists.

Maybe gifts like this just came with the territory.

After seeing my last client of the day, I opened my laptop again. Keith had let me know he planned to work late, so I determined I'd do the same and finish at least the first chapter of the new book and hopefully make some headway on the second chapter.

"Later, Deni. I gotta run." Jay swished by my office on her way out.

I relished the quiet — it was conducive to writing. But before I settled in, I got up and went to check the front door to make sure Jay had locked it on her way out. Then I made myself a cup of decaf and got to work. The only interruptions during the first hour came when my office line rang a few times, but each time the caller hung up rather than leaving a message. Not too unusual in a counseling office. It could take time to muster the courage to leave a message for a counselor.

But sometime during the second hour, a rustling sound drew my attention to one of the two large side-by-side windows in the office. Night had fallen, making it difficult to see outside except for the dim beam of light thrown from the streetlamp at one end of the parking lot. I glanced back to the screen and reread the last sentence I'd written when something rustled again, this time accompanied by a squeal, like something scratching glass. A branch from the bush in front of the window, maybe?

I got up from my desk and walked to the window. The bush in front of the window shuddered as I approached, and again came the squeal. The sharp tip of a branch moved against the glass. The wind must have picked up. I cupped one hand on the window and peered out. The fog had thinned but still haloed the light from the streetlamp, which shone on a group of redwoods at that end of the parking lot. But as I watched the trees, not a bough swayed.

When the bush below me rustled again, I

stepped back from the window and quickly closed the blinds. If it wasn't wind that shook the bush, what was it? I paced my office until I came up with a reasonable explanation — a cat or maybe even a raccoon or opossum was likely in the bush. The office complex was just a few blocks up from the American River, and it wasn't unusual to see wildlife occasionally.

I chided myself for my anxiety and sat back at my desk. It was then I recalled the charm in my drawer and the sound of someone coming into the office earlier in the day, not long before Jaylan found the box on the reception desk. Had someone delivered the gift again, or had it come with the mail this time? I bent and pulled my trash can out from under the desk and pulled the crumpled paper out. I checked it for a postmark, as I had after opening the first box that held the bracelet.

Again, just my name and address were scrawled on the paper. No postmark, and whoever it was from hadn't wasted money on postage this time. I crumpled the paper again and tossed it back into the can. Whether or not the boxes were postmarked didn't change anything. The gifts were nothing to fear.

Though, alone in the suite of offices, the

nonchalant stance I'd adopted over the last week didn't offer much comfort.

There was something odd about the gifts, wasn't there? *Weird,* as Jay had said.

I sat back at my desk and stared at the screen of the laptop, but the focus I'd enjoyed in the warmth of my office earlier in the day had fled. Instead, clarity was elusive. The fog that had lingered most of the day seemed to have seeped into my mind. I shivered, so I got up and went to check the thermostat in the hallway. As I reached to turn up the heat, something rattled. I dropped my hand from the thermostat and froze.

Someone was outside the office door rattling the handle. Were they trying to get in? The whooshing sound of my pulse in my ears was dizzying. I crept down the hall and peeked around the corner to the front door. The handle rattled again, and this time I could see the slight movement of the handle on the interior side of the door. Why hadn't I set the alarm when I'd made sure the door was locked?

I dashed back to my office, reached for the phone, and punched 9-1-1 into the keypad. When the operator answered, I reported my emergency.

■ ■ ■ ■

"Ma'am, if you're ready to leave, I'll walk you out." The deputy who'd taken my statement waited as I grabbed my purse and set the alarm before we left the office.

After locking the door, I pointed to my car in one of the spaces across from the office suite. "That's it." The other deputy was sitting in the driver's seat of the squad car where he'd gone to make a call.

When we reached my car, I got inside and the deputy leaned down before closing my door. "If we receive complaints from others in the office park, we'll let you know."

I appreciated his comment, though I felt a little foolish. As they'd taken my report, they asked if it was possible a client who'd made a mistake about an appointment time had tried the office door. Of course it was possible. Jaylan and I both saw clients one evening a week. But I hadn't considered that possibility when I made my call. Actually, there were several possibilities, all of them harmless, but they hadn't occurred to me at the height of my anxiety.

And although I'd told them about the gifts I'd received, and even mentioned the man I'd seen at the book signing and church, they had little to go on, and really no reason to link those events to someone outside the office door.

"Give us a call if you need anything or if anything else comes to mind." He gestured toward their car. "We'll follow you out."

"Thank you."

He pushed my door shut and walked back to the squad car. Once I could see that he was inside, I backed out of the parking space and drove out of the parking lot. They followed me several blocks to the eastbound on-ramp to Interstate 50, where I turned off to head home.

I'd called Keith before I left the office, and he'd said he would meet me at home. I was grateful I wouldn't walk into an empty house. Some time at home together would also give me an opportunity to talk with him about what I was feeling.

Although I wanted to believe, as he did, that everything was all right. I knew otherwise. I wasn't all right, and that was something we'd both need to deal with, whatever that looked like. I suspected a generalized anxiety disorder triggered by the stress of a year filled with change and increased demands.

When I pulled into the driveway of our

home, the house was dark, inside and out. Neither of us had thought to leave the porch light on when we left that morning. I clicked the garage door opener and remembered the bulb on the opener had gone out over the weekend.

The fog that had burned off closer to the city was still a thick fleece blanketing our suburban neighborhood. I sat in the driveway, headlights shining into the empty garage, and hoped the headlights coming down the street were Keith's, but the car drove past our house. I reached for my phone and called him, but there was no answer.

Still shaken from my earlier experience at the office, I didn't look forward to walking through the dark garage and into the dark house alone.

But it was that or drive around the neighborhood until Keith showed up. I was tired and ready to soak the tension I held in my body in a tub of hot water sprinkled with lavender bath salts. I sighed and pulled into the garage.

With the headlights off, the garage was black as pitch. I sat in the dark car for a moment, then gathered my belongings and got out of the car. I used the flashlight app on my phone to light my way to the door into the house. Once at the door, I flicked off the flashlight on my phone and dropped the phone into my purse. I couldn't hold the phone, my purse, briefcase, keys, and open the door. In the dark again, I felt for the door handle and keyhole as though reading braille. I thought again about the movement outside the window of the office and the way I'd seen the door handle turn, and my heart beat more rapidly and my breaths became shallow.

I fumbled with the key, working to insert it into the lock as quickly as possible. As I did, frustration with Keith simmered. Not only had he promised to meet me at home, knowing I was shaken, but he'd also said he'd change the bulb when I mentioned it last Sunday afternoon.

He'd done neither.

When I finally got the door unlocked, I tapped the switch to close the garage door, and then I stepped inside, flicked on a light switch, and turned and locked the door to the garage. I dropped my purse and briefcase and leaned against the door to catch my breath.

Was my frustration justified? Yes, but I also knew I was on edge, so I turned a deaf ear to the accusations running amok in my mind. As my heart rate slowed and my breathing returned to normal, I walked through the downstairs and flipped on lights, including the porch light so at least Keith wouldn't arrive home to darkness.

When my phone rang, relief surged. Surely it was Keith calling with an apology for not getting here before I did. But when I pulled the phone from my purse, I didn't recognize the caller's number, so I let voice mail answer.

When the phone dinged, letting me know I had a message, I checked it to make sure it wasn't Keith calling from another number. I stood at the kitchen counter and listened to the voice mail, but no one was there. Just as I was about to hang up, a sound on the recording caught my attention. I strained to hear the faint, rhythmic sound, which I soon identified as someone breathing.

The "message" went on and on.

Hands shaking, I ended the call before the message finished playing. An anxiety disorder? Maybe. Or was I deluding myself? Was it possible the person who sent the charm bracelet also knew my middle name and had my cell phone number?

As much as I wanted to ignore the thought, it pestered.

CHAPTER TWELVE

Adelia
May 6, 2017

It's just before eight on Saturday morning when I pull into the gravel lot of Ride the Kaweah, one of the most popular and respected white-water adventure companies on the river. As I pull the Jeep up next to the group of storage units where rafts, kayaks, and gear are stored, the illusion of déjà vu threatens to overtake me.

As I get out of the Jeep, I expect to see Ryan's truck parked off to the side of the property. He'd already be here by now, checking his watch as I pulled in, that wry smile on his face, Ray-Bans hanging from a cord around his neck.

But this is no time for illusions.

There is, however, little that distinguishes the property from the last time I was here more than a decade ago, and today. The old school bus, painted blue, used to transport rafters to the commercial put-ins, sits just where it always sat, and Mick's truck, as old as the bus, outfitted with racks for kayaks, is parked at an angle in front of the office.

I grab my backpack and make my way to the ramshackle building that houses the office. When I enter, Mick is on the phone taking a reservation. He pushes a couple of forms across the counter in my direction, along with a pen.

I pick up the papers — a W2 and an emergency contact form — and quickly fill them out. When I glance back at Mick, I see him eyeing me as he talks — his eyes rove over my bare shoulders and biceps exposed by the tank top I'm wearing. The look he gives me when our eyes meet is neither lascivious or embarrassed. Instead, his quick nod assures me he thinks I can still handle the physically grueling job of navigating a raft down the narrow chutes and rapids of the Kaweah or pulling an involuntary swimmer back into the raft.

When he hangs up, he doesn't say anything in the way of greeting. Neither of us has much to say, we covered the necessary ground late yesterday afternoon over drinks on the deck of The Gateway where the pounding rapids beneath us drowned our words to all but our ears, which is why I'd suggested we meet there.

I hand him the forms I've completed, along with copies of my first aid, CPR, and swift water rescue certifications, all of which I updated over the last six weeks. He takes the copies, then glances at the forms I completed. After reading what I've filled in, he looks back to me, his weathered face pale, but still he says nothing. He turns and shoves the forms into the top drawer of a rusted metal filing cabinet, then comes around the counter and heads out the door. He looks over his shoulder at me. "You coming?"

Outside he gives me a brief tour, opening the storage units and another shed, pointing out PFDs, helmets, paddles, oars, splash suits, and the like.

"Nothing much has changed," I observe.

"A lot has changed, including the locks." He tosses me a key. "That fits the padlock on the gate and the locks on the storage units and sheds. When you get here in the mornings, unlock everything."

I tuck the key into a zippered pocket in my shorts.

"You remember the orientation drill?"

I consider his question for a moment. "Mostly."

"You do it this morning. I'll check you."

I help Mick, who's owned Ride the Kaweah for almost three decades, pull out gear as the other guides show up and then customers who've made reservations for today. We'll send out two groups: one this morning — experienced rafters who've paid for a guide to take them down the almost nonstop class IV rapids, and a second group later in the day for the lower section of the river only, made up of mostly class III rapids.

At 9:00 a.m. Mick puts fingers in his mouth and lets out a shrill whistle. "Gather up!" He walks to a large cottonwood shading one edge of the property and waits until everyone has joined him under the tree.

"This here is Adelia." Mick jerks a thumb my way. "Or . . . Addie, as she's known around here."

My breath catches upon hearing the nickname, and my eyes meet Mick's. He stares at me a moment and then continues. "You call her whatever you want. The important thing is that you listen to her now, and listen good."

Listen well, I think. But then I remember it isn't my education that got me here. It's my experience. I hesitate, but only briefly, then step forward.

I look over the group, a mix of men and

women, friends come to add to their own list of experiences, and a handful of guides. All the guides are new to me and young. So young. Or maybe it's just that I've aged and I'm more aware of that here than anywhere else.

"Good morning. Looks like a great day for a trip down the river — blue skies and high, fast water." I smile, but I can't hold the expression. "But never forget, the Kaweah is a killer. Drowning is the number one cause of death in Sequoia National Park. Take that stat seriously. Thus far, I don't know of any . . . deaths" — my eyes meet Mick's again — "on a *commercial* trip. Let's keep it that way."

A couple of guys who've already established themselves as the clowns of the group stand at the back. One of them mutters something, and they both laugh then slap high fives. It's clear they aren't listening and are distracting those around them.

I pick up one of the PFDs. "Excuse me." I point to the guy who made the remark, whatever it was. "You, in the plaid shorts, join me up here, please."

His buddy slaps him on the back. "Way to go, bro!" A few others laugh.

The guy, his chest bare, saunters up to me, looks me up and down, gestures to the bandanna tied around my head, and lifts one eyebrow. "Blond or brunette?"

"Put this on." I hand him the PFD.

"That's going to make for some awkward tan lines."

"If you're here to work on your tan, you're in the wrong place. See those wetsuits and splash jackets?" I point to the pile of suits and jackets. "Those are going to ensure you don't get tan lines. Happy?"

"I'm just messing with you." His teeth gleam in his tanned face as he smiles at me. "You didn't answer my question." He points at the bandanna.

"Oh, right." I pull off the bandanna. "Neither." I turn so he can see the tattoo. His eyes widen. "You're messing with the wrong woman," I hiss under my breath.

He raises his hands in surrender, but the smirk on his face suggests he wouldn't mind messing with me. But he complies and slips into the life vest.

"Buckle it up." I tell him loudly enough so the group can hear. "People, this is your PFD, or personal flotation device. If you're taking this trip, you're experienced rafters, so you're familiar with the device. But just to refresh your memory, you want the vest to fit snugly." I pull the straps on the guy's vest, making sure it's tight enough. "If you

141

can lift the vest up to your ears, it's too loose. You will wear the vest at all times while on the river."

As I go through the orientation, I'm surprised by how naturally the information still flows. I talk about the necessity of the suits in the frigid water, footwear, and the inevitable, falling out of the raft.

"When one of you falls out, and more than one of you will, you need to immediately assume a defensive position. Roll to your back and keep your feet up — toes out of the water. That way, if you hit a rock, your feet take the blow. Never, under any circumstance, do you want to try and stand up in the water. The rocky bottom of the river can entrap your foot, and the current will pull you under. As soon as you're able, swim aggressively back to your raft or the raft nearest you."

Twenty or so minutes later, I wind up the spiel and turn to Mick. "Anything else?"

"Nope." He turns and walks away.

As rafters clamber out of the bus at the put-in, I pick up one end of a raft, another guide at the other end, and we lift it over our heads and make our way down the river's bank, stepping across rocks and boulders. We put in just above Gateway Rapid. Within minutes of getting into the raft, we'll have to paddle as a team to slalom our way through a 250-yard, boulder-strewn rapid, then work to avoid the hydraulics at the bottom — those churning, foamy holes below the drop of the many ledges the Kaweah is known for. Holes that can trap a raft full of people in their powerful grip.

The Gateway churns below, spray from the crashing rapid carrying on the breeze, creating prisms of color as the sun shines through the airborne droplets. I survey the rapid and then turn to see Moro Rock and Alta Peak, and take strength from their immovable stance. The easy part of my day has already passed. But I didn't return to Three Rivers for ease.

I turn back to face the Kaweah, a river I haven't rafted since that last fateful day almost eleven years ago.

I vowed I'd never step foot in this water again. But today I will conquer the Kaweah once more.

I have come to conquer.

And the Kaweah, with its parade of power, is a weak adversary compared to the other I've come to defeat.

The one I must defeat.

But I have not come alone.

I cannot do this alone.

CHAPTER THIRTEEN

Denilyn
January 26, 2017

After my morning class, I take advantage of a break in the weather, slip into my coat, and head across campus to the coffeehouse attached to the cafeteria. When I come out from under the shelter of trees, the sky expands before me — dark thunderheads to the east set the backdrop for patches of azure, brilliant in-between white puffs of clouds in the foreground. The air is crisp, clean. I relish the rare moment of peace and vow to work harder to keep my mind from spinning through my memories as it has for the past few weeks.

When I swing the door open and step into the Bean, I'm met by the aroma of coffee mixed with the warm scent from a wood fire crackling in the large, rock fireplace. Students sprawl on the upholstered chairs and sofas set in front of the fire, while others sit at tables, books or laptops open, heads down. The mood is relaxed as students and faculty alike have settled into the new semester. The murmur of voices, punctuated by occasional laughter, adds to the welcome the place extends.

I set my briefcase on an empty table, take out my wallet, and get into line to place my order.

A voice behind me speaks just above a whisper near my ear. "Let me guess — a medium half-caff, low-fat latte with a swirl of caramel."

I laugh as I turn around. "You English professors have great memories."

"It's all that reading we do — it's good for the mind."

"It serves you well, obviously. But I was planning on having the latte fully leaded. It's still early in the day."

"Ah, that's right. You only cut back on the caffeine after, what is it, 2:00 p.m.?"

"It depends on how the day is going."

"I see." Jon places his hand on my shoulder and nudges me around. "You're up."

As I place my order, he steps forward and hands the young woman at the register his credit card. "I've got this."

"No, I've got it. But, thank you."

"C'mon, allow me a small pleasure."

Before I can protest again, he's placing his own order. Coffee. Black. When he's finished paying, I follow him to the counter where we'll pick up our drinks.

I pick up a few napkins. "Are you staying? Or do you have a class?"

"I have thirty minutes before a meeting with a student. My next class isn't until after lunch."

"Would you . . ." I hesitate, not wanting to give him the wrong impression, but I enjoy his company, and he's seemed clear during our last couple of conversations that I'm only able to offer him friendship. "I have a table if you'd like to join me for a few minutes."

"I'd like that." The barista hands him his cup of coffee. "Have a seat. I'll wait for your latte."

I start to argue with him, but I know it's useless. He's a gentleman through and through. "Thank you, I'll do that."

As I take my seat, Ryan enters the Bean. He stops to talk with a student briefly, then walks toward the counter. When he sees me, he detours and comes over to the table.

"Hey, you here for a few minutes? I'll join you. Can I order something for you?"

"Oh, I . . ." I glance from Ryan to Jon, who's coming our way, and then back.

146

"Sure, join us."

"Us? If you're meeting with someone —"

"Ryan. Good to see you." Jon sets my latte on the table then holds out his hand to Ryan.

Ryan hesitates for just a second before shaking Jon's hand, or was that my imagination?

"I invited Ryan to join us."

"Great. Can I get you something?" Jon sets his cup of coffee down.

"No, thanks. Actually, I need to get back to my office." Ryan looks to me. "Deni, I have a situation with a student I'd like to discuss with you. Do you have time this afternoon?"

"Sure. After my last class?"

"See you then." He turns and walks back out of the café without ordering anything.

Jon pulls out a chair. "Did he seem a little tense?"

"Ryan?" I laugh. "*Intense.* It's his middle name. We're old friends."

"Ah, I don't know him well. Seems like you have a great group of people in your department."

"We do. I'm very fortunate."

"It's more than fortune. You're good at what you do, Deni. You're a gifted leader who's developed a strong team."

147

I wrap my hands around the warm latte cup. "Thank you. I haven't felt like much of a leader recently, so I appreciate the reminder."

He studies me a moment. "Are you okay?"

The gentleness of his tone and the compassion I read in his expression are like rainfall on parched land. Not that others in my life don't care, but beyond Jaylan and Heather, I haven't opened up much.

Before I catch myself, I sigh, exposing more than I'd intended. "I'm so-so, I guess."

Again, the response I see in his expression, his body language, is one of understanding, and I realize how much his own pain, the grief he's still dealing with, has impacted him — changed him.

"I'm just" — unexpected tears prick my eyes, and I look down at the table — "struggling a little bit."

"I'm here to listen if you'd like to talk."

I dab at the corners of my eyes with one of the napkins and give myself a moment to consider my response. Then I look back up. "You're familiar with the flight or fight response, I assume?"

He nods.

"I'm flying high and fast." I try to smile, but the effort proves feeble.

"So you'd prefer not to talk about it?"

"I often know what's helpful emotionally, but that doesn't mean I always do it." I shrug. "But . . . I would like to find some balance or middle ground. So if you're game . . . ?"

"I'm game."

"Okay." I reach for another napkin. "After the attack" — I've told him enough that he knows what I'm referring to — "I suffered with symptoms of post-traumatic stress disorder for quite some time. Therapy helped. Applying techniques to stay present helped." I look up from the napkin I've folded into quarters. "But . . . recently, the symptoms have returned and I'm not sure why. Actually, I'm . . . afraid. Afraid of why the symptoms have returned and what they may mean."

I take a deep breath and lean back. It's the first time I've named the fear out loud. I am afraid of what's behind the symptoms. Afraid my instinct is accurate. That my body is alerting me to something my mind knows but that I've yet to process or accept. Something I've experienced before, I remind myself. Again, the implications of that possibility threaten to overwhelm me, as they did in Heather's office two weeks ago and as I drove home that night. I haven't let my mind go there much since then.

"May I ask you a question?"

I nod.

"Suppose you landed, just for a few minutes, what would that look like?"

"Are you sure your doctorate's in English and not psych?"

He laughs. "Very sure."

"That's such a wise question. It might look like . . . stillness. Rather than flight, running from my fear, or fight, confronting my fear, it's maybe just . . . sitting with my fear for a time, or maybe even relinquishing the fear?"

"Sometimes in stillness, when we've quieted our minds, we hear from God."

There's no judgment in Jon's tone, nothing accusatory. Just gentleness. Maybe it's that gentleness that leads me to consider what he's said. And it's something I haven't considered in a very long time.

"I used to believe that. Or maybe I still believe it, but I just haven't practiced it much."

"Listening for God?"

I nod. "It's not as easy as it used to be." I look away, and again I expect an admonition, but none comes. Then I look back at Jon. "May I ask you something now?"

"Anything."

After your wife died, how did you still

believe in God's goodness? How did you, how *do* you, trust Him?"

He ponders my question a moment, then leans forward and rests his arms on the table. "I made the choice to trust Him. It's a choice I still make, every day."

"Even when you don't feel like you can trust Him?"

"Especially on those days. But honestly, Deni, I don't think trust is a feeling. I believe it's a choice. And on those days when doubt plagues me, I ask for His help to believe what I can't see. That's faith, believing what we can't see. And in this world, we can't always see goodness."

Again, I have the sense of having lived in a dry land for much too long, and Jon, through his words, his faith, has offered me a glass of cool water to slake my thirst.

"Thank you," I whisper.

After my last class, I spend almost twenty minutes talking with two students about a group project I've assigned. When we've finished our discussion, I make my way upstairs to my office. When I get there, my office door is open and Ryan is sitting in the chair across from my desk.

"How'd you get in here?" I come around the desk.

"Your door was open."

"What? Open or unlocked?"

"Both. Just like it is now. I figured you forgot to close and lock it when you left. When I realized you weren't here, I thought maybe you'd just run out for a minute, so I sat down. When you didn't come right back, I decided to sit here and keep an eye on things."

"Thanks." I look around the office. Everything seems to be in its place. "I've never forgotten to close and lock the door. In fact, I remember locking it because I had to come back in and get my keys out of my coat pocket."

"Is it possible you grabbed the keys but forgot to close and lock the door?"

"No." It wasn't possible, was it? I'm hypervigilant about that kind of thing.

Ryan shrugs. "I don't know what to tell you. Janitor, maybe?"

"In the middle of the day? That makes no sense."

I drop into my chair and reach for the phone. "Give me a minute. I need to check with facilities."

"I can wait in my office."

"No, no." I put the phone down. "I'm sorry. I'll call them when we're finished. I've already kept you waiting." Again, I survey the office. Had someone come in? If so, why?

"Deni?"

"Yes, sorry. You mentioned a situation with a student . . ."

"Yeah, but listen, really, if you'd rather do this later —"

"No. Now is good."

Ryan looks around the office, then looks back at me. "Oh, this rattles you, right? I'm sorry, I should have realized."

"I'm not . . ." I sigh. "Yes, it's a little unnerving. Since coming back to school last week, I've had several odd occurrences. Things like this. I'm sure I locked the door."

"I believe you. But we all forget things once in a while. Isn't it possible —"

"No. I've doubted myself enough. This time I'm certain."

"Okay. Listen, why don't you check it out. Make that call, and we'll talk later."

I exhale my frustration. "Okay. Thank you." As Ryan gets up to leave, I reach for the phone again. "Hey, wait a minute. What happened at the Bean this morning? One minute you were going to join us, the next you had to get back to your office. What was that about?"

He pauses at the door and turns back toward me. "I didn't want to interrupt." His tone is tight.

"You weren't. I told you to join us."

He looks down at the floor. When he looks back up, his emotions are no longer curtained and there's misery in his eyes. "I've seen the way you look at him, Deni."

I shake my head. "No, there's . . . we're friends. That's all. We're just friends."

"Whatever you say. I'll catch you later." He turns and walks out.

Phone still in my hand, I look down at the desktop. I forget sometimes how well Ryan knows me. Maybe better than I know myself.

But it's more than that, isn't it?

While we seem to maneuver around it fairly well most of the time, it's always there, the issue between us. Ryan has expressed his feelings for me through the years. Once was just about a year after Adelia left us, although — I close my eyes and let the memories wash over me — that wasn't the first time.

I open my eyes, set down the phone, and reach up and massage my temples.

Adelia . . .

She and Ryan had such a tumultuous, passionate relationship. And ultimately so tragic. When Ryan told me he was in love with me after all he'd gone through with

Adelia, I was certain his feelings were just confused. In the same way I'd felt certain he was confused the first time he confessed his love for me.

But I didn't, I don't, feel that way about him.

So we've choreographed an intricate dance that allows us to remain friends and continue to work together as we sidestep the issue. But I know it's a dance that costs Ryan. And occasionally, like today, I see the price he pays when, for just a moment, he lets down his guard and I see the pain in his eyes.

Whatever it is he has felt for me, it's still there.

Grief, like an angry sea, tosses, and its waves crash over me. So much grief over the last decade. So much loss for all of us. Perhaps the greatest loss was that of our innocence.

Sometimes I fear I'll drown in the churning waves of grief.

But as I stare at the empty office, what I can only describe as a vision comes to me. A hand reaches for me in that sea. A strong hand, the hand of One offering to save me.

I swallow the ache in my throat as I recall Jon's words. *Trust is a choice.*

But is it a choice I can make again?

■ ■ ■ ■

After speaking with individuals in both the facilities and security departments of the university, I have no answer about my office door. No one in the facilities department had any reason to be in my office, and the janitorial staff, as I know, won't come in until tonight. And because this building is the oldest on the campus, it's one of the few that doesn't yet have security cameras. At least not upstairs where the offices are housed. Only classrooms downstairs are monitored. Cameras for the upstairs offices and hallways are part of next year's budget.

There's no way to know if I left the door open or if someone else unlocked it.

Ryan is probably right — I grabbed my keys and walked out without locking the door. Honestly, I can't imagine it. But neither do I specifically remember locking it — it's such an automatic action. The last thing I remember was going back to get the keys out of my coat pocket. Was I interrupted after that? I don't recall. My mind was likely elsewhere. Which means it is possible I didn't lock the door.

I get up from my desk where I've spent the last hour either on the phone talking about the door or stewing about it. I walk out of my office and poke my head into Ryan's office. "Have a few minutes now to talk?"

He pushes away from the computer and rubs his eyes. "Yeah."

"Do you mind coming back to my office? I left the door open."

He chuckles. "Good one." Then he gets up and follows me next door. "Did you find out anything?"

"No. You're probably right. Maybe I was preoccupied and never closed it."

"Well, as long as nothing's missing, no damage done, right?"

"I suppose." Ryan takes the chair across from my desk again, but this time I pull up the chair from the corner of my office and sit in it so we can talk without the barrier of the desk between us. "So, back to the student you wanted to talk about . . ."

"Yeah, it's Willow. That's why I wanted to mention it to you."

"Willow? That surprises me. What's going on?"

"She didn't show up for my classes this week. Second week of the semester? Seemed odd. As a TA, she's supposed to let me know if she can't be there. Which, obviously, you know. I haven't seen her since last Friday.

Have you heard anything? Talked to her?

I shake my head. "No. I did have a conversation with her last week, but she didn't mention anything related to school. Have you checked with any of her other instructors?"

"No. If it were anyone else, I might not think much of it. But because of your recommendation" — he shrugs — "it seemed worth asking you about."

"Let me do a little checking. I'd like to give her the benefit of the doubt — she does have some things going on, but I don't know the impact they're having."

"Yeah, all right." He hesitates. "So . . ." His gaze shifts from me to the window. When he looks back, he appears troubled. "Does Willow remind you of anyone?"

I'm slow to respond, but then I nod. "I wondered if you'd see it."

"Adelia." Her name is just a whisper on his lips.

"Yes. She reminds me of a young Adelia." Or at least what I imagine she looked like at that age. She was several years older when we met her. "Actually, I was just thinking about her."

"Yeah, me too."

"How does that feel — that reminder?"

He stares past me for several seconds then

gets up. "Let me know what you find out about Willow, okay?" When he reaches the door, he pauses, his back still to me. "Have a good weekend."

"Ryan?"

He walks out of the office and doesn't turn back. Maybe that answers the question I asked him. I get up and move the chair back to the corner of my office, then go and stand at the window. A sprinkling of rain spatters the walkways and parking lot below, and dark, thick clouds blanket the sky above. But as I let my mind wander back, all of that recedes and I see Adelia, as she was when we first met. Long, dark hair, flawless creamy complexion, and her eyes — green, but a deeper shade than my own.

Ryan used to say her eyes were the color of the deep pools of the Kaweah and mine were the lighter color of the water as it plunged over boulders and rocky ledges.

I always wondered if there wasn't something more to that analogy.

Adelia and I were often asked if we were sisters, so alike were our looks. Me of Italian descent, Adelia Latino. Yet the similarities, at least physically, were striking. Well, except for the tattoos — we didn't share those in common. I smile at the memory.

Willow, with her blond hair and light

complexion, doesn't physically resemble Adelia, as much as her mannerisms; and her inflections when she speaks are a reminder. But more than that, there was a look I'd see in Adelia's eyes — a look I also recognize in Willow's eyes.

It's the same look I've seen staring back at me from my own mirror.

Has Ryan recognized that look?

It's the look of fear.

But what did Adelia fear? And what about Willow?

I may never know.

CHAPTER FOURTEEN

Denilyn
December 2009

Keith and I were in the process of buying our home when I received the advance for my first contracted book, which enabled us to pay for a few upgrades. The extra Keith was most interested in was wiring for a surround sound system in the bonus room upstairs. In my mind, granite countertops in the kitchen were the nonnegotiable upgrade. As it turned out, after the advance, we could afford both.

I wiped the speckled black granite countertops, flecks of copper flashing like licks of flames ready to devour. Then I rinsed my hands at the sink, dried them, and went to the base of the stairs and yelled up to Keith. "They'll be here any minute. Can you come down and help?"

I felt more than heard the edge in my tone, and I didn't like it. We'd argued when he didn't meet me at home as he'd said he would after the incident at the office several days ago. His excuse that he'd stopped to talk with someone on his way out of the office and "got caught up" in conversation about the Sacramento Kings point guard hadn't sit well. Hadn't I made it clear how distressed I felt?

Wasn't I a priority, or my security a priority?

I'd continued to wrestle with those feelings, along with my rising anxiety, since that evening, and we'd had little time together since then to make amends. We needed to work through the issues, and I also needed to forgive him, I knew.

"Keith?"

I climbed the stairs and found him sitting on the floor of the bonus room, earphones on his head, a movie on the big-screen TV. Irritation bubbled, but I turned down the burner and placed my hand on his shoulder. When he looked up at me, I bent down, intending to give him a lingering kiss — an act of forgiveness.

But I hesitated.

Could I trust Keith to consider my needs?

Instead of kissing him, I lifted the headphones off one of his ears. "Hey, they'll be here any minute."

"Yeah, okay." He pulled the headphones off and hung them around his neck. "Maybe we can try out the sound system and all watch this" — he gestured to the movie on the screen — "after dinner. The base will rock the whole house."

I glanced at the screen where an explosion had ignited a nighttime sky. "We'd have to sit on the floor."

Keith looked around the almost completely unfurnished room. "Good point."

It was the first time in almost a year of marriage that we'd invited friends for dinner. We'd meant to do it sooner, but time hadn't allowed. Or, more accurately stated, we hadn't made the time. But entertaining wasn't the only thing we'd neglected. The house was just barely furnished. We'd joked that we were going for a minimalist look, but the truth was, we were both so focused on work, we hadn't taken the time to make the house a home. The stark walls of the bonus room mocked me. I made a silent vow to slow down and shift my focus.

I needed to focus on our marriage, including the home and family we hoped to create together.

I hoped Keith could do the same.

"You want that on the table?" Jay stood at

the island in our kitchen as I pulled the chicken dish I made out of the oven.

"No, thanks. I'll take care of it."

Ryan sauntered in from the family room. "You go sit down; I'll help her," he said to Jay.

"No, I'm helpin' her."

"You're the one always talking about equal rights for women, yet a man steps in to help and you —"

"Oh, now you're gonna pay attention to —"

"Will you two never stop? Both of you go sit down." I pointed to the dining room — the table and chairs were some of the few pieces of furniture we'd purchased. "I've got this covered. But thank you."

When we were finally all seated and dinner was served, I relaxed and smiled. Despite our bare walls, this was what a home was meant for, sharing a meal with your closest friends.

"You been holdin' out on me? This is fantastic. I need this recipe." Jay took another bite of the chicken I'd made.

"I found the recipe online. I'll email you the link."

"Reminds me of something Mrs. Westerville used to make when I worked their farm. She'd serve their big meal at lunchtime, remember?"

Ryan wiped his mouth with his napkin, then dropped it back into his lap. "Do you ever hear from the Westervilles?"

"They sent us a wedding gift and a card at Christmas. I keep meanin' to get back there for a weekend and introduce them to Gabe. But . . ." Jay shrugged then met my eyes across the table.

I knew what her shrug meant. *But it's hard to go back.*

"Yeah, I'd like to meet them sometime." Gabe speared another bite of chicken with his fork.

"I'd like to check out the famous Three Rivers," Keith added. "Sounds like you three had some great times there." Keith looked from me to Ryan and back. "You two could take us down the river."

"My days on that river are over." I shot Keith a look that I hoped implied this wasn't a topic to pursue.

"Well, you don't have to act as our guide. Ryan could take us down, or we could go with that company you worked for. What was it called?"

I was learning that Keith often missed the subtleties I hoped he'd understand.

"Ride the Kaweah," Ryan responded. "Actually, I talked to Mick recently." He looked at Keith and Gabe. "He's the owner." Then he addressed all of us again. "I'm was thinking of going back this summer to lead trips for a month or two, depending on how long the water lasts."

I stared at Ryan, my mouth agape. "What?" I was stunned as much by Ryan's nonchalant tone as I was by the idea that he could so easily return to Three Rivers.

"How could you . . ." Jay shook her head. "I will never understand you."

"I didn't ask you to understand. I just thought that while I'm still" — he raised his eyebrows at Gabe and Keith — "*unencumbered,* I may as well do what I enjoy. As it turns out, Mick can't use me, so I'm not going. But maybe next year." Then something flickered in Ryan's eyes, a flash of emotion I couldn't discern. He looked down at the table, then back to the group, but as he spoke, it was clear he was speaking to Jaylan and me. "It's time to face some things. Demons, if you will. At least it's time for me to do so. We each handle things in our own way, right?"

It was Gabe who responded. "Right, man. Do what you need to do." Then, sensing the tension at the table, I guessed, Gabe redirected the conversation. "So Deni, I hear you met some of Sac County's finest at the office the other night. Had a little action over there?"

Ryan reached for his water glass. "Action?"

"Not action, exactly." Embarrassed, I laughed. "More like an active imagination."

"You don't know that." Jaylan came to my defense. "That wasn't the only odd thing you've had goin' on lately."

"What do you mean?" Ryan asked.

"It's nothing, really." I glanced at Keith. "Probably just an overzealous reader. Someone who identified with the book maybe."

"She saw some guy at the beginning of her book tour — at a bookstore in Menlo Park, and then we ran into him at church a few weeks later. She's received a couple of anonymous gifts and some hang-up calls. But there's nothing to connect those to that guy. And the officers who came to the office didn't find anything to suggest someone had tried to get in." Keith leaned back in his seat. "I don't think it means anything."

Gabe set his fork down. "You're probably right, man. But she needs to pay attention. Could be a reader who's getting obsessive, or maybe a former client or someone else. We take stalking seriously."

"Stalking?" Keith shook his head. "It's a little premature to call the guy a stalker, don't you think?"

As the four of them continued to talk about the gifts that had shown up and the calls I'd received, my mind latched onto what Gabe had said about taking stalkers seriously. A breeze of unease sent a chill through me. I glanced at Keith — had he heard Gabe's advice? Had he taken it to heart? While Keith was right, nothing connected the man I'd seen at the signing and again at church to the gifts or hang-up calls, my intuition had been screaming something else at me for several days. I'd worked to continue denying what I felt because, as I realized again, I longed for Keith to be right.

Yet I couldn't ignore what Gabe said.

"Deni, do you have my cell phone number in your phone?" Gabe's question pulled me back to the conversation.

"I don't think so."

"I'll send it to you." Gabe pulled his phone out of the holder on his belt. "You call me anytime. I'm here for you, got that?"

I nodded.

"We're all here for you." Ryan reached over and gave my hand a quick squeeze.

"That's right," Gabe said. "You did the right thing the other night when you called 911. If something happens again and it's an emergency, you do the same thing. Then you call me. Better safe than sorry, right?"

As Keith and I cleaned up the kitchen that night after everyone had gone home, I debated about whether to bring up the conversations that were replaying in my mind. I was tired, which was rarely a good time to discuss a topic that was bothering me. But if I didn't say something now, I knew I might not have another opportunity for several days as we both immersed ourselves in our work again.

I turned off the faucet at the kitchen sink, dried my hands, and then turned to Keith who was loading the dishwasher. "So, I was surprised by the white water rafting idea. Three Rivers?" I began. "I don't understand."

Keith, a plate in hand, stopped what he was doing and looked at me. "What do you mean?"

How could he not know what I meant? But I didn't want to argue again, so I tempered my response. "Well, you know what happened there and how painful it was."

"I just thought it might be fun." He put the plate in the dishwasher. "Babe, it's been a few years. Even Ryan's ready to go back. Like he implied, it could be healing."

"But as Ryan also said, we each deal with things in our own way, and I had to deal with a lot that last summer. We all did. And since then we've each had to deal with the emotional toll that loss took. For me, returning to Three Rivers isn't going to further my healing. Not at this point. Instead, it would be like ripping a scab off a wound that's just begun to heal."

"Okay. I get that, but sometime I'd love to see you in action, on a river, you know? It's hard to imagine you guiding trips down class IV and V rapids."

"Why is that hard to imagine?"

He shrugged. "Guiding groups of people down some of the most difficult rapids in the state takes courage."

"The American River has some great white water. There's no need to go all the way to Three Rivers. We just need to take the time to do it." I was stalling as I considered Keith's statement. I had a feeling we were headed to the second part of the conversation that had bothered me. "But that's not the point. What *is* your point?" My earlier irritation had returned.

"Let's not make a big deal out of this, okay? My point is that we used to have fun. You were adventurous, enjoyed a good time, loved a good risk — or that's what I thought.

We laughed together. Lately, I don't know — it's like you're afraid of your own shadow."

"Afraid of my own . . . Is that how you see me? Did you hear what Gabe said tonight?"

He leaned his head back, eyes closed, and exhaled. He stood that way for a moment, figuring out what to say, I assumed. Then he looked back at me. "Like I said, when I met you, when we married, you were a strong, confident, adventurous woman who loved a good laugh. But somewhere over the last month or so, that person has vanished. Not completely, but maybe doing something fun and adventurous, you know, will . . . empower you."

There was something to consider in the point he made, but I couldn't move beyond the anxiety I felt, nor could I understand why he wasn't more . . . What? What was it I wanted from him? I couldn't pinpoint it — fatigue muddled my thoughts.

"You see no reason for me to feel anxious." It was a statement, not a question. He'd made that more than clear when we argued several days ago, and again just now. "I know you don't give a lot of credence to intuition, but what if I'm right? What if that guy, the gifts, the phone calls . . . What if,

as Gabe suggested, someone is stalk —"
Could I admit what I'd feared and denied?
Not only admit it to Keith, but to myself? I
took a deep breath. "What if someone *is*
stalking me? You said yourself that because
I'm known now, people follow me. What
if . . ." I shook my head. "You know what I
mean."

"See, babe, that's exactly what I'm talking
about. I knew Gabe's comments would
freak you out. Gabe's a cop. He's seen some
bad stuff — he looks for bad stuff. But that
doesn't mean everything is bad. And yeah,
maybe I'm not the most intuitive guy, but
I'm looking at the facts, and so far they
don't add up to much. You may have someone interested in you, following you even,
but no one has done anything to endanger
you. Right?"

I left the sink and dropped onto one of
the barstools at the island. My head ached
and my eyes were heavy. "Right. No one
has threatened me."

Keith was technically right, and his confidence that my concern was unfounded
nearly snared me, but this time I pulled
away from what felt like a trap. A trap set
by my husband? It made no sense. But I no
longer had the energy to analyze it.

I got up from where I'd just sat and made

my way to the bottom of the stairs. Then I turned back to Keith. "I am suffering from some anxiety. But afraid of my own shadow? Hardly." My tone was firm, despite my fatigue. "It's time I pay attention to that anxiety and figure out the root cause. I believe there's something behind it. Someone behind it. Do I have concrete evidence? No."

Keith just shook his head again.

"I also respect Gabe's position and consider him an authority when it comes to this kind of thing. If he tells me to pay attention, I'm going to pay attention. It's time I took steps to ensure I feel secure, including trusting myself and what I'm feeling. If those feelings prove to be the result of a general anxiety disorder, I'll know that soon enough and deal with it. But I truly believe there's something else going on." I waited, hoping Keith would say something. When he didn't respond, I turned and walked up the first few stairs but then stopped and turned back. "I love you, and I hope we can respectfully agree to disagree and work through this."

I climbed the rest of the stairs and went through our bedroom into the bathroom, where I removed my makeup, washed my face, and brushed my teeth. Then I went into our closet and changed into my pajamas.

Fifteen minutes later I went to bed.

Alone.

On the following Wednesday, Jay and I walked out of the office together at dusk. It was one of those icy evenings, and with the sun just setting, the cold felt as though it went through my coat, straight to my bones.

I climbed into my car, started it, and immediately turned on the heat, wishing I had driving gloves or a heated steering wheel. I blew on my hands to warm them, then backed out of my parking space. As I pulled around the corner of our building and headed for the parking lot exit, something caught my eye along the side of the building. I slowed, cognizant that Jaylan was behind me.

In the planter area surrounding the building, a man stood alone directly underneath one of the outdoor lights attached to the building. As I slowed the car, he leaned against the wall. He wore a thin jacket over his clothes, and each breath he took crystallized in white puffs of air. He wore no hat or gloves, and my first thought was that he'd freeze to death out there. Then my heart lurched. I'd seen that jacket — khaki green, army style — and that same posture before.

The last time I'd seen him, he was leaning against the trunk of a heritage oak.

I came to a stop just past where he stood, and I looked back at him. He didn't flinch as I stared at him. In fact, he returned my look and held it.

His stare bore into me, and I was certain. It was him.

He knew where I worked. I swallowed the fear rising in my throat. The bracelet and charm were from him — he'd walked into our office and left the gifts for me. It was him outside my office window that evening last week, and it was him who'd tried to come into the office after Jay left.

I couldn't prove any of it.

But I knew it now, just as I'd suspected it last week.

Seeing him at the book signing and then again at church may have been coincidental. I'd chosen to believe it was a coincidence, even though my gut had told me something else. But his presence here wasn't a coincidence.

No, this was planned. Calculated. Not only did he know where I worked, but he wanted me to see him here. I was sure of it.

I glanced in my rearview mirror and could see that Jay was also looking at him. Should

I confront him? Pull over and get out of the car and demand to know what he was doing?

Lord, what do I do?

As soon as I lifted the prayer to God, I knew this wasn't the time for courage — it was the time for wisdom. I stepped on the accelerator and pulled out of the parking lot. About a block from the complex, I pulled over to the side of the street. Jaylan, as I hoped she would, followed me. Before I could get out of the car to talk to her, she'd called me.

"That's him, isn't it?"

"Yes. Definitely."

"Call 911. I'll call Gabe."

"What am I supposed to say? He hasn't really done anything that I can prove."

"You tell them the man who's stalking you is outside your office. Tell the dispatcher that officers were here last week. Call!"

The urgency in Jay's tone spurred me on.

This affirmed, at least in my mind, that I could no longer afford to hope that Keith was right. I knew better now. Just as I'd known better all along. As Gabe said, it was time I pay attention.

I dialed 911.

CHAPTER FIFTEEN

Denilyn
December 2009

My second encounter with the Sacramento County Sheriff's Department proved no more fruitful than my first. They took the information I offered and conducted an exterior search of the office complex. Beyond a few footprints in the soft dirt under the light where Jay and I had seen the guy standing, there was no other evidence that he'd been there.

Nor had he threatened me in any way.

Again, I felt a little foolish.

And again, after that event, I came home to an empty house.

Keith had flown out of Sacramento International Airport Monday morning for a weeklong business trip. I pulled into the driveway of our home, dreading another dark entry into the house alone. But when I clicked the garage door opener and the door lifted, light flooded the garage. Keith had replaced the bulb. Something about his simple act brought tears to my eyes.

I wished he was here to welcome me home.

I parked the car, got out, and then walked out of the garage door and down the driveway to the mailbox. I grabbed the stack of envelopes and flyers from the mailbox, and as I was walking back up the driveway, I noticed a package on the porch. It was a box addressed to me — something I'd ordered, I assumed. I set the mail on top of it and carried it through the garage and into the house. As the door between the garage and the house swung closed behind me, the sound echoed through the empty rooms, and a pang of loneliness echoed through my soul.

I locked the door and flipped on lights as I went to the kitchen, where I set the pile of mail on the island, and my briefcase and purse on one of the barstools. Then I went straight to the range where I set the teapot to boil. A cup of chamomile tea might help calm my frayed nerves.

As I pulled a mug from an upper cabinet, my phone rang, startling me, and the mug went crashing to the tile floor.

I put my hand over my pounding heart.

"Oh no . . ." The mug was a favorite — hand-painted Italian pottery. We'd purchased two of the mugs in Tuscany while on our honeymoon.

Now there was just one.

I sighed, turned off the range, and set the teapot aside, then stepped over the shards of pottery and grabbed my phone.

Keith and I had spoken little since our discussion on Saturday night. When he'd left for the airport before dawn Monday morning, I was still asleep.

I answered his call, relieved we'd have a chance to talk. "Hi there."

"Hey. Thought I'd check in. I saw you called earlier."

Keith was talking so loud over the clamor in the background that I held the phone away from my ear.

"Where are you?"

He laughed. "Yeah, it's loud. We're bowling! There's this great place with music and food, and I just hit two strikes in a row."

No one appreciated a good time like Keith. If there wasn't a party, Keith created one. It was part of what drew me to him when we met as I pushed toward completion of my doctorate. My list of priorities hadn't included fun for far too long, so when Keith unleashed his enthusiasm and ability to make any situation an occasion, I was drawn like a moth to a flame.

But now . . . I needed his support and I needed him not only to consider my feelings but to take them seriously.

However, feelings, at least those he considered negative or intense, weren't high on Keith's list of priorities, I'd learned.

I heard Keith laugh and then let loose a whoop. Someone else had scored, I assumed.

"Keith?"

"Yeah, yeah, I'm here. Hey, can we talk later? It's hard to hear you."

I needed to tell him about what had gone on tonight at the office. But something about his tone made me want to tuck my emotions away someplace safe while at the same time I wanted to fall apart, secure in my husband's arms. He felt so far away. Physically and emotionally.

My emotions were like a knotted skein of yarn, one I couldn't seem to unravel.

I cleared my throat. "Sure. Call me later, okay? I need to talk to you."

"What?" He laughed again at something I could neither hear nor see.

"Never mind."

"Yeah, okay. I'll call you tomorrow if I get a break."

"Wait. Keith . . . ?"

He'd already hung up.

I set my phone back on the island and then looked down at the mug, fractured beyond repair.

What was happening?

The next day passed without a call from Keith. I'd had a tight schedule myself, including seeing clients late into the evening. I assumed he was working long hours too. He managed the sales team for a booming software company, and long hours were part of the job he loved. When I hadn't heard from him by midday on Thursday, I left him a message.

He returned my call while I was with a client and left a message with a brief apology for not calling. No explanation. No excuse.

I decided I'd wait until I got home that evening to call him back. I hoped I could catch him after he was finished with work and commitments to his team.

When I walked into the house that night, I dropped another pile of mail onto the growing stack on the island. I needed to go through it and decided I might as well get it over with. I pulled a letter opener from a drawer in the island, sat down on one of the barstools, and with my phone cradled between my shoulder and ear, I called Keith and then began slitting open envelopes. My call went straight to his voice mail.

"Hi, it's me. Give me a call before you go to bed tonight. I want to make sure you're okay and see how your time is going. Maybe we can catch up and talk through some things."

I ended the call and then began putting the mail into piles. Bills. Things to respond to. And trash. It was ten minutes or so before I reached the box at the bottom of the pile.

I'd forgotten about it.

I glanced at the front of the box to see who had sent it, but there was no return address. Just a white printed address label affixed to the box. Across the top of the box was a row of stamps haphazardly placed.

The postmark indicated the package was sent from Seattle.

Had Keith mailed something to me?

I slit the packing tape and then pried open the box, anxious to see what was inside. I dug through packing peanuts until my hand landed on something soft. When I pulled it from the packing material and saw what it was, I dropped it as though it had scorched my hand.

On the kitchen counter, almost invisible on the black granite, sat a small, black velvet jewelry bag.

If Keith had sent it, it was a cruel joke.

I walked around the island to the kitchen sink, grabbed a glass out of the cabinet, and filled it with water. I turned, leaned against the sink, and sipped the water while eyeing the bag. I assumed it held a charm — the letter *C* for my last name. Our last name. *Costa.*

But I wouldn't know for sure unless I opened it.

I finally set the glass on the counter with the intent of going back to open the bag. But dread, like shackles around my ankles, immobilized me. Who was sending these gifts? And why? I'd felt sure the bracelet and charms I'd received at the office were from the man I'd seen outside the office. But now . . . Doubt, a rude intruder, settled within.

"Just get it over with," I whispered.

Slowly, I made my way back to the island and picked up the bag. I loosened the drawstring and emptied the contents into the palm of my hand, then closed my hand around the cool, smooth metal of the charm.

I held the charm a moment, then took a deep breath and uncurled my fingers, opening my hand. There in my palm was the charm, but it wasn't the letter I'd expected to see. I stared at it. Then, like the uncoiling of a venomous snake as it strikes, understanding hit my consciousness and I dropped the charm on the island and backed away from it.

"No. Oh Lord, no." My voice broke with a sob. "Help me . . ."

Hand trembling, I reached for my phone and searched through my contacts for the number I needed.

He answered after the first ring.

"Deni?"

"G . . . Gabe . . . I . . ."

It wouldn't occur to me until later that I hadn't even considered calling Keith.

"What's wrong? What happened?"

The gold charm winked in the light from above the island.

"Deni, talk to me."

"He . . . he knows where I live. Gabe, he knows. And" — I gasped then sobbed again — "he's going to . . . kill me. Gabe, he's going to kill me!" I cried.

The first two charms that I assumed were my initials were anything but. The third charm made that clear. The letter *E* sat on my kitchen island, conveying the sender's message.

He wanted me to D-I-E.

CHAPTER SIXTEEN

Denilyn
February 3, 2017

As I merge onto Interstate 80, I join the Friday evening mass of vehicles heading east toward the Sierras. When I made the appointment to check in with my psychiatrist, Dr. Bauer, to see how the medication adjustments he made have impacted the anxiety I've dealt with recently, I didn't consider weekend traffic.

I stay in the slow lane, biding my time until I reach my turnoff a few miles up the road. Just as I approach the exit, a dark swath of clouds lets loose their hold and dots of rain speckle my windshield. I flick on the wipers and then tune the radio to an oldies station. The music sets the tone for the weekend. I look forward to time at home with those I love, only a few papers to grade, and time to relax. Something I've done little of the last few weeks.

Dr. Bauer and I agreed that the medication adjustment has been effective. For the first time in weeks, I'm sleeping well, and the nightmares and flashbacks have eased. I'm present, and there's plenty in the present to deal with.

Willow comes to mind again as she has repeatedly over the last week. After doing some checking, it seems she's missed a couple of other classes in addition to Ryan's classes. My email to her has gone unanswered. I wasn't checking in as a school authority, only as a friend, and made that clear. I'm concerned about her.

The music irritates rather than relaxes me, so I turn it off and listen instead to the rhythm of raindrops — the sound once again familiar after such a long absence. There's something soothing about the patter on the roof and windshield.

By the time I reach the canyon, darkness has descended and the sprinkling has turned to a deluge. I glance at my rearview mirror, where I'm grateful to see headlights, like prisms, through the rain on the back window. The vehicle is several car lengths behind me and somehow reassures me. I prefer not to travel this section of road totally alone. As the road dips into the tight valley, I check my speedometer. I'm ready to be home, but it isn't worth the risk of speeding, especially in this weather.

When I slow for a curve, the headlights behind me brighten and illuminate a portion of the steep canyon wall ahead. The lights bounce back behind me as the vehicle, much closer now, follows me out of the curve.

Why did the driver turn on his brights? Does he want me to pull over so he can pass?

I have an eerie sense of familiarity as I recall the truck that nearly ran me off the road a few weeks ago. I lean forward and peer out the front windshield. The sheer canyon wall borders the road to my left, and on the right the road hugs the rushing river. There is only a narrow shoulder between the road and the river along this section.

When I glance in the mirror again, the reflection of the bright lights behind me is almost blinding.

Mouth dry, I swallow as I adjust the mirror to keep the lights out of my eyes, then I step on the gas as I come out of another curve.

My heart rate accelerates with the SUV.

As the road straightens, I slow again, giving the driver ample time and space to pass me. My eyes dart from the rearview mirror to the road and back again. Rain pounds now, and my wipers, nearly useless even with new blades, obscure my view. The reflective line on the road to the right of me wavers as I view it through the water the wipers are smearing across the windshield.

When the truck doesn't pass, I step on the gas and increase my speed again in a vain attempt to put some distance between us. But the driver of the truck does the same, staying with me.

I tighten my grip on the steering wheel and consider tapping my breaks as a signal to back off, but he's so close now that even a slight decrease in speed could cause him to hit me.

What is he doing?

Oh Lord . . .

Knowing there's a scenic viewpoint ahead, a turnout in the road, I turn on my blinker, indicating my intent to pull over and let the driver pass, but we're going so fast I fear pulling off the wet road too quickly will cause me to slide through the turnout and into the churning river.

As I consider that possibility, my SUV lunges forward at the same time I hear the crash and crackle of breaking plastic and the screeching of bending metal. My head jerks forward and then whips back. Just as I realize the truck has hit me, the SUV jolts forward again accompanied by the same crunching, screeching sounds.

I look in the rearview mirror again just in time to see the truck rev and come careening toward me.

My scream ricochets inside the car as the truck hits me hard, causing the SUV to jettison across the road toward the sheer rock wall of the canyon. I have no time to consider what to do. Instead, I instinctively brace for the impact as I try to locate the brake with my foot. Shattering glass sounds behind me, and I scream as I slam into the wall. Something seems to explode in front of me, then slams me back in my seat and holds me there as the SUV does a frenzied spin.

The moments are a dizzying blur.

But finally, all movement and sound stop.

All is still.

And I'm . . . alive. It's my first thought. I am still alive.

Breathless, I realize what I thought was an explosion was the airbags deploying. It's too dark to see where on the road I've landed, but ahead of me two red taillights glow, accelerating up the road. I track the lights as they ascend up and out of the canyon.

I gasp, too shocked to do anything more. Cold wind and rain blow in through the broken back window, and the driver's side door is concave and pressed against me. My neck, left shoulder, and arm ache.

The SUV's engine is still running. It appears only the headlight on the passenger side is working now. It throws just enough light onto the road that I can see the dotted double lines between the lanes. I'm in the middle of the road. The car is still in gear, so I push the now deflated airbag away from the steering wheel as best I can, grip the wheel, and slowly depress the accelerator to see if the SUV's too damaged to move off the road. The car limps forward, bumping and screeching. It's clear there's damage to at least two of the wheels, among other things. I'm able to pull to the side of the road next to the river, where I shift into Park and turn off the ignition. Then I collapse against the steering wheel, heart pounding, body shuddering.

As my mind grasps what's just happened, anger bubbles and I pound the steering wheel with my fists. "Haven't I had enough? Haven't I?" I scream my question at God. Then I lean my forehead against the steering wheel. "Why?" I whisper. "Why have You abandoned me?" I choke out my question through sobs, voicing the fear that's plagued me for almost eight years. "Why?"

When my tears are spent, still trembling, I open the middle console and reach inside for my cell phone. Hands shaking, I press 9-1-1.

When nothing happens, I remember where I am.

I search the darkened road ahead of me and behind me. My head throbs. What do I do now? I've pulled my battered vehicle as far off the road as possible, but I'm still partially blocking the lane. I check my phone again to see if, by some miracle, I have service. But I know better. I swipe the tears from my cheeks.

Think. I have to think.

What if he comes back?

I know he won't come from behind — it would take hours to circle back from another route. If he intends to come back for me, he'll have to turn around up ahead somewhere. I'd see him coming, though that thought offers little comfort. There's nowhere to go except down the embankment and into the river.

"Help me, please help me." I cry out through my tears — though I have little, if any, remaining faith that my prayers are heard.

Darkness presses in on me, the seeming

weight of it suffocating. Rain pounds on the roof and windshield, wind howls through the broken window, the noise deafening. I take a ragged breath, then another. My thoughts are muddled. "Breathe, just breathe," I whisper.

If a car comes by, surely the driver would see me and stop. But I'm a sitting duck. With the way I'm sticking out in the lane, it's more likely another car would hit me. Hazard lights. Where are they? I search the dashboard until I see the dimly lit triangle. I push it and then turn around in my seat to look out the back window — the red lights briefly illuminate the area just behind the car each time they flash.

Is sitting here waiting for a car to pass, and hopefully stop, really the best choice? I consider my options. Either I walk along the almost nonexistent shoulder up and out of the canyon, or I wait here and hope someone else doesn't hit me from behind.

Walking poses its own risks. If whoever hit me before comes back, I'm exposed and vulnerable walking along the dark road. At least in the car, I can lock the doors, which offers little comfort, but it's something. And if he hits me again, at least the SUV offers a small measure of protection.

It's at least a half mile uphill before I'd

have phone reception again. I peer out the front windshield again — the rain shows no sign of letting up.

Just as I decide to wait for a few minutes more, headlights crest the top of the canyon. The vehicle makes a slow descent on the canyon road coming toward me.

Is he coming back for me?

I reach for the door handle, pull it, and then push against the door. It won't open — it's too damaged. I unlatch my seat belt and scramble across the console to the passenger side, wrestling the airbags. I'm prepared to jump out of the car if it appears he's going to hit me again.

Then a question I haven't considered occurs to me.

Who is *he*?

■ ■ ■ ■

Part Two

■ ■ ■ ■

Only when you drink from the river of
silence shall you indeed sing.
KHALIL GIBRAN

CHAPTER SEVENTEEN

Denilyn
February 4, 2017

Shattered glass flies through the darkened interior of the SUV as it spins wildly, creating a tornado of the shards. I close my eyes to protect them from the slivers of glinting glass.

"Open your eyes, Denilyn."

I spin around to check the backseat. Where is he?

"Open your pretty eyes."

"Where are you?" I cry.

A cackle of laughter sounds, and I cover my ears.

Then the car slams into the wall again and a scream reverberates . . .

"Denilyn."

Something scratches my arm, and I try to shove it away.

"Wake up!"

I jerk upright and open my eyes.

"Wha . . ." The room is shrouded in dim light. "Where . . ."

"You're okay. You're home. You're okay, darling."

My mother sits on the edge of the bed, and Max paws at my arm. I bury my hand in the thick fur around his neck. "I . . . was dreaming?"

"I was making coffee and thought I heard you crying. When I came in, Max was trying to wake you. And then you screamed."

Pain radiates from my neck up the base of my skull. "My head . . ." I lie down again, my head, left shoulder, and arm throbbing. She reaches over, and like I'm seven years old again, she brushes the hair from my face and concern etches her features. "Whiplash?"

"Maybe. And . . . I don't know what else."

"You were hit hard last night. Did you sleep much?"

"A couple hours, I think." I sit up, slower this time, push my pillow behind my back, and lean against the headboard. Max shifts and rests his muzzle on my thigh, his golden-brown eyes appearing worried as he stares at me.

My mom reaches over and pets him. "He takes good care of you, but he takes up a lot of the bed."

"He stays on his side." I reach for him again. "Well, mostly."

She gets up, goes around to the other side of the bed, and straightens the blanket I keep on top of the covers for Max, then looks down at me. "Now, what can I do for you?"

I begin to shake my head but think better of it. "Nothing." I knead the base of my neck and shoulder. "I have to get going. Get in the shower, and . . ." My eyes are heavy, my head heavier.

"Where do you think you're going?"

"I have to work."

"It's Saturday, darling."

My mind swims through sludge as I try to make sense of what she's said. "Are you . . . sure?"

"Very sure. The only thing you need to do is take care of yourself today."

As my mind clears, memories flash like the lights of the California Highway Patrol cars and ambulance as they arrived at the scene last night after someone stopped to help me and called 911.

"They'll have more questions for me today. The officer said they'd want to talk to me."

"That's fine. When you're ready, you can talk to them. But first" — her tone is firm now, and I know I'm in for a lecture or at least a strong suggestion — "you need to see a doctor. I know you refused a trip to the ER last night when the ambulance arrived, but I'm your mother, and you will not get away with that with me."

"Mom —"

"Of course, I will respect your choices, but if your doctor can't see you today — and I expect that will be the case on a Saturday — then we will make a trip to the ER ourselves. Also, if you don't already have an appointment scheduled with your therapist, I strongly suggest you call her first thing this morning and at least leave a message for her. You sustained not only physical injuries last night but additional trauma too. Of course, I don't need to tell you that. You'll also need to call whomever you need to speak with at the university and let them know you're taking several days off next week."

"Glad to know you'll respect my choices." I toss the covers off, not letting her see the pain that simple movement causes. Still feeling like that seven-year old, I scoot to the edge of the bed and drop my legs over the side. "Oh . . ." I close my eyes and let my head hang. Max, my fearless German shepherd, whimpers at my side. I lift my head and look at him. "I'm okay, buddy." Then I look at my mom. "I can't take several days off. I've never missed a day of teaching."

"Well, that's fortuitous, isn't it? You have a strong track record and plenty of sick time, I assume."

She's right, of course. She's always right.

I concede and realize I'm grateful to do so. "Thank you," I whisper as I crawl back into bed.

"No need to thank me."

I place my hand on her arm. "No, Mom, really. Thank you for being here — for all you do. I don't know what I'd do without you."

"There's no place I'd rather be. If your dad were still alive, he'd be right here with us, you know that. We both would have moved in with you. After what you went through, and I'm not just talking about last night, he wouldn't have let you out of his sight."

"I know." I swallow the ache in my throat. "I miss him."

"I know you do. So do I."

As tears well, I know my mother is right — I need to take care of myself and the details following last night's accident. Is that what it was, an accident? It hardly seemed accidental. I rub my temples. "I'll make calls later. I just want to sleep a little more. Do you mind taking over the morning routine?"

"That was my plan. I'll make breakfast and take care of everything." She gets up and goes to the large window in the room and pulls the drape across the louvered blinds where morning light is seeping through the slats, and then she turns back. "Maxwell, you come with me."

Max's ears perk, and he looks from my mom to me.

"Go ahead. Go eat, buddy."

That's all the encouragement he needs. He jumps off the bed and follows my mom to the bedroom door, where she pauses. "You sleep, love. I'll take care of everything."

I lie back down, rumple my pillow, and shift from one side to the other, attempting to find a comfortable position. I want nothing more than to lose myself to sleep for several hours. But just as I drift off, the sensation of being hit from behind jolts me again and I jerk back up, heart and head pounding.

I stare into the dark room where the events of last evening replay, as they did throughout most of the night and early morning hours. I reach over and pull the chain on the lamp on my nightstand and diffuse the memories with soft, warm light.

I suspect sleep will elude me.

The question that swarmed my mind all night returns. Who tried to run me off the road? There's only one person I can think of, but he's in prison serving a sentence for assault. If he were released early, I'd have received notification. That's my right as a victim and witness.

The earliest he's eligible for parole is June 1.

As of today, that's still more than one hundred days away.

February 6, 2017

After spending several hours in the ER on Saturday afternoon, I was told what we already suspected — I'd sustained a whip-lash injury. Fortunately, it's nothing rest and time won't heal. I spent most of the remainder of the weekend in bed or on the sofa, letting my mother take care of me.

But this morning I need to make a call. Still in my robe, I slip out of my bedroom, Max trailing me, and cross the house to my home office, where I gently close the door so I have some privacy.

I sit at the desk — the mission-style oak desk that was in my office when I was still seeing clients. Its straight lines and heft seem to offer strength. Max curls himself on top of my feet, offering warmth and comfort. I open my laptop to google the number I need. I've waited until just after 9:00 a.m. when I'm sure the government offices are open. So when my call is transferred to the appropriate department and I get a recording asking me to leave a message, I sigh in frustration.

"This is Denilyn Rossi — D-e-n-i-l-y-n R-o-s-s-i — I'd like to check an inmate's status and confirm the date of an upcoming parole hearing." I leave my phone number and times I'm available to take a call. After I end the call, I follow up with an email requesting the same information.

It's time I stop obsessing about his parole hearing and date of release and, instead, take a healthy step to put my mind at ease by ensuring nothing has changed.

To make certain he is still incarcerated.

Especially after what occurred Friday evening, although, as the detective I spoke with yesterday assured me, they will also verify that information.

But this was a step I needed to take for myself.

Just as I'm about to get up from my desk, my phone rings. I pick it up and see that it's Ryan calling. "Hi there."

"Where are you? I was worried about you

when you didn't show up this morning. Are you sick?"

I hesitate. "Not sick, not exactly, anyway."

"What's going on? I don't remember you ever missing a day of work."

"Actually, I was in an accident on Friday evening. I'm nursing a case of whiplash and some bumps and bruises. Nothing major. But the doctor, along with my mother, of course, advised me to take a few days off to rest."

"Wow . . . What happened?"

I take a deep breath. "Someone ran me off the road — into the canyon wall."

"Intentionally?" His tone is incredulous.

"Yes, it appeared it was intentional."

"They targeted you?" I can almost feel his anger, fire-poker hot, through the phone line.

Part of me wants to lay my head down on the desktop and cry, but I'm not sure I have the energy for even that. "I don't know. But because it appeared intentional and because of my history, they're assuming it was targeted until they can prove otherwise."

"Is Mathison out?"

"I . . ." Hearing his name tossed out trips me up. "No. I . . . don't think so. I'm supposed to receive notification of parole hearings or a release date. I haven't heard anything, but I did call to confirm that nothing's changed. I'm waiting to hear back."

"Okay." His tone softens. "Keep me posted."

"I will."

"In the meantime, what can I do for you? What do you need?"

What do I need? The list is endless. I need security. To know I'm safe — my family is safe. I need to move on with my life, to put that horrendous year, that horrific night, behind me. I need to know there isn't someone trying to kill me again. I need everything to go back to the way it was.

Before.

Long before any of this began.

I rub the back of my neck, trying to ease the ache there. "Nothing, really, but thank you." Then something occurs to me. "Oh wait. There is one thing. As far as anyone at work is concerned, this was just a car accident. I don't want a lot of speculation and conversations —"

"No, no, of course you don't. I understand."

After ending the call, I stare at the desktop and follow the grain of the oak with one finger. *Mathison. Bradley Mathison.* The name is branded on my mind, never to be forgotten. He'd been right — I had known his name, but I couldn't place him the first time he confronted me. And it was several months before I did place him. It was Ryan who finally named him — who reminded me of how I'd known him. Of how we'd known him.

I sit at my desk for a long time staring out the window where the day has dawned in muted tones of gray again, as though the rain has washed the earth of all color. A fine sprinkling, like lace, veils my view. Trees are barren. Silence is sovereign. Not a bird sings. The landscape, all of life it seems, is bereaved.

"Trust is a choice."

Yes, but when death reigns, it is a difficult choice to make.

CHAPTER EIGHTEEN

Adelia
May 7, 2017

I toss in the still unfamiliar bed, in the dark, unfamiliar room. I throw the sheet off me and move to a spot where my body hasn't yet warmed the sheet and mattress. I keep my eyes closed, willing myself to sleep, but the constant muffled roar of the river in my ears, like a lion stalking its prey, disturbs. Finally, I push myself up and pull the earplugs from my ears and throw them, one at a time, at the wall across from the bed, an action I regret when pain ripples through my upper arm.

Despite the rigor and discipline of getting my body ready for this mission, my muscles ache from my first trip down the Kaweah. A strap of pain crosses my back. I get out of bed and slowly lift my arms above my head and reach for the ceiling, stretching the muscles in my back. I do the stretch several times, working to loosen the muscles and relieve the pain.

I yawn, look at the bed, and decide it holds no comfort for the moment. Although I left the air conditioner on, the room is stifling. There are no vents in the master bedroom, which appears to have been an addition to the original house. I kept the windows in the room closed in an attempt to shut out the thunder of the river, but it's always present.

Sleep won't come anytime soon.

Instead, I wander out of the bedroom and through the house to the kitchen, where I get a glass of water. After I've quenched my thirst, I open the slider and step into the ink of night. It takes a moment for my eyes to adjust to the dark, but soon I see the ghostly shapes of the trees — sycamores, willows, and cottonwoods, branches stretched wide — along the bank upriver.

Somewhere above, the face of the moon blooms almost full. According to the lunar calendar, the moon will reach its fullest two nights from now.

When the moon is full . . .

I consider the invitation a few of the guides issued to me as we carried rafts to the storage units at the end of the day. "Hey Adelia, you up for a moonlight trip down the river?" I'd heard one of the other female guides snicker when she heard them include me.

I glanced back at her, eyebrows raised. "Wouldn't be the first time." Then I looked at the guys. "Sure, I'm in."

He'd laughed. "Okay. We go Wednesday."

I didn't let them see what I was feeling as my pulse pounded in my ears. Perhaps the invitation was issued to the *old lady* as a joke — I have more than a decade, at least, on most of the guides. But it's an invitation I couldn't decline. Instead, I silently gave thanks for the opportunity, one I knew I needed to take advantage of to refresh my skills.

I'm not sure what's coming; I only know it will occur when the moon is full.

Only the best make it down this river at night, and only when the moon is full and the sky clear. I look downriver where light reflected from the moon shimmers on a deep pool that sits atop one of the rocky ledges the river falls over. Beyond the ledge, the water churns, its white froth visible even in the dark. There the water becomes a swirling hydraulic — a place where the Kaweah can hold those without strength and experience in its sucking grasp.

"But I have both strength and experience." I speak the reminder to the river and myself.

The only reply I receive is the steady rumble of the tumbling water, and my fury for this river rises. Not only has it pulled me back here, but it has pulled me from what matters most.

I close my eyes and see his dimpled cheeks and hazel-colored eyes. Those eyes with a smile in them, always. How I long for the innocence behind that smile to last forever. Yet I know better. It's only a matter of time. Already, just over the last year, he's grown two more inches and he's traded "Mama" for "Mom."

My little Nicky . . .

I've spent each day since his birth, if not at his side, no more than a few minutes' drive away. Now it would take the better part of a day to get to him. I won't see him for more than a month. The sacrifice feels like too much.

Yet he is why I'm here, I remind myself. He is why I allowed this river to pull me back. But it isn't just the river . . .

It is time for death to give way to life. More than time.

My life since his conception has focused on protecting him. Every thought, every choice, every action. I would give my life

211

for his. I will give my life for his if necessary. But that protection has come with an unforeseen cost. A toll. One which, for his sake, I can no longer pay.

I've created a prison, and it's time for freedom.

I am here to fight for his freedom.

That is my singular focus. My only goal.

But . . .

With the river's roar reverberating in my ears, and that churning hydraulic yearning to yank me in, doubt tempts me.

I can say I still have the strength, mental and physical, to navigate this river with the light of the moon as my only guide, but is that true? Will I be ready by the next full moon, June 9th? Suddenly it feels as though the days are slipping away, dragging me under, and my breath catches. Then my breathing ceases, as though water has filled my lungs.

I gasp once and then again. Then I draw deep of the night air.

"No," I whisper. I turn away from doubt. "You have no place here!"

As soon as the words are out of my mouth, peace settles my soul. And with it, knowing dawns . . .

I've long seen the Kaweah as my foe, my adversary. But tonight I understand for the first time that I must make it my ally.

I must fight this battle *with* the river, not against it. For it isn't the river that's held us hostage. The river only played a role, but it was not and is not my adversary.

That title belongs to another.

I watch the ever-moving river awhile longer.

It is never static, always changing, the water level rising and falling, dependent on nature, the Creator, for its being.

Just as I am dependent.

I close my eyes once more and raise my face toward the heavens, an acknowledgment, again, that I have not come alone. If I am still, there is another who will fight for me. Then I open my eyes and take in the firmament above — points of light as far as the eye can see dot the black canvas — another reminder of the power that upholds me.

"Thank You," I whisper.

Then I turn and walk back into the house, shut and lock the slider, and return to the bedroom, where I open the shutters and push open the windows in the room. I leave the shutters open so the cool breeze of the night stirs in the stagnant room.

I climb back into bed, the roar I've worked

so hard to shut out now the song that lulls me.

The river will be my ally.

CHAPTER NINETEEN

Denilyn
December 2009

It was close to midnight by the time the detectives left the house with the only evidence I had to give them — a charm bracelet with the single charm attached, two additional charms, and the mailing box and label. I answered question after question, although most of them I had no answers for.

Jay stood at my kitchen island. "You're comin' home with us."

Although Jay's tone was emphatic, I wanted nothing more than to fall into my own bed. I glanced at the clock on the microwave, then looked at Gabe. "You said Keith was trying to get a flight out of Seattle, right?"

Gabe pulled his phone out of his back pocket. "Yeah, but I haven't heard back." He looked at the screen. "He hasn't let me know if he's on his way or not. And Jay's right — you're not staying here alone."

As much as I wanted to assure them I'd be all right, what if . . . I didn't want to consider the possibilities. My shoulders sagged with fatigue. "Let me just grab a few things." I turned to head upstairs then looked back. "Thank you both for being here and for . . ." — I didn't have the energy to say more — "you know."

"We do know. Get up there." Jay looked almost as tired as I felt.

I dragged myself up the stairs, stuffed a pair of pajamas, a change of clothes, and a few toiletries into an overnight bag, then went to my nightstand where my phone was charging. I'd run upstairs sometime while the detectives were here to plug it into the charger. I hoped I'd find a message from Keith, but there was nothing from him. He was scrambling to get home, I reasoned.

Instead, I had two missed calls from Ryan and two texts. HEY, I REMEMBERED KEITH WAS TRAVELING THIS WEEK. CHECKING IN TO SEE IF YOU NEED ANYTHING.

Then about an hour later: LET ME KNOW YOU'RE OKAY.

I glanced at the time and decided Ryan would want a response regardless of the hour. THANKS FOR CHECKING. LONG DAY.

I'LL CALL TOMORROW.

Was it just that Keith had rushed to find a flight, check out of his hotel, and get to the airport that kept him from calling or sending a text? Had he wanted to come straight home, or had Gabe persuaded him to do so when he called him to let him know what had happened?

I wanted to believe the best — needed to believe the best of Keith. But doubt niggled.

I unplugged the charger from the wall and tossed it into the overnight bag, along with my phone. Then, rather than climb into bed to fall asleep in the comfort and security of my husband's arms, I went back downstairs and told Jay and Gabe I'd follow them to their house.

Nothing felt right or certain.

Nothing.

After a restless night, I finally fell into a fitful sleep sometime before dawn and then woke with the sun. I tossed in the unfamiliar bed, ultimately landing on my back and staring at the ceiling. When it was clear I was awake for good, I reached and turned on the lamp on the nightstand and then picked up my phone. I was grateful to see a text from Keith letting me know he was on his way. Whether that meant on his way

217

from Seattle, on his way from the airport, or on his way to Jay and Gabe's, I had no idea.

All that mattered was that he was coming.

Chilled, I pulled the down comforter over the blanket already covering me and snuggled under its warmth. I took in the decor of the guest room as I lay there. Bright batik prints and black-and-white photos from Ethiopia, where Gabe and Jaylan spent their honeymoon working with a relief organization, hung on the walls. Proud of their African American heritage, they wanted to give back to the country of their ancestors. I respected their selfless act. Both Gabe and Jay had also chosen careers that allowed them to serve others in selfless ways.

But, in addition to respecting them, I also envied them. The feeling wasn't one I dwelled on, but I'd often recognized a partnership, a melding of passions and purpose between Gabe and Jay, something my relationship with Keith lacked.

That awareness, once again, left me standing on a precipice overlooking a stark void.

The slow swoosh of the bedroom door pushing open over the carpet in the room pulled me from that edge. A large familiar hand holding a Starbuck's cup appeared around the corner from the hallway.

I smiled when Keith poked his head into the room.

"Grande latte with whip."

"Whip?"

"Thought you might need a little something extra." He came and sat on the side of the bed.

I scooted up and leaned against the headboard. "Thank you for coming home. And for the whip."

He leaned over and planted a kiss on my forehead, then handed me the latte. "Sounds like you've had an action-packed week." He smiled, though I could see the shadows under his eyes. He'd likely been up most of the night.

"You want adventure, I'm here to provide it."

He raised his eyebrows and got up. He came around the other side of the bed, kicked off his shoes, climbed in, and put his arms around me. I sat my cup on the nightstand and then nuzzled into him. "I'm so glad you're home. I was so . . . scared. I am so scared." My voice caught. "What are we going to do?"

When he stiffened and pulled away from me, I realized I'd misread his intent, or he'd misread mine.

"We're going to let law enforcement do

their job. Speaking of which, why do I have a message from a detective? He said they need to talk to me today."

"The charm was mailed from Seattle."

"Yeah, I know. Gabe filled me in. But what does that have to do with me?"

I sat up. I knew Keith hadn't sent the charm. He wasn't a suspect, of course. He'd never do anything like that to me. But couldn't he see why they'd have to question him? Again, his attitude surrounding all of this baffled me. I trusted him implicitly, but . . . "Well" — I sighed — "like you said, we have to let them do their jobs. I'm sure talking with you is just a formality. Because, obviously, you were in Seattle at the same time the package was postmarked. Maybe talking with them will trigger a memory — something or someone you saw." I shrugged. "I don't know."

"They'll probably figure out it's all just a sick joke."

"A joke? But that guy was at the office and —"

He pulled the covers back and got up and reached for his shoes.

I hesitated. "You don't want to talk about this?"

"I just don't want you making a bigger deal about it than it is, okay?" He bent to put his shoes on and then looked over his shoulder at me. "I'm starving. Let's go get brunch at that place downtown that makes great southern food —"

"Keith . . ."

"— their beignets are the best. Remember the pork belly benedict they make? Maybe Gabe and Jay can join us. After brunch we can catch a matinee. What's playing?" He pulled his phone out of the back pocket of his pants and pulled up movie listings. He began reading titles and times to me.

As I listened to him ramble on, it occurred to me . . .

He couldn't face what was happening.

Couldn't or wouldn't? I wasn't sure.

What I was sure of was that he was as afraid as I was.

One afternoon several days after I'd received the final charm, I sat in my office where I'd just finished rearranging my client schedule to coincide with Jay's schedule. Gabe had suggested that neither of us should spend time alone at the office until the "situation," as he called it, was resolved.

I was grateful for his suggestion, while at the same time more aware than ever of how the *situation* was encroaching on my life. Like a hamster in a cage, I felt small and confined, running on a wheel to nowhere. And it wasn't just my life that was impacted; it was the lives of all those around me.

The hypervigilance — the constant looking over my shoulder, watching for that one familiar but still unknown to me face wherever I went, the adrenaline spikes when the phone rang or the mail arrived — proved exhausting. The nightmares had also begun and were disrupting not only my sleep but my peace.

I was both weary and overwhelmed.

And I couldn't talk to Keith about any of it.

Nor could I depend on Jay or Ryan or other close friends to help me work through the feelings I was having at any given moment. I needed to process with a therapist. I was quickly reaching the point where I'd need medical assistance too. An examination and prescription to relieve anxiety.

I got up from my desk and stretched, trying to relieve some of the tension in my back and shoulders.

How long could I keep up with my client list? I wasn't sure. I'd caught my mind wandering several times as a client was talking. I was struggling to stay present and focused.

When the phone on my desk rang, my

heart stuttered. I dropped into my chair, looked at the caller ID, and then picked up the call.

"This is Denilyn Costa."

"Mrs. Costa, this is Daniel Neibuhr from the sheriff's —"

"Yes, hello. Do you have any news?"

"Nothing much. Until we have an ID on the guy you've seen, there's not much we can do. We did, however, discover where the bracelet and charms were purchased. Through a search online, we found a jewelry store chain that carries the exact bracelet and charms. There are two stores in our area, so we checked with both of them. The second store has record of selling the bracelet and two charms a few days before you received the first package. But whoever purchased the bracelet and first two charms paid cash for them, which isn't a surprise.

"The third charm was sold by the same retailer, but through one of their shops in Bellevue, outside of Seattle. Again, the customer paid cash. The fact that whoever made the purchases used cash may indicate that they didn't want the sales tracked. Or it could mean nothing. It's a dead end at this point, unless an employee from either store can remember making the sale and give us a description of the customer. But so far we haven't had that kind of luck."

He went on to clarify something we'd discussed over the weekend and then asked me a few more questions, but I had nothing more to offer.

"Just one more thing, Mrs. Costa. As I'm sure you know, I did speak with your husband earlier this week. I know you've said he didn't send that final charm. I can't prove whether he did or didn't, but it seems like a pretty big coincidence that he was in the same city where the charm was purchased at the same time it was sent. I'm not questioning your judgment; I'm just saying it's odd. Okay?"

I nodded, though I knew he couldn't see me. But I wasn't sure I could speak. He may not have directly questioned my judgment, but he wasn't convinced that Keith hadn't sent the charm.

He cleared his throat. "Any questions for me, Mrs. Costa?"

"Um . . ." Did he really suspect my husband? "Did you . . . did you ask Keith if he'd told anyone on his team about the bracelet and the first two charms — anyone who was in Seattle with him?"

I'd asked Keith that question myself, of course. I was grasping, but then I wondered what my question revealed about me? What would the detective think it revealed? Was I questioning what Keith had told me? Of course not. I trusted him. But doubt had begun to take root.

"Yes, ma'am, I asked him that. He said he doesn't remember telling anyone about the bracelet, but he couldn't be sure."

That's what he'd told me. *"How can you not remember?"* I'd pushed. *"You have to remember whether you said something or not. Is there anyone on your team who would want to set you up, make you look bad, play a perverted joke? Think, Keith. Think. Please."* But he'd shut down, walked away. I was seeing, for the first time since we'd met, that in the face of hardship or stress, his habit was to escape. "Okay, thank you." I leaned back in my chair, wishing I too could escape. "What do you suggest I do now?"

"I suggest you keep your eyes open. And if you haven't already done so, install a security system in your home, and let us know of any new developments."

I'd called a couple of alarm companies on Monday and set appointments for them to give us bids. It was money we didn't want to spend, but it was also money we couldn't afford not to spend. Keith agreed, and I was grateful not to have a disagreement over finances in the midst of everything else.

Perhaps an alarm would provide a measure of comfort.

After the call, more than ever I wanted the bracelet and charms to be nothing more than the sick joke Keith had suggested they were. I'd written a book for those traumatized by bullies. Clearly someone was now bullying me.

Maybe the bracelet was as far as it would go. I prayed that was so.

But that theory didn't answer the question about the man who seemed to be stalking me, even if the stalking was benign in nature, at least thus far.

Who was he? And why did he seem familiar to me?

I'd asked myself those questions a hundred times over.

But I still didn't have answers.

January 2010

A few weeks later on a Friday evening, just as Jay and I were leaving the office, I received a text from Keith saying he was still working but would leave his office within thirty minutes. I didn't like the idea of walking into an empty house, so I texted him back and told him I would stop at the grocery store so neither of us had to go over the weekend.

As I pulled into the parking lot of the store, I felt a moment of freedom. The simple act of wandering the aisles of the busy grocery store felt both safe and normal. I hadn't sensed either safety or normalcy in the last week, and I vowed I'd enjoy the time.

I grabbed a cart on my way into the store and made a slow circle around the produce department, marveling at the array of colors — purple eggplants, golden and crimson beets, and every shade of green imaginable. I chose a head of broccoli and some salad greens and then went to grab a couple of russet potatoes to have with our dinner the following evening. As I placed the potatoes in a produce bag, I sensed someone behind me. I turned, and I was face-to-face with *him.* I dropped the bag, and the potatoes rolled across the floor. I took a step back, hitting the shopping cart with my hip.

"What . . . what do you want? Why are you following me?" I reached for the cart and maneuvered it so I was behind it — a blockade between us.

He looked at my wrist then back to my face. "You're not wearing the bracelet. I thought you'd like it. *D* for *Denilyn.*"

My breath caught and my heart raced.

"*I* for *Isabelle.* But you don't like it? You

227

don't like the bracelet?" There didn't seem to be any malice in his tone, only what I perceived as disappointment.

I gripped the handle of the cart, trying to steady myself, then glanced around to see if anyone was watching us, anyone witnessing him talking to me. But no one was paying attention. People were focused on their shopping lists or reaching for items they needed. It was Friday night and shoppers were anxious to get what they needed and get out and go home or to wherever it was they were spending the evening.

My mind raced. Should I try to engage him, or should I run? "What . . . what about . . . my last name?" I hadn't considered the question. It was out of my mouth before I could stop it.

His dark eyes bore into me, and he slowly shook his head. "Denilyn Isabelle . . ."

I took another step back, but there was nowhere to go. I was trapped in a corner between two displays and the cart.

He took another step closer to the cart. "*R* for *Rossi*. Would you like that?"

Was he really concerned about pleasing me?

"No . . . that's not my name" — as I was talking, I realized what I needed to do — "now."

His brow furrowed, and he said something else. Something about a *C.* He was shaking his head. I maintained eye contact with him, but I couldn't absorb what he was saying. My focus had shifted as I reached into my purse sitting in the top of the cart. I tried to make the action look natural, as though I was still listening but had remembered something I needed out of my purse. I dug through the contents until my fingers landed on the cool smooth case of my phone.

Just as I pulled the phone from my purse, a woman walked up to us. "Excuse me. May I?" She pointed at the displays of potatoes behind me.

"Oh . . ." I looked at him. "You'll have to move." His eyes darted from me to her and back, but he didn't move.

I kept the phone down low, behind my purse. I tapped in my security code then looked back to him. He kept looking from me to the other woman.

"Excuse me," she said louder. "I just need a couple of those." She pointed again.

Finally, he took a few steps back, giving me room to move the cart. But first I glanced at the screen of the phone again, tapped the icon I wanted, and then lifted the phone and pointed it at him. I had to work to steady my hand, and then I snapped his picture.

His eyes widened in surprise, then narrowed with what I assumed was anger. He stared at me for a split second before he turned and ran.

Hands shaking, I dropped the phone back into my purse and doubled over.

"Are you okay?" the woman asked.

I'd been holding my breath. I gasped then pointed toward the doors of the store. "Catch . . . him!" I cried. "Someone catch him!" But no one moved. The few people who heard me looked confused.

Trembling, I pushed the cart out of my way, stumbled past the woman and her cart, and then ran for the door. It slid open as I approached, and I ran out into the already dark parking lot. Cars, headlights blinding me, maneuvered through the lot, looking for parking spaces. Others were headed toward the parking lot exits. Frantic, my eyes roved through the parking lot, looking at each person. When I saw a man getting into a car, I headed that way and stepped into the lane that ran in front of the store. A car honked as it slammed on its brakes, stopping just before it hit me. Rooted, I turned and looked at the driver. A woman about my age, hands in the air, glared at me.

When the car I thought I'd seen the man getting into came up the row toward me, I ran to it only to discover it was an elderly woman at the wheel.

I had to find him — had to see what he was driving. Get a license plate number or something that could be used to track him. I had to stop the madness. Make it end. But there was no sign of him.

He'd vanished into the crowded lot.

Or somewhere else in the shopping center.

He was gone.

CHAPTER TWENTY

Denilyn
January 2010

The picture I'd taken was a clear shot, straight on, of his face. I'd transferred the photo from my phone to my laptop, where his dark eyes, surprised, stared at me from the screen. With time to really look at him, to consider what about him was familiar without the stress of his presence, I was surer than ever that I did know him, or at least had seen him, possibly met him, somewhere.

But where? The answer still eluded me.

I attached the photo to an email and sent it to Daniel Neibuhr, as he'd asked me to do when I'd called him. They could run it through a facial recognition program of some sort and see if it matched photos of offenders in their data bank. If this guy had a record, there was a chance they'd make a match and identify him.

We now knew for certain that he'd sent the bracelet and was responsible for the threat that came with it. But the question as to why the third charm was mailed from Seattle remained unanswered. Had the guy following me wanted to frame Keith? If this was a case of erotomania — the delusion that he was in a romantic relationship with me — he could want Keith out of the picture.

In which case Keith could also be in danger.

There was still so much we didn't know, including the guy's identity.

After I sent the photo, on a whim, I opened a new email, attached the photo again, and then wrote a brief note:

Dear Friends,

I am trying to identify the man in this photo. Do you know him? If so, please contact me as soon as possible. This is an urgent matter, one I will explain at a later date. In the meantime, I appreciate your respect of my privacy until the issue is resolved.

Denilyn

I then sent the email and photo to everyone on my contact list, both personal friends and professional acquaintances. I had nothing to lose and everything to gain. I closed my mail app and stared at the photo still open on my screen.

"That's him."

I turned and looked up at Keith. I hadn't heard him come in. He was much later than the thirty minutes he'd predicted in his text before I left the office, but I was growing used to his absences.

"Yes." I looked back at the screen.

"Where'd you get the picture?"

I clicked the photo so it closed and then pushed back from the computer and swiveled in the chair. Keith had plopped down in the upholstered chair in the corner of the den. He ran his hand through his hair. He had dark circles under his eyes. "I took it tonight. At the grocery store. He . . . was there."

Keith said nothing, his expression blank, so I continued. "He'd followed me, I guess. Maybe from the office. I don't know. I was shopping, and suddenly he was behind me. He wanted to know why I wasn't wearing the bracelet."

"So it was from him."

"Evidently."

"Well, that answers that." He got up and headed out of the room.

"Keith, wait."

He stopped at the door of the den and turned back.

"Can we talk about this? How you feel?"

It seemed odd that I was the one asking how he felt. Shouldn't it be the other way around given the circumstances? But I told myself not to overthink it. To offer what Keith needed.

He shrugged. "Nothing to talk about."

"You don't have any feelings or concerns or" — I shrugged — "anything?"

The pulse in his neck throbbed, but he offered nothing and then turned to leave again.

He stopped in the hallway and looked back at me. "I'm going to take a shower and go to bed. I'm beat."

"Wait a minute. I need to talk with you about this. I know you're tired — so am I, believe me. I had a long, stressful evening. Please, just come back and sit down. Just for a few minutes."

If I couldn't offer what he needed — and it was clear I couldn't — then I would seek what was best for me. For us, I believed.

His jaw clenched, but he came back in and sat in the chair again, though obviously he wasn't at ease there.

I leaned forward, my tone gentler. "Babe,

I'm . . . struggling. I'm scared, and I need you. I need your support. Your help through this. How can we get through this — together? What do you need me to do differently, or what do you need in order to support me?"

He stared past me and shrugged. "I don't know. It's just a lot of drama, you know? I can't handle the drama." There was tension in his tone that I'd rarely, if ever, heard.

"Drama? It's more than drama. That implies —"

"You know what I mean."

"Are you angry?"

"I'm tired, okay? I don't want to get into all this now."

I wanted to hurl words at him like darts. I wanted to hurt him as much as I was hurting. *You never want to talk about it,* was what I wanted to say. *You never want to deal with anything important.* And that was just the beginning. I took a deep breath. "When would it work for you to talk about it?"

"I don't know." He got up.

"What about with someone? What if we made an appointment with a counselor who could help us navigate —"

"Of course, that would work for you, wouldn't it Dr. Costa?"

"What? Keith, this is me. What are you

doing? Are you trying to hurt me?"

"You know, Deni, not everything is about you." With that he turned and walked out.

Who was he? The man I'd just seen was as unknown to me as the stranger in the store tonight. Both were only vaguely familiar. I'd never heard that type of sarcasm or accusation from my husband. Never. My throat ached, but I knew crying would drain any remaining emotional energy I had. I leaned back in the desk chair, closed my eyes, and swallowed my tears. I had to preserve myself, my energy. Had to protect myself in any and every way I could.

Protect myself from Keith? When had that become necessary?

Just as I was pulling myself out of the chair to follow Keith to bed, my laptop dinged, indicating an email had just arrived in my inbox.

Then my phone rang.

I slumped back into the chair and saw Ryan's name on the screen of my phone. As much as I cared about Ryan and our friendship, he required energy I didn't have right now. I let the call go to voice mail and opened my email app instead.

The email was also from Ryan, a response to the email I'd just sent. I opened it, and even before I'd finished reading it, I grabbed my phone and called him back.

"You know him? How?" The fatigue I'd felt just moments before was replaced with adrenaline. "Who is he?"

"Brad. That's all I remember, but I'll figure out his last name. He was a kayaker who hung around Mick's sometimes. Or at the bar at The Gateway. Remember? Quiet guy. Like he was hiding something."

I searched my mind but came up blank. "No, I don't remember. I knew him too?"

"Remember the guy I had the run-in with that night at The Gateway? With Adelia?"

"The guy who had a thing for her? The guy who . . . Oh Ryan!"

The memories flowed like an engorged creek — so many details they threatened to flood my mind. Several of us had met at The Gateway late one evening. They had live music — a band from Southern California was playing, and we'd gone to hang out, listen to the music, and cure the nighttime boredom we often suffered in the small town. Most of Three Rivers shut down about 7:00 p.m. The Gateway was the "hot spot," if there was one.

That night Jaylan and I met Ryan and Adelia there. It had become clear early that summer that they had something going on besides the friendship we'd all shared. Ryan was clearly infatuated, though why it had taken him so long to figure out he was drawn to her, who knew. But all that intensity of his was redirected to Adelia, or Addie, as we called her then — the nickname Mick had given her. Even Jay agreed that Ryan had softened, or was *"at least easier to bear."*

Because the place was jammed that night, we'd grabbed the only open seats, stools at the bar. We ordered drinks, though none of us were big drinkers, and turned the stools to watch the band and the action on the dance floor.

The music was so loud that talking was pointless, but soon it became clear that the guy sitting on the other side of Addie was trying his best to have a conversation with her. I only noticed because I saw a look of agitation on her face as the guy tried to engage her. I was on the other side of Ryan, so I nudged him and pointed out what he'd missed.

It was a nudge I regretted.

As soon as Ryan saw what was happening, he'd stood, and Addie had looked at him and put out her hand, as if to ward him off or hold him back. I couldn't see Ryan's expression, but I could imagine it. Ignoring Addie's cue to back off, he got in the guy's face, pointed a finger, and unleashed a tirade of some sort. I couldn't hear it, but again, I could imagine. I'd seen Ryan angry, and it was clear whatever he'd said was heated.

When Ryan grabbed the guy by the shirt, Adelia grabbed Ryan's arm, and the guy lifted his hands, as if surrendering, and backed off, literally. He'd grabbed his beer off the bar and moved somewhere else. Or left. I didn't know, and at the time it didn't seem to matter.

It made sense now why my memories of him were vague. The bar was dark, the music blaring. Though I'd seen him, I hadn't recognized him as someone who'd hung around Mick's. At least not until the next day when I saw him again. This time from a distance, across the property. He'd stood in the shade of a cottonwood near the fence and stared at something. When I followed his gaze, I realized he was watching Adelia as she helped load rafts into one of the storage units.

In hindsight I recognized the expression he'd worn that day. It was the same expression I'd seen on his face as he watched me, both at Kepler's and again as he leaned against that tree in the church courtyard.

That was the beginning of the end of that

horrific summer.

"Ryan, why . . . me? What is he thinking?"

"I don't know. You barely remember the guy. Does he remember you? I don't get it."

"He knows my name. He's done his research, that's for sure. First name, middle name, last name. The first time I saw him was at a signing — he had my book. He definitely knows me, or thinks he does. He must remember me from Three Rivers. There's a link. There has to be."

"Wait, Deni. Where'd that photo of him come from?"

"I took it. Tonight. I was at the grocery store, and he was there, following me." In a torrent of words, I told Ryan everything that happened, about the questions the guy had asked, about the woman who interrupted us, and then about trying to find him in the parking lot. I told him how I felt, the fear that consumed me, and how when I'd finally gotten back into my car, I was so nauseated I was sure I'd be sick.

I told him how when I'd come home, I'd walked in alone and felt adrift, bereft, with nothing to keep me afloat. Like water tumbling over a spillway, I spilled all the emotions I'd dammed over the last few weeks.

I told him everything I'd wanted to tell Keith.

I talked until the river of emotion had run dry.

Or almost dry.

I stopped short of sharing my growing doubt about my husband, and my marriage.

"Why didn't you call me tonight? If Keith wasn't there, I'd have come over until he got home. You know that. I'm here to help. Whatever you need."

I wiped my damp cheeks, grateful Ryan couldn't see my tears. "Thank you. But I have to get through this — I did get through it. Keith would have been here if he could. He just . . ." Was I really going to cover for him? "Anyway, thank you. And thank you for listening."

"Hey, that's what friends are for, right?"

After Ryan and I said our goodbyes, I sat in the silence of the den for a long time considering all Ryan had offered me. His viewpoints, personal and professional when I asked, his understanding, compassion, and support. All the things I'd desired and needed from my husband but that Keith was either unwilling or unable to give, Ryan gave freely.

But it wasn't fair to compare the two men. Their experiences of my circumstances were entirely different, and each would process them in his own way. God had provided a friend when I needed one tonight. I was grateful, and I'd leave it at that.

I had to leave it at that.

CHAPTER TWENTY-ONE

Denilyn
February 15, 2017

As students filter into the classroom and take their seats, I'm grateful for what I anticipate will serve as ninety minutes of both normalcy and distraction. If only I can discipline my mind to focus — although I know there's more to it than discipline.

A few minutes before it's time for class to begin, Willow walks into the room and makes her way to the front where I'm seated. I stand up as she approaches. "I am so glad to see you. How are you?"

Her fair skin tinges pink as she looks from me to the floor and back again. "I'm okay. I know you don't have time to talk right now, but I just wanted to tell you I got your email. Sorry I didn't respond. I've just been, like, sort of overwhelmed. I made some changes to my schedule, so . . ." She shrugs. "That'll help."

"Thanks for letting me know. I was just concerned about you."

"Thanks. So, okay, I'll see you later." She turns to go, then looks back and waves.

I watch her as she walks out of the classroom. Her thin frame looks almost brittle. Was her timing intentional? Did she come now knowing I wouldn't have time to talk or ask questions? Though I'm glad she connected with me, something about the brief encounter unsettles me.

But then, unsettled is my most frequent state of being these days, so I take that into consideration.

I switch on the projector and then find the PowerPoint presentation on my laptop that supports my lecture. When I had one of the university's IT guys look at my laptop to see if he could find the missing file with my presentations and the syllabi for my classes, there was no sign of it. Although the file was easily restored from my backup drive, I still don't understand what happened. The missing file is more than an annoyance; it's baffling. One more event I can't explain.

I turn to the class. "Before we get started, are there any questions based on the reading I assigned? Or did anything strike you?"

Several students look at me, eyes wide,

terrified I might call on them. It's an expression I'm very familiar with. Others dig through backpacks so they won't have to make eye contact with me. Then there are those whose blank stares make me wonder if they've even heard me.

"So the chapter enthralled you, I see." A few students offer sheepish smiles. "Let's see if I can pique your interest, but in order to do that, you'll need to participate. Don't leave me all alone up here, people."

I reach for my mug, take a sip of my lukewarm coffee, and wish I could infuse caffeine directly into my system and, come to think of it, into my students too. Early morning classes have their drawbacks.

I glance at the screen then turn to the class. "Who, based on the reading, can give me an example of a psychological influence on aggression?"

I wait until finally a student raises his hand. "Sanji, go ahead." I can always count on Sanji to get things going.

"Personality traits." His tone is confident.

"Yes. Give us an example."

"Someone who either lacks empathy or has low empathy for others."

"Thank you. How about another example of a personality trait that may lead to aggressive behavior?"

Another hand goes up. "Yes, Meghan."

"Impulsivity."

"Good. Give me an example of how someone who lacks empathy or is impulsive might display aggressive behavior."

Meghan thinks for a moment. "Like, bullying?"

I nod, and another student raises his hand. "Jason . . ."

"Cyberbullying. Like that guy whose ex just offed herself because of the stuff he said about her on social media."

"She committed suicide. Yes, that's an example of how someone who lacks empathy and may also be impulsive might demonstrate aggressive behavior that leads to tragic consequences. It's also an event that's become all too common."

A young woman in the back of the class raises her hand. Her name has slipped my mind, so I point. "Yes?"

"My sister went out with a guy — they only went out once — she wasn't that into him. So when he asked her out again, she said no. Then he started harassing her and following her everywhere, like stalking her. She finally had to get a restraining order against him. That's aggression, right? Kind of like bullying?"

I take a deep breath and then address the

class. "What do you think?"

Heads nod in unison, and another student speaks up. "That also demonstrates both a lack of empathy and impulsivity, right?"

"Definitely a lack of empathy. Anytime someone forces unwanted attention or behaviors on another person, which a stalker certainly does, it's a form of bullying. Oftentimes there's an imbalance of power between a bully and the person they're bullying — it may be social power, physical power, or even financial power."

"Aren't you kind of an expert on that?" Jason asks.

"An . . . expert?" I've never had a student in the classroom directly ask me about my experience. "Actually . . . I guess you could say that." I have nothing to lose here, only something to offer, I remind myself. "I had a man stalk me over the course of a year. Perhaps similar to what your sister went through" — I'm grateful when her name comes to me — "Kassy."

There isn't a student whose attention isn't completely focused on me now.

Kassy is the first to respond. "What happened?"

I run my hand through my hair, the raised scar on the side of my head a permanent reminder of exactly what happened. But I won't share the details. "He was arrested, tried, and is serving a sentence in one of our state's corrections facilities."

"Deni?"

"Yes, Jason."

"Sorry. I mean, I'm sorry for whatever you went through, but that wasn't what I meant, exactly. Aren't you an expert on bullying? You wrote a book, right?"

"Oh yes . . . The book was based on research I did for my doctorate. I'm not sure I'm an expert, but I've researched the topic extensively. And, like Kassy's sister, I also have some personal experience with an extreme form of bullying, or aggression."

I glance back at my presentation on the screen and then click ahead several slides until I reach a brief quiz I've developed. "There are other psychological influences on aggression, including environmental influences, as you know if you've read the chapter. Take out a piece of paper and go through the questions on the screen, listing your answers, and then we'll go through the questions. I'll give you about ten minutes."

The quiz provides the breather I need to assimilate my thoughts and gather my emotions. While I've never intended to hide my past from my students, neither have I offered to share it. Speaking about it brings it all rushing back. I rub the back of my neck and take a few deep breaths. As I do, my phone dings somewhere in my briefcase. I forgot to turn off the volume.

I reach for the briefcase and pull out the phone to glance at the screen. I type in my security code and then open my texts and see I've received something from an unfamiliar number. When I open it, the text includes just one letter: *D.*

Before I can turn off the volume, another text arrives: *I*

No. Please, no . . .

Then comes the third, and what I know will be the final letter: *E.*

As the phone crashes to the floor, I reach out and grip the edge of the table, rattling the projector.

When I look up, all eyes are on me.

February 21, 2017

I hug the pillow tight to my chest. "It's starting all over. How can it all be happening again?" I sob.

Heather gets up from her seat, grabs a box of tissues, and comes and sits next to me on the sofa. She hands me the box, then rests her hand on my shoulder.

I take a few tissues and wipe my eyes. "I can't do this again. I can't!"

"I'm sorry, Deni. I am so sorry."

Heather lets me cry, and I realize it's the first time since the accident that I've allowed myself to fully feel the impact of what's happening. At home I felt the need to remain strong, to keep my fear to myself. At work I had to remain focused. But here I can let go of all I've held inside and trust Heather not only to handle it but to help me work through the feelings. Still, we both know there are no easy answers.

She gently pats my shoulder, then goes back and sits across from me. "Do you want to tell me what's happened?"

Though we exchanged messages after the accident, I didn't schedule an additional appointment to see Heather. The doctor advised me not to drive for several days — to give my neck and shoulder time to begin healing. Then there was the issue of having to secure a rental car while waiting to find out if my SUV was repairable or declared a total loss. And I knew I'd have my hands full once I returned to work.

I share the details of the accident and the myriad emotions it evoked. "Until Wednesday I thought there was a chance it was a fluke — that rather than someone targeting me, it was a case of road rage. That I was just the person in the way." I wipe my eyes again.

What I don't say, what I can't bring myself to say out loud is that because of where the accident, or attack as I now see it, took place, on the road to my home, I'm certain that whoever is doing this knows where I live. Should that surprise me? No. But I'd clung to the hope that Mathison, who was sentenced before I purchased the property and home, wouldn't know where I lived now.

I've felt safe in my home, a rare gift. It's become my refuge. But now . . .

"What happened Wednesday?" Heather's question pulls me back to the moment.

"I . . . received three texts while I was teaching. The sender used a smartphone app that generates untraceable numbers. Each text included just one . . . letter." I bend at the waist and sob again. "I can't do this again. I can't."

"Take your time, Deni. You're okay. You're safe here."

When I've caught my breath again, Heather continues. "I suppose I don't need to guess the letters."

"D-I-E."

"Oh Deni . . . What have the police said?"

"Bradley Mathison is still incarcerated.

Parole hearing scheduled the first week of June. Nothing's changed."

"So . . . ?"

"Who knows?" I shrug. "I was told it's possible he hired someone, or . . . maybe there's someone else. Which I can't even begin to process."

"Were the details of the bracelet and charms ever released publicly?"

"Not that I know of."

"And the vehicle that ran into you?"

I shake my head. "Nothing so far. They haven't located it." I lean back into the soft down of the sofa. "All these years I've never felt like it was over. Like . . . I couldn't get over it because it wasn't over, even though it appeared, when Mathison was sentenced, that it was over. But that sense of peace I'd waited for never came. Now, if nothing else, I feel less crazy. Though that's a very small consolation."

"You're not crazy," Heather says quietly. "I know you've felt that way, but you're one of the strongest, healthiest women I know. Are you still struggling? Yes, but not without reason. The recurring PTSD symptoms may make more sense now. You were right — this isn't over. But you will get through this. You will."

I want to believe, Heather, I do, but I can't

claim that assurance for myself yet. "You'll have to keep believing that for me."

"I will, Deni. I will."

Before I left Heather's office, we discussed things I might do to help myself feel safe — at work, at home, and everywhere else. Though I can't ensure my safety, it helped to discuss a few concrete choices I can make.

A simple choice is to remind myself that I'm not in this alone. Not only am I surrounded by family and friends who will support me emotionally, and physically if I need them, but I also have law enforcement behind me working on my case.

As Heather suggested, it's time I have a few conversations and put some plans into place. I press a button on the steering wheel and speak, "Call Jay." The voice-activated system dials her number, and within moments her voice fills the inside of the rental.

"Hey, I was just thinkin' about you. How you doin'?"

"Honestly?"

"That's the only kind of conversation I want, you know that."

"I was counting on that. I'm okay but not great. I just left Heather's."

"How was your session?"

Fatigue, like an anchor, threatens to pull me under. I shift in the driver's seat. "Exhausting but helpful. I've done the equivalent of holding my breath since those texts on Wednesday. It was good to exhale and get all the emotion out, at least for the moment. We also came up with some plans. Have a few minutes for me to run something by you?"

"I got all the time in the world. Gabe's workin'. He'll want to hear whatever you have to say too, you know. But I'll fill him in."

"Thank you. I decided it would help me to know I have a place to go on the spur of the moment if necessary. If" — I take a deep breath — "something's going on at home. If I don't feel it's safe for us there for some reason and we need to get away quickly. I know it's a lot to ask, but how would you and Gabe feel about making your place available? We wouldn't stay more than a night or two, but your home has always been a safe place —"

"Don't say nothin' more. I'll talk to Gabe, and then I imagine we'll have a key made for you. And what's this about not staying more than a night or two? You think anyone's goin' to come after you here? They better think twice before they go up against Gabe."

"Thank you. I can't imagine that happening, but I realized . . ." I falter.

"What? What'd you realize? Spit it out."

I have to say it. I have to face it. "Whoever this is knows . . . where I live. Most likely, anyway. I just . . . I'd just feel better having a place to go, if . . . You know."

"You've got it. We've got your back, sister, you know that. We'll do everything we can. Gabe is all over those guys workin' your case too. Of course. We're here for whatever you need."

"Thanks, Jay."

"But listen, that's not all. I'm here for you. You need to talk through something, you need to cry or yell or scream, you know who to call. Unless I'm with a client, I'm available. Don't forget that. I'm prayin' for you too, and I know that may not be what you want to hear, but it's the truth."

After talking with Jay, I call Ryan and get his voice mail. I leave a message asking if he can have coffee or lunch tomorrow on campus, and explain it's a personal matter rather than professional.

Finally, I make the most important call.

One I should have made after the accident, but I realize now that talking to him

256

would have it made it all too real.

But he has to know.

When I hear his voice, a lump lodges in my throat and the road ahead swims. I swipe at my tears as I find my voice, "Hi, it's me . . ."

CHAPTER TWENTY-TWO

Denilyn
February 22, 2017

Ryan jabs a piece of chicken with his fork and lifts it from the salad he's eating. "So, what's up? You said it was personal? You okay? How's your neck?" He takes the bite and chews.

I reach for my neck and knead it. "It's okay — healing, I think." I stir my soup, steam rising. "I know we've both had a lot going on, so I wanted to catch up and ask a favor." I set my spoon down and lean back in the chair. The cafeteria bustles with activity, and I trust our conversation will be lost to the surrounding noise. "Last week, during my early class . . ." I take a deep breath.

"What? What happened?"

I recount receiving the texts. His reaction is what I expected.

"What? Are you kidding me?" He sets down his fork. "Who's working your case?

Is Gabe involved? It has to be Mathison, doesn't it? Who else would know to send those exact texts? He's still locked up, right? Isn't that what they told you?"

I smile, though it takes effort. "Which question would you like me to answer first?"

The lines in his forehead deepen. "How about all of them?"

I lean forward. "No, I'm not kidding, a couple of very capable, I assume, detectives are working my case with Gabe checking every detail, and yes, I was notified that Bradley Mathison is still serving his term. Satisfied?"

"No. Are you?"

I sigh. "No, I'm not. But I do believe — I have to believe — that the sheriff's department is doing everything they can to find out who is threatening me. The texts, if nothing else, confirm that the *accident* was anything but accidental. It was intentional, just as it seemed. I'd hoped otherwise. But, it is what it is." I say all of this to Ryan with little emotion. I can't let myself feel this. Not here.

"Yeah, okay. So what's the favor? By the way, my answer is 'yes,' whatever it is. You know that, right?"

"Yes, I do know. Thank you. I need someone here, on campus, I can call if anything happens or if I suspect anything may happen. I know I don't need to ask that of you. But I wanted to ask. Also, just . . . keep your eyes open. If you notice anything —"

"Of course."

"Thank you. And the next time you offer to walk me to my car, I may take you up on it. My pride has to take a back seat to my safety."

"Good. Now we're getting somewhere. What else can I do?"

"Honestly, I don't know. I've been reluctant to depend on my friends again. It feels like asking a lot, but I realize now that I need to surround myself with those who will support me until all of this is over." I push the soup away. "If it's *ever* over."

As we cross the campus from the cafeteria to the psychology and science building, Ryan pulls up the collar of his coat against the chill in the air. "Hey, the other day, that thing with Jon at the Bean, and then later?"

He slows his pace, and I turn to look at him.

"I owe you an apology. If you're seeing him, that's your business."

"Thank you, but an apology isn't necessary. I was serious when I said that Jon and I are just friends." I stop on the pathway.

"Ryan, I can't get involved with anyone right now. Can you imagine? With all I have going on personally? More importantly, I don't want to confuse . . ." I shake my head. "You know. We've been over this many times." I wrap my arms around myself. "Let's get inside."

"Yeah, okay." As we begin walking again, at a fast clip this time, Ryan continues. "Well, for what it's worth, I am sorry. Oh, by the way, I don't know what you found out about Willow, but I did receive notification that she's dropped my class — her TA position."

"She did?" We climb the steps to the building. When we've reached the doors, I pause. "She told me she'd made some changes to her schedule, that she was feeling overwhelmed. But I'm surprised she'd leave you without a TA."

"I'll get by."

Again, something about Willow's actions leave me unsettled.

February 24, 2017
After my morning class, I leave the classroom with the intent of returning to my office to grade papers, but just before I reach the stairs, I see Willow heading for the doors to leave the building. "Willow . . ."

She turns, sees me, and pauses.

"Do you have a few minutes to catch up?"

"Um, sure. I don't have another class until this afternoon."

"Great. Want to follow me to my office?"

She looks toward the stairs and seems to hesitate. "I was going to the Bean for coffee. Could we go there?"

She has dark semicircles under her eyes, and the pack on her back seems to weigh her down. I want to provide an opportunity for her to talk if she chooses to do so. "Sure, I can always drink another cup of coffee."

As we cross the campus, we talk about events at the university — the spring choral production, the theater department's production of *Oklahoma,* and the new dorm building due for completion next fall. Small talk.

When we enter the Bean, there's only one table available. "Why don't you grab the table and I'll order our coffee. What would you like?"

She reaches into her backpack and pulls out her wallet. "Just a small, black."

I smile. "Put your money away. My treat. Would you like something to eat too?"

She shakes her head. "No. I'm good."

I order our coffees and then take them to the table, where Willow stares at the screen of her phone. I set the cups on the table, and she looks up. "Thanks. I mean, you didn't have to do that."

"I'm paying it forward." I sit down across from Willow and take in her appearance. "Willow, are you taking care of yourself? Are you eating and getting enough sleep?"

She lifts one thin shoulder. "Sort of."

"What does 'sort of' mean?"

"I'm just stressed, I guess, so I'm not eating as much. But it's not like I have an eating disorder or anything like that. Really."

"I believe you. I'm just concerned."

"Thanks, there's just stuff going on." She reaches for a packet of sugar. "Um, remember when you asked if I was talking to anyone?"

"I do."

"Could you, maybe, give me the name of someone I could . . . see?" She looks down at her coffee as she speaks. "My sister might help pay for someone. I talked to her a little, and she and her husband could help, at least for a few appointments."

"That's a positive step, Willow. I'm happy to refer you to someone. In fact, when I was practicing, I had a partner I shared an office with. She's a wonderful therapist. I also have names of other therapists I recommend. You can call and chat with a couple of them if you'd like, and see if they feel like a good fit. Sometimes it takes a few appointments before you're comfortable with someone; other times you click right away. How does that sound?"

"If I see one of them, will they . . . tell you . . . ?" She bites her bottom lip.

I give her a moment to finish her question. When she doesn't, I help her along. "Are you wondering about confidentiality?"

Her fair complexion colors as she nods.

"A therapist will protect your privacy. What you talk about will remain confidential."

Willow doesn't share anything more, but she doesn't need to. I agree to email Jaylan's contact information to her, along with the names of a couple other therapists I recommend. I am grateful she'll see someone. If she does choose Jay, I'm hopeful she'll feel at ease with her. If anyone can put a new client at ease, it's Jay.

After we part ways, I make my way back across campus and consider our conversation. What was it exactly Willow had asked — or not asked? *If I see one of them, will they tell you . . . ?* Was it me specifically she wondered if a therapist would share information with? Or did she intend her question to be more general in nature? Maybe

she just referenced me because I know the
therapists.

It doesn't matter, of course. Willow has
every right to privacy.

But still, I wonder.

"Will they tell you . . . ?"

Will they tell me what?

CHAPTER TWENTY-THREE

Denilyn
January 2010

Several days after I'd taken the photo and Keith and I had argued — or not argued; I wasn't sure what had happened — I once again arrived home to an empty house. Daily I was more thankful that we'd installed an alarm. I'd also purchased timers for several lights, upstairs and downstairs, so I no longer walked into a dark house when I returned home alone.

I came in from the garage, deactivated the alarm, and then went upstairs to change my clothes.

Keith and I had spoken little since that night, so when I heard the garage door open shortly after I came in, I hoped we could spend some time together working through things.

When Keith came into the house, the door slammed behind him. "Deni? Where are you?" It was clear by his tone that he was angry, which was an emotion I'd rarely seen him exhibit. But lately he'd become someone I didn't know.

"I'll be right down." As a therapist, I understood anger, but I'd never grown comfortable with it personally. I finished changing as quickly as I could and made my way downstairs, where Keith was pacing between the kitchen and family room. "What's wrong?"

"Why'd that detective show up at my office this afternoon?"

"I don't know. What did he say?"

"He wanted to ask me more questions about Seattle — what I did there, where I'd gone." Keith grew ugly in his anger. "You name it, he asked it. All questions he'd already asked me. He couldn't have called or sent an email to set a time for that conversation? Instead, he embarrasses me by showing up at my place of work? Just in case you're not clear on this, I did *not* send that charm!"

I worked to keep my tone level. "I know you didn't."

"Really? Did you share that news with your detective friend?"

I bristled. "Keith" — I took a deep breath — "how is this my fault? I'm not sure what you want me to do about any of this. I'm frustrated. Actually, more than frustrated. I'm really hurt. I need your support through this, not your blame or anger. Can't you see that I . . . need you? I need your help." I wiped tears from my cheeks.

He stared at me a moment, expression blank, and then he turned and walked back out to the garage, the door slamming behind him again.

I stood stunned, not knowing what to do.

But as it turned out, I didn't have to do anything.

He'd left.

"Hey, Deni. That guy's name is Bradley Mathison. M-a-t-h-i-s-o-n. I called a guy I knew in Three Rivers — he used to work for Mick. I remember seeing him with the guy a time or two. He said Mathison used to rent kayaks from Mick — never had one of his own. The guy hasn't seen Mathison in several years but said he lived in the area at one time — grew up there. Hey, the guy told me something else too — something this guy claimed. When you have a few minutes, call me."

Ryan had called sometime after I got home and Keith left. But I'd missed the call. I listened to the voice mail again, this time writing down the name. Then I called Daniel Neibuhr and left him much the same message that Ryan had left me. I hoped I'd hear something back from him soon.

My next inclination was to call Keith and tell him. Hope had surged with Ryan's message, and I wanted to share it with Keith. But after all that had transpired, I didn't think even a step toward resolution of this case would be welcome news.

It was clear he wanted nothing to do with the case or the circumstances surrounding it.

What had happened to the man I'd married? Or to the marriage itself? Even if Bradley Mathison was found and arrested, how could we mend the fissure between us? It grew wider by the day.

How would we ever traverse that canyon? We'd both have to agree to do a lot of work — work I wasn't certain Keith would choose to do. How had my life crumbled so quickly?

I rambled through the empty house, finally standing for a long time in front of the open refrigerator, knowing I should eat something, but nothing appealed. In fact, food seemed to repel me. When my phone rang, I grabbed it, hoping it was Keith. But instead, it was Ryan calling again.

I decided I might as well talk to him and

see what other information he'd garnered. "Hi there. I got your message. Thank you."

"Yeah. Let's hope they find him and put an end to this, right?"

"Exactly."

"I wanted to tell you something else the guy I talked to mentioned. Do you have a minute?"

I pulled out one of the barstools and settled there. "I have more than a minute."

"Are you okay? You sound beat."

I swallowed the ache in my throat. "Yes, I'm okay. Thanks for asking. This is all just . . . taking a toll."

"I can imagine. I'm sorry. How's Keith handling it?"

"I . . . don't really know. You'd have to ask him."

Ryan was silent a moment. "Is he home? There with you?"

I hesitated. "No, not right now."

"Are you comfortable alone? If you want someone there, I can come over."

I looked around the empty house and at the darkness beyond the windows. He, Bradley Mathison, could be out there right now, watching the house, watching me. "I'm okay, but thank you."

"Deni, this is me. I know you, remember?"

"I know you do. I appreciate the offer,

really. This is wearing, but . . . I'll get through it." I knew I needed to keep the conversation on track for both our sakes. I couldn't let my vulnerability lead me somewhere I couldn't go. Didn't want to go. "So, what did you find out?"

"Yeah . . . So, I guess Bradley Mathison used to brag about his relationship with Adelia — made a big deal about seeing her and taking her out behind my back."

"What?"

"C'mon, you must've known. I *knew* she cheated on me."

His tone, his words, chilled me.

"Ryan, you're not serious. Adelia would never have —"

"You don't have to protect her anymore."

"Protect her? I'm not protecting her. She wasn't unfaithful. Mathison is delusional. He's mentally ill. Isn't he proving that now? When I saw him in the grocery store, he couldn't understand why I wasn't wearing the bracelet he'd sent me. Think about that . . . Bragging to anyone about a relationship he wasn't actually involved in sounds like an erotomanic delusion. He likely thought Adelia was in love with him. He may think I'm in love with him. He isn't healthy, Ryan."

"Yeah, maybe."

"There's no maybe about it. Listen, as I said, I'm a little worn, frazzled, by all of this. I don't mean to sound unsympathetic, but I truly believe Adelia loved you and was faithful to you. If she wasn't with you, she was with me or with Jay. There wasn't anyone else."

"Yeah, okay." I wasn't sure he was convinced. "Hey, I called to offer you support, not the other way around. Sorry I went off. You know me — I get a little intense, right?"

"On occasion, maybe. But it's part of your charm." My comment didn't lighten his mood as I'd hoped.

"Sure it is. Listen, I'll let you go. I assume you've reported the guy's name?"

"I did. I hope to hear back from one of the detectives soon."

"Okay, let me know what you find out. You know I'm here if you need me."

"I know. Thanks."

After the call with Ryan, I got up and walked around the house to check each of the doors again to make sure they were locked. I paused at the front door. Was he out there? I turned away and walked back to the kitchen, stopping on my way to set the alarm. I couldn't let myself dwell on the "what ifs." Detective Neibuhr assured me they'd have a car patrolling our neighborhood.

As I set the teapot to boil for what had become my nightly cup of chamomile tea, something occurred to me. I went back to the island where I'd left my phone and called Daniel Neibuhr again. When I didn't reach him, I left a second voice mail.

"Hi Dan, now that I know who sent the bracelet and charms, and know a little more about his background, I think it's possible he, Bradley Mathison, knew Keith was in Seattle when he sent that last charm. I have reason to believe he may have set out to frame Keith. Give me a call when you have a minute, and I'll explain. Thank you."

It seemed plausible that Mathison might have tried to frame Keith to get him out of the picture so he could — I shuddered at the thought — have me to himself. Or maybe he thought he was helping me in some way by framing Keith. Either explanation could fit within the context of an erotomanic delusion, I reasoned. While it may sound far-fetched to those not familiar with erotomania, the mention of the name John Hinkley Jr. — the man who shot President Ronald Regan in order to impress an actress, Jodie Foster — helped people understand the lengths someone might go in the midst of such a delusion. My theory seemed worth sharing with those working my case.

After the teapot whistled, I poured the boiling water over a tea bag in a mug. Then I picked up my phone again.

This time I called Keith.

But there was no answer.

Close to midnight, when Keith still hadn't come home, I texted him: GOING TO BED. THE ALARM IS SET. DON'T FORGET TO ENTER THE CODE WHEN YOU GET HOME.

Would he come home? I couldn't imagine him staying out all night without letting me know. But then, I couldn't have imagined his behavior the last few weeks either.

After I readied myself for bed, I climbed between the sheets and pulled the blankets over me. I lay there for several minutes listening to the sounds of the house — the refrigerator running in the kitchen, the ice maker dropping cubes in the freezer, the roof creaking. Outside a gusting wind blew.

Never had I felt so alone.

I reached over and turned off the lamp on the nightstand. I rolled over, praying sleep would come yet certain it wouldn't.

Where was Keith? *Lord, please protect him. Help him . . .*

I tossed and turned until it was clear sleep

would indeed elude me. I sat up and reached for the bedside lamp again. Maybe reading would make me sleepy. But just as I was about to turn the lamp on, I heard a car on the street below. I got up and pulled the drape back from the window by our bed in time to see a police cruiser pass under the streetlamp just beyond our house. I watched as the car slowly made its way up the street.

They were watching, I assumed, for the man who'd terrorized me.

The man who'd turned my life inside out.

I woke the next morning, groggy after finally falling into a deep sleep sometime in the early morning hours. When I rolled over, I saw that Keith's side of the bed was empty. Was he traveling? No, that wasn't it. A weight in my chest reminded me that something was wrong, but the details were lost in the haze of slumber. I sat up and looked around our bedroom. As I did, the memory of Keith's anger the night before returned, and with it came a wave of nausea.

How could this be happening?

Had he really stayed out all night?

I climbed out of bed, pulled on my bathrobe, and peeked into our guest room, hoping I'd find Keith asleep there, but it was empty. Instead, I found him, still dressed in what were now rumpled clothes, curled under a throw on the sofa in the family room.

He stirred when he heard me. "Hey," he mumbled.

"What are you doing down here?"

"I didn't want to wake you when I got home." He pushed the throw back and sat up. "I'm an idiot. I'm sorry." His voice was still thick with sleep.

I went to the sofa and sat next to him. As I leaned into him, he pulled away. "Deni . . ."

I pulled back and looked at him.

He ran his hand through his mussed hair. "Listen, I heard what you said last night, and I get it, but I don't know if I can . . . give you what you need. I know this isn't your fault. But it's just" — he shook his head — "it's just a lot. I'm a happy-go-lucky guy, you know that. I can't . . ." He shrugged.

"What are you saying?"

He got up and walked into the kitchen and grabbed the coffeepot and filled it with water. Then he turned back and looked at me. "I don't know what I'm saying, except that I know this isn't your fault. And I know I can't be what you need. You deserve more, but I don't have more to give you. Maybe it's a character flaw or immaturity or . . . I don't know what. But I can't do this."

"I can't change what's happening, so where does that leave us?"

"I don't know." He turned around, opened the canister where we kept coffee, and added several tablespoonsful to the maker, then set it to brew. When he turned back, a look of resolution etched his features. "I love you, but . . ." His broad chest rose and fell with the breath he took. "I feel trapped. I thought I was ready for marriage, but I was wrong."

"Wrong?" I whispered. "What do you mean?"

"Listen, I need some time . . . apart. I need to just take some time. I need to figure out what I mean. This isn't your fault — it's me. I just have to do this. I'm sorry." He turned away and headed for the stairs.

"Keith, wait . . ."

He paused at the bottom of the stairs.

"What are you doing?"

"I'm leaving. I'm going to go stay with a buddy, or . . . I don't know. I'm just going." He turned back and went up the stairs.

I sat on the sofa trying to assimilate what had just happened — what he'd just said. He couldn't mean it, could he? He couldn't be serious. Bile rose in my throat. I got up from the sofa and dashed to the downstairs powder bath, where I leaned over the toilet and heaved, my stomach, like my life, turning inside out.

CHAPTER TWENTY-FOUR

Adelia
May 10, 2017
Wednesday morning, before leaving to unlock the property and give the safety spiel to rafters, I make the call at the designated time to exchange information. We don't dare meet in person — this town is too small for us to go unnoticed together.

"Anything I need to know?" I ask him.

"Just stick with the plan. At this point, nothing has changed."

"Where is he?"

"Not here yet. But he'll come."

"I hope you're right."

"Hey, this was your idea, remember?"

I hesitate. "I remember. Okay, listen, I'm going on a night run tonight with some of the guides."

"Why?"

"You know why."

"No. It's too dangerous. Too big a risk

right now. If we lose you, we never get him. You know that."

"And if I'm not ready by this time next month?"

He's silent, then I hear him blow air through his teeth. "You can do this?"

"I have done it, I can do it, and I will do it. Another run will ensure that all goes well when it's necessary."

"Remember why you're here. Remember your motivation."

"I never forget. I think about him every day, every minute of every day."

"Okay. Be smart. Check with me in the morning so I know you're still alive."

"Very funny."

"I'm serious. Call me."

He ends the call before I agree.

From the beginning, this plan was all or nothing, black or white. It will either work or fail. There are no in-betweens. It's a risk I'm willing to take. "It is a risk I am willing to take." I speak the words aloud, needing to hear them for myself. And I will speak them as many times as necessary.

Is the risk wise? Whether I live or die, the risk facilitates the safety of those I love.

"It is a risk I am willing to take," I whisper again.

Then I grab my backpack and head out

the door to Ride the Kaweah, where Mick's mood, whatever it is this morning, will greet me. The moods he reserves for me alone, I understand now.

The moon, straight overhead now, illuminates the raft as we climb in. Chase has planted himself to hold the raft, and Daphne pushes past me to get in before me.

It was clear and is clear that inviting me wasn't her idea. I suspect she's enjoyed her status as the only female who keeps up with these guys. She can have her status. I'm not interested in fitting in or being accepted. Those days passed long ago. I have just one purpose here, and that's to test and refine my skills.

I take my place, tighten my PFD, and grab the paddle one of the other guys hands me. We put in just above the Gateway Rapid so we're sure of a chaotic and strenuous beginning to our adventure, but one we're accustomed to, I remind myself. I used to make this run at least once a day, five or six days a week. And I've done it several times since arriving back here less than a week ago. Of course those trips were made in daylight.

But tonight isn't any different.

■ ■ ■ ■

"Keep the line!" Chase yells above the roar of the rapids. We position our paddles and then dig in, directing the raft down the familiar line where the water funnels through a series of boulders.

"Line!" Chase yells again.

We work as a team. Whatever Daphne felt about my presence here doesn't matter now. We're a crew.

"Forward, forward!"

We each paddle, fast and hard, working both with and against the river.

"Stop!"

As one, we lift the paddles from the water.

The boulder strewn slalom of Gateway Rapid, a bucking bronco, lurches beneath us. As we approach the bottom of the rapid, the back end of the raft kicks out.

"Back, back-paddle!" Chase yells.

Before I can do anything to help myself, I'm plunged into the torrent. No time to think or act, the construction of the PFD does its job and flips me to my back and brings me to the surface like a buoy. On my back, I do what comes naturally after so many trips down rivers. I pull myself into a sitting position in the water, let my feet float to the surface, and then I straighten my legs a little but not too much, as I may need them to act as shock absorbers. Then I make sure my toes are out of the water.

But before I can look to find the raft, I realize I'm turning in circles. Swirling. Twirling. And just as the strong arm of the river grabs me and pulls me under, I suck in a gulp of air and close my mouth.

I hold my breath.

And hold it.

I open my eyes but can see nothing but the soupy complete blackness. Nothingness.

And hold it.

My body spins, and I try to swim out of the powerful hydraulic, but it doesn't feel as if I make any progress. I flail and fight against the river.

And hold it.

My lungs burn, and I'm not sure if the dizzying sense is from the circular motion of the water or from a lack of oxygen.

Oh God, help me. Help . . .

How long have I been under? Seconds? Minutes? I flail again, trying to loose myself from the river's grip. But it's too strong.

My lungs ache, burn. There's no hope. I will die here. The river will take me, as it's taken so many others. *Oh Lord . . .*

I have nothing left, no fight left.

My head throbs.

Work with the river. Work with it.

Work with it? Work with it. The river, my ally . . .

I stop fighting and instead fumble for the clasps on the vest of the PFD. With fingers numbed from the icy water, each clasp is needles in my fingers, but I work to undo them anyway.

Hope offers a burst of energy, and I struggle out of the vest.

I have no way of knowing which way the bottom of the river is and which way the surface of the water is — I am lost, completely. At the mercy of the water.

But then I remember, it doesn't matter which way the surface is, or the bottom.

Lungs on fire, I use the last of my strength to pull my knees to my chest. I wrap my arms around them, then release any remaining air in my lungs.

I begin to drop, to sink.

I sink, and sink.

Just when I'm sure it's over, when I know I'm about to pass out, my back hits something hard, and then what feels like sand and pebbles swirl around me, chafing me.

I've reached the bottom, and suddenly my ally propels me beyond the hydraulic.

With my pulse roaring in my ears, the

river spits me out.

As I break the surface of the water, I gasp, cough, and wheeze, and gasp again. I fill my lungs, exhale, and fill them again. Sputtering, I inhale and exhale again and again. I roll to my back, letting the river carry me. I breathe deep, over and over.

"Adelia!"

Did someone call my name?

A light flashes, then it's gone. The sloshing, churning water is in my ears, surrounding me in every direction, the tumult constant. I'm sure I've imagined it. I have nothing left. Nothing. The river begins tossing me to and fro, sloshing over me, pulling me down again.

It will take me where it will.

The light flashes again. They're looking for me. Suddenly something jerks my shoulders from above, causing my dry suit to cut into my neck, and I'm lifted out of the water, pulled from the current. Hands wrap around my upper arms, and I'm flung over the side of the raft.

They've found me and pulled me in. I'm on my back, on the bottom of the raft, legs still draped over the side.

"Is she conscious?" A female voice yells above the din.

I open my eyes and see the faces above

me, young faces, worried. And then I know what I must do regardless of the effort it takes.

I smile.

I open my mouth, take one more breath, and then force a laugh. "Whoa . . . Great ride." I will myself to move, to roll myself over, every inch of my body screaming as I do. That done, one of the guys reaches for my elbow. And with him steadying me, I get myself in a sitting position.

One of the other guys is leaning over the side of the raft, the stick end of the paddle in the water. When he pulls the paddle in, my vest is hooked to the handle, its reflective tape shimmering in the moonlight.

Arms like noodles, I struggle into the vest, just as I'd struggled out of it. I get back into position and someone hands me a paddle, and although my arms are limp, I look at Daphne, seated at an angle across from me on the other side of the raft, and I lift the paddle and hope she can't see my arms trembling from the exertion. "Like I said, it's not my first rodeo," I yell.

The bravado I work to convey is false.

I am alive by no feat of my own.

I am alive only because God has spared me.

Again.

CHAPTER TWENTY-FIVE

Denilyn
January 2010

After Keith left, I spent the next two days alone. I didn't leave the house. I didn't speak with anyone. I couldn't bear the thought of telling anyone what had happened. It was more than wounded pride. Maybe it was hope — the hope that Keith would change his mind or come to his senses. Hope that he'd miss me. That he'd realize he'd made a horrible mistake. But with each passing hour, hope waned like the warmth of the setting sun and was instead replaced with the icy realization that my husband had left me when I needed him most.

He hadn't completely abandoned me. He'd sent one text letting me know he was staying with a friend from college and would be in touch. He asked me to let him know when would be a good time to come by and pick up more of his things.

But that was it. No remorse. No regret. Or so it seemed.

I'd canceled my clients and texted Jay, feigning illness. Which wasn't much of a stretch. I felt ill. More than sick. I could barely function.

Finally, on the third day, after two sleepless nights, I called my mom.

Sobbing.

And asked if I could come home.

Someone had threatened my life, and my husband was gone. Staying at the house alone wasn't only unwise; it wasn't healthy. I needed help.

I'd stuffed a few clothing items and toiletries into an overnight bag and made the ten-minute drive to my mom's. When I pulled up in front of her house, she was standing on the porch waiting for me. She came to the car, and when I got out she folded me into a hug and held me tight. I stood there on the street in my mother's arms and cried like a wounded child.

She finally pulled back from me and brushed the hair off my face. Keeping one arm around my shoulders, she took my bag and walked me to the house, never letting go of me.

My mother's home, my parents' home until my dad died, was the house I'd grown up in — a rambling ranch on an acre-plus lot, with towering liquid ambers in the front yard and a heritage oak in the back, its branches stretching above the roofline. The trees had dropped their leaves like tears and now stood barren against the cloud-streaked sky.

Walking into the entry hall was like stepping into the past. I'd had that sense every time I returned since I left for college, which seemed so long ago now. My mom set my bag in the entry and led me into the kitchen, where she sat me at the old oak kitchen table.

"Wait here. I'll be right back."

She returned with a box of tissues and a warm washcloth. "Wipe your eyes, blow your nose, and wash your face. You'll feel better."

I followed her instructions. And she was right, of course. I got up from the table and went to the laundry room, where I tossed the used tissues into the trash and dropped the washcloth into the washing machine. My eyes were swollen and my nose stuffed, but just being here, rather than sitting at home alone, was restorative.

I went back into the kitchen and sat at the

table again.

My mom stood at the stove, stirring something in a pot. "I pulled some home-made potato soup out of the freezer. I know it's one of your favorites."

My stomach rumbled. How long had it been since I'd eaten anything?

"You ready to talk about it? Tell me what happened?"

I shrugged. "I don't know what happened. When this whole stalker thing started, Keith turned into someone else. He . . . couldn't handle it."

My mom set down the spoon she had been holding, turned and faced me, and put her hands on her hips. "*He* couldn't handle it?" She started to say something more but seemed to think better of it. She turned back to the stove, lowered the flame on the burner, then turned back to me. "Darling, I am so sorry. I cannot imagine what you're feeling. What you're going through."

"When it rains, it pours. Isn't that what you always said?"

"Yes, but with all that's happening, it's more like you're in the midst of a hur-ricane." She reached into a cabinet and pulled out two bowls and then two plates. She set them on placemats on the table. "I'm going to feed you, and then I'll let you tell me what you need after that."

"I don't know what I need."

"That's all right. We'll figure it out together." She took my face in her hands. "You're not alone in this, Deni. You are not alone."

Tears welled again. "Thank you," I whispered.

When she ladled the steaming soup into my bowl and placed two pieces of homemade buttered bread on my plate, I wasn't sure I could eat them. But after the first bite of the soup, my stomach rumbled again, and I ate all of what she'd given me plus a second bowl. The food not only nourished me but also offered comfort I hadn't had the strength to afford myself while alone.

Sated by the meal, I wanted nothing more than to sleep. Though it was only mid-afternoon, I pulled on the flannel pajamas I'd stuffed into my overnight bag, crawled into the bed in my old bedroom, and slept straight through the afternoon and night.

When I woke the next morning, the room was already bright, and the scent of coffee wafted from the kitchen. I still woke with the dread of knowing something was wrong, and then I recalled what had happened. But at least I'd slept soundly, secure in the knowledge that my mother was nearby and that, hopefully, Bradley Mathison had no idea where I was.

When I left home, I was watchful, making certain no one followed me. Or, at least as certain as possible.

I got out of bed and padded to the kitchen.

"Good morning, darling. Coffee?" My mom got up from the table, where her Bible lay open and her own cup of coffee stood by.

"Please, but I'll get it." I pulled a mug from the cabinet and filled it with the strong coffee.

"Did the phone wake you?"

"I don't know — I wasn't aware of it if it did."

"Ryan called. He said he'd called your cell phone several times over the last few days but hadn't heard from you. He was worried."

"What did you tell him?" I'd seen his messages but hadn't had the energy either to listen to them or return his calls.

"I told him you were here and that I'd relay the message that he was trying to reach you."

"I guess it's time I told him. And Jay too. I don't know when I can work again." I sat down at the table with my mom. "Even after a full night of sleep, I'm exhausted. I've never felt so tired."

"You have a lot on your plate, Denilyn. Give yourself some time. What can I make you for breakfast?"

"This is fine." I lifted the mug.

"If you want to get your strength back, you need to take care of yourself, including eating. How about scrambled eggs? I'll scramble in some vegetables."

My stomach roiled at the thought. "No, no. I can't. Maybe just a piece of toast?" I knew I needed to eat something to appease her, but nothing I could think of sounded good. "But I don't need you to wait on me. I'll make it when I'm ready."

"I'll let you do that." She smiled. "Is there anything new on the case?"

I sighed. "No. I gave his name to the lead detective, but they haven't tracked him down yet. The last address they've found for him is in Three Rivers. But hopefully they'll have him soon."

"Yes. Then we will all rest easier."

"I thought about that — about how Keith will feel once they make an arrest. Will he come back then? It isn't as simple as just walking back in the door. Surely he knows that."

"No, you'll have quite a bit of work to do, I'd imagine. How do you feel about that?"

I set my mug down and leaned back in the chair. "Honestly? I don't know. I can't predict what Keith will do, but after what he's said, I have a hard time believing he'd do that kind of work. I'm committed to him, to our marriage, but I want a husband who can offer emotional support when something goes wrong. Daddy never would have walked away when you needed him."

"No, he wouldn't have. But you can't compare the two — they're different men. Though I don't think your expectation, or desire, is unreasonable. Having a spouse who will stand by you when life throws you something unexpected and difficult, extremely difficult, is part of what marriage is about. 'For better or worse . . .' "

I stared past my mom for a moment, remembering something Keith had said. Then I looked at her. "He told me he feels trapped. Maybe there's more going on than he said. Maybe there's . . . someone else."

"Denilyn, speculation isn't helpful. Deal in the facts as they're presented to you."

She was right, but I struggled to remain focused on the facts. It seemed too many were missing.

■ ■ ■ ■

After making a piece of toast and forcing it down, I excused myself to make phone calls. I'd get them over with before I showered.

With the aid of a good night's sleep, a dose of caffeine, and the conversation with my mother, a measure of clarity returned. I wouldn't let Keith leave me hanging. It was time I stood up not only for myself but also for our marriage. I picked up my phone and called him, but when he didn't answer and I heard his voice on voice mail, my resolve wavered.

"It's me. Please call me when you can. We need to . . . work through some things." That was an understatement.

Next I left messages for both Jay and Ryan and asked each of them if they could co-ordinate a time to get together and talk. I asked Jay to include Gabe. My reserves were low, so meeting them together seemed best, and I preferred time with them rather than a phone call.

I needed my closest friends to surround me.

Two nights later I stood at my mother's kitchen sink, which faced the street, as I rinsed our dinner dishes and loaded them into the dishwasher. We'd had a simple meal, an early dinner, before my mother would leave for her book club gathering and I would leave to meet Ryan at Jay and Gabe's. When Jay offered to have us at their place, I welcomed the invitation. I didn't want to share the news of Keith's leaving in a coffee shop or restaurant.

As I rinsed the last pieces of silverware, headlights on the street outside drew my attention. The car seemed to make a slow pass by the house. I turned off the faucet and stood watching. Was it someone who was lost and looking for an address? Or was it him? Had he found me somehow?

I bent down and placed the silverware in the dishwasher, then reached up and flipped the switch to turn off the light over the kitchen sink. I also turned off the other overhead lights in the kitchen. I returned to the sink, where I could watch the street. Just as I'd decided I was making something out of nothing, what appeared to be the same car came again, this time from the opposite direction, as though the driver had turned around at the end of the street.

The car slowed and then came to a stop in front of my mother's house. The driver didn't pull over or park the car. Instead, he stopped in the middle of the street. Because it was dark, I couldn't see the driver's face. But I could see his silhouette. He was lit from behind by the neighbor's porch light across the street.

It appeared his head was turned in my direction. Was he watching the house? Watching me? Had he seen me standing at the sink when he made his first pass?

"Mom." When she didn't respond, I called her again, louder this time. "Mom."

"What is it, Deni?" She called from her bedroom.

Just as I was going to respond, the car rolled forward, then drove away. Was it him? I didn't know. I couldn't tell from the little I saw of him. It could have been anyone. "Never mind."

My heartbeat pulsed in my ears. There was no way to know who was in the car. Maybe it was him. Maybe it was someone admiring the house or looking for someone or — anything. There were several possible explanations.

But just in case, I pulled my phone out of the pocket of my sweater and called Detective Neibuhr. When I'd let him know I was staying with my mother, he'd told me to report anything that seemed out of place or suspicious. At the time, I wondered if all I was reporting was my own paranoia.

But later I'd know otherwise.

We sat in Jay and Gabe's family room, where a fire crackled in the fireplace and copper mugs filled with steaming cider sat on a tray on the coffee table.

"What do you mean he left?" Gabe sat with his elbows on his knees. "For the evening? Or what?"

"So, you haven't heard from him?" I asked Gabe. "I hoped he'd talk to you."

Gabe shook his head. "Not a word."

Ryan sat nearest me on the L-shaped sectional in front of the fireplace. He reached over and put his hand on my shoulder. "He left? For good? Or . . . ?"

"He said he couldn't handle everything that was going on. He feels trapped." I shrugged. "I can't tell you more than that. I don't know more than that. He packed some things and is staying with a friend. I guess we're . . . separated." It was the first time I'd said the word or even let myself really consider it. "I left him a message the day before yesterday, but he hasn't called me. I tried again this afternoon, but . . . nothing. I'm hoping he just needs some time. I don't know."

"You're not staying alone at the house are

you?" Gabe asked.

"She's staying at her mom's." Ryan looked from Gabe to me. "What do you need from us? What can we do?"

"You're doing it right now. I just need your support. I'm not even sure what that means at this point. I'm confused. I'm scared. I'm spent."

"You know you've got our support — whatever you need." Jay had remained silent until that point. "But Keith?" She shook her head. "No. He best not be comin' around here."

"Jay, he's . . ." I hesitated. I didn't know what Keith was thinking or feeling. I didn't know him at all, it seemed.

"I'm angry. I'm sorry if that's hard on you right now. But just allow me my anger. If Gabe wants to talk with him, that's up to him. But I'm supporting you. You got that?"

"Yes. And . . . thank you."

"I'm not takin' sides. I'm just angry right now. That's mine to own and work through."

I reached for a mug of the cider and warmed my hands around it. The scent of cinnamon and cloves swirled in the steam rising from the mug. But what normally offered comfort, instead annoyed. I set the mug back on the tray. "I should go. I'm exhausted."

"I'll walk you out." Ryan got up from the sofa.

Gabe and Jay followed and walked us to the door.

"Is your mother's home secure?" Gabe asked as we stood at the door.

"I feel safe there. Although . . ." I told him about the car I'd seen earlier in the evening. "I reported it to Dan Neibuhr, but I'm sure it was nothing."

"Deni, you need to flip your thinking right now. Everything is something until you *know* it isn't. This is no time for denial. Keep your eyes open. Pay attention. Report anything that doesn't look right or feel right." Gabe pulled my coat off the rack in their entry hall and handed it to me. "Got it?"

The tide of fear rose, threatening to drown me. "Yes."

"Your mama gonna be there when you get back?"

"She's out, but she won't be too late."

"I'll follow her home," Ryan said to Jay and Gabe.

"That's not —"

"It is necessary, Deni. We're close to picking up Mathison, but we don't have him yet. Let Ryan follow you and get you into the house." Then Gabe gave me a hug. "This part is almost over. We'll get him."

Whether I wanted to believe that level of caution was necessary or not, I knew the three of them wouldn't let me leave and go back to my mother's house alone.

This was what support looked like in practice.

This was what I'd wanted, what I'd needed, from Keith.

I stood on the sidewalk next to my car in front of Gabe and Jay's, a cold wind scattering a few crisp leaves. "Look . . ." I pointed overhead, where the stars looked like someone had tossed diamonds across a sheet of black velvet.

Ryan stood close. "Reminds me of some of those moonless nights in Three Rivers. Remember?"

"I do." I shivered. "But it was warmer there."

He put his arm across my shoulders and pulled me close. "You're right."

Just as I was getting uncomfortable with his gesture, he dropped his arm and stepped back. "So, I'll follow you."

I sighed. "I feel like a child. Really, I'll be fine. It's out of your way. You don't have to —"

He reached out and put one finger on my lips to silence me. "You know I'd do anything for you." He moved his hand to my cheek and let it linger there. Even in the dark I could see or sense something sparking in his eyes.

I stepped back, and he dropped his hand. "Don't." I shook my head. "Really. Just don't."

Ryan had always towered over me. Now he looked down at me. "Deni . . ."

I turned and opened the door of the car and got inside, but before I could close the door, he stepped into the space between the door and the car.

He shook his head. "I'm sorry. I know the last thing you need right now is . . ." He shrugged. "Sorry. I know you're vulnerable, and it makes me want to . . . take care of you. But . . ."

"I just need to go. Please don't follow me. Please. Just let me go, Ryan. Let me go. Once and for all. Please?" We both knew I was talking about more than letting me drive away alone.

He looked back at the house, then down at me again. "Listen, I said I'm sorry. And you heard what Gabe said. You shouldn't go home alone."

"I'm fine. I am. I can take care of myself." Tears brimmed. "Please . . ." I pleaded. Move. Please. Just let me go."

He lifted his hands in surrender and stepped back.

I pulled the door and closed it, started the car, released the emergency brake, and put the car in gear, all while Ryan stood on the sidewalk and watched. As I drove away, I glanced in the rearview mirror. He still stood in the same spot.

As I drove out of Gabe and Jay's neighborhood, I watched to make sure he wasn't following me.

It seemed he'd respect my wishes.

Yes, while I longed for someone to support and protect me.

It was Keith I longed for.

Not Ryan.

CHAPTER TWENTY-SIX

Denilyn
February 2010

With Keith gone and me having moved in, at least temporarily, with my mother, everything felt off. Wrong. And I began to doubt myself. Had I overreacted to Ryan's touch? Had I misread his gesture? As I returned home from Jay and Gabe's, I pulled into my mother's driveway and then reached into the console for the garage door opener and pressed the button. The three-car garage had more than enough room for both our cars, and my mother had insisted that I was safer parking in the garage and walking directly into the house from there.

If I'd overreacted to Ryan or not, I wasn't sure. I was too tired to unravel the myriad strands of our longtime friendship. Ryan had likely overstepped a boundary, and I'd likely overreacted. I hoped it was nothing we, our friendship, couldn't endure.

The garage lit up as the door lifted. Before pulling in, I glanced in the rearview mirror and looked out both side windows one more time to make sure no one had followed me. I longed for the day when I'd no longer have to look over my shoulder. Although, maybe I always would. This experience was, I suspected, marking me in permanent ways.

My mother's neighbors' porch lights were on, their homes warmly lit inside. The street was quiet, and the neighborhood was an area where crime was infrequent. The car I'd seen earlier was nothing to worry about. Or at least nothing I could do anything more about.

The tension I'd felt on the drive home and the earlier fear Gabe's warnings evoked had at least eased, if not dissipated. Gabe was right, I knew, this wasn't a time for denial. But I also couldn't live in a heightened state of anxiety forever. Somehow I had to find a balance.

I'd taken most of the prescribed precautions — we added the alarm to the house, I'd purchased a personal alarm that I attached to my key fob, my cell phone was always within reach should I need to make an emergency call. I was mindful, watchful, and attentive. I'd reported anything suspect, even when I'd felt silly doing so, as I had earlier in the evening.

Since receiving that third charm and the threat it implied, at the recommendation of the detectives working my case, I'd also canceled speaking events and public appearances, much to my publisher's dismay. But they did seem to understand, and I assured my editor that the lighter schedule afforded me more time to work on the second book. However, I hadn't written a word in several weeks. Focus was hard to come by.

And while I anticipated returning to my counseling work, it felt good to be away from the place where I'd seen Bradley Mathison, and where he'd delivered the bracelet and the second charm. The office was located in a busy area of town. With so many cars and people on the streets and in the parking lots, it seemed impossible to watch for him.

I couldn't do much more to protect myself and still live my life.

This man had already taken too much from me. I couldn't let him take all of me.

I eased the car into the bay of the garage and parked. I turned off the ignition, grabbed my purse, and got out of the car. I looked behind me one last time, but the street was empty. Tree branches swayed in the wind, and yard debris — leftover leaves and clippings — swirled in the street. Otherwise, all was still.

I started for the door into the house, keys in hand. I planned to take a hot bath and then go straight to bed. I hoped another good night's sleep would lift the malaise that had plagued me. Although, until the stress lifted, a few physical repercussions might remain.

As I crossed the brightly lit garage, everything suddenly went dark. "What — ?" I stopped walking, unable to see anything. *What happened?*

Darkness closed in, suffocating in its descent.

My pulse rushed. Was there a power outage? I turned, heart pounding, and looked out the still open garage door. The neighbors' lights still shined. I gripped my keys and turned back as something sounded near me, movement of some sort. *Help me . . .* A gust of wind rattled something. *That's all it was. That's all.* My eyes still hadn't fully adjusted to the dark, but I took a couple of stilted steps toward the door and reached my hand out to feel for it. But the door wasn't what my hand landed on. My heart leaped from my chest to my throat, and I jumped back.

"Denilyn . . ." A familiar voice spoke my name.

I fumbled with my keys, feeling for the alarm. That's when I saw him lunge toward me, just a shape in the dark. Before I could find the alarm, the keys were batted from my hand and clattered to the floor.

He was too fast for me to put up any fight. He grabbed me, spun me around, and held me from behind, his hand around my neck.

"I waited for you," he whispered, his breath hot against my ear.

There was a scream on my lips, but he tightened his grasp on my throat.

"Let go!" I hissed. But then the vice around my neck tightened again and a bright light shined in my eyes, blinding me. I closed my eyes tight against the glare.

"There you are. Now I can see you."

I reached up and pulled on his arm, digging my fingernails into him, but he didn't flinch, only tightened his grip on my neck, closing off my airway.

I struggled against him, kicking back at him, but he was too strong for me.

"Please, Denilyn, please. I don't want to hurt you," he seemed to plead. "Just let me look at you."

Panic surged as my head began to swim without air. I stopped fighting, willed my body to relax, or at least go limp, so he'd let go of me or loosen his grip.

For just a second, his hand moved off my throat and I gasped, sucking air into my lungs. Then his arm was around my neck and he pulled me back against him. "I won't hurt you. I don't want to hurt you," he whispered again, his voice hoarse, his tone oddly gentle.

I breathed in and out, filling my lungs again and again. As I did, he seemed to bury his face in my hair and breathe deeply.

I shuddered. He would kill me. He'd come to kill me.

With his arm still looped around my neck, he shifted behind me, and even with my eyes closed, the light shone bright again.

"Open your eyes, Denilyn. Open your pretty eyes." He tightened his arm around my neck. "Let me see your eyes," he whispered.

I squinted against the beam of light until he moved it so it wasn't directly in my eyes. "You're pretty. So pretty."

"Please . . . please" — I whimpered — "let me go."

"Let you go?" He sounded confused. "I've just gotten you. We're finally alone together. This is what we've wanted. Just the two of us."

My pulse roared in my ears. *Think. Focus.* I needed to focus.

I nodded.

"That's right. That's why you took that picture of me. You wanted my picture. You're the only one who's ever wanted my picture. I didn't understand. That's why I ran. But now I know. I know."

I swallowed. "Ye . . . Yes," I whispered. "Yes." His hold on me relaxed but just barely. "I . . . I wanted to . . . remember you."

"I have your picture. On the back of that book. So pretty."

I bit my lip and nodded again. "Thank you." *Oh God, please, please . . .*

His arm slackened a bit more, and I moved slightly, turning toward him. But as I did, he pulled his arm tight against my neck again.

"I . . . want to see . . . you." A wave of nausea flowed over me, and I was sure I'd be sick. I took a deep breath and the sensation ebbed. "May I . . ." I tried again to turn toward him rather than pull away from him.

He loosened his arm, and with the hand that still held the flashlight, he nudged me around so that I was locked in a face-to-face embrace, of sorts, with him. Sweat snaked down my spine.

"Look at me," he urged. "Look at me." He dropped his arm from around my neck, stepped back, and lifted my chin.

Each breath I took was labored, my heart pounded, and the dark was dizzying, disorienting. *Focus. Stay focused.* I had to focus.

I slowly lifted my hands and reached for his waist, where I rested my hands. Then I took a slow step back, as if to see him better.

I stood still for a moment as he brushed my cheek with the back of his hand. Again, nausea threatened. I closed my eyes and waited for it to pass. Then I opened them again. The flashlight hung down at his side, its light bouncing off the floor, distorting his face. But I forced myself to stay still. To look at him. For just a moment longer.

Then in one fast move, I pushed him away from me with all my strength, hoping he'd fall backward. Then I spun around, intending to run for the open garage door and to one of the neighbor's houses.

I took a step, then another, I'd make it.

I would.

But just before I reached the door, a loud crack sounded somewhere, and pain . . . searing pain . . .

I felt myself falling . . .
Falling . . .

CHAPTER TWENTY-SEVEN

Denilyn
March 3, 2017

As I pull into a parking spot at the Roseville Galleria, I check the clock on the dash. I have twenty minutes until I meet Jaylan for a late afternoon cup of coffee at a new place just outside the mall. I have just enough time to run into the mall to purchase a small birthday gift for Jay — something I should have done days ago.

I get out of the car, lock it, then begin the long walk from the parking lot toward the mall. Though I prefer small boutiques over the bustle of the large shopping center, there's a shop in the mall that I know Jay favors. As I reach the crosswalk leading to the department store I'll enter through, my phone rings, but rather than dig through my purse for the phone, I decide to let the call go to voice mail. I walk into the warmth of the store, where a lilting melody from a grand piano sets a luxuriant tone. I slow my pace as I cross the store, taking in the array of rich colors, designs, and a shoe department that seems to span at least half of the ground floor of the store. When my phone rings again a few minutes later, I stop and pull the phone from my purse to make sure the call isn't important.

When I see that it's my mother, I answer. She rarely calls during the day unless necessary. "Hi, what's up?"

"Deni, I need you to meet me at the vet."

The urgency in her tone startles me. "What's wrong?"

"I need you to come now!"

"Mom, what? What happened to Max?" I turn around and jog back the way I came, shoppers staring at me as I go. "Is he okay? What happened?"

"Just get here, Denilyn. I'm here now. I have to go." With that, she hangs up.

When I reach the crosswalk again, I look quickly, then run across the street, not waiting for the signal to change.

After making a quick call to Jay to cancel our plans and what feels like an interminable drive to the veterinary clinic through Friday afternoon traffic, I pull into the lot, park, and then rush inside. I stop at the reception desk. "Excuse me." I step in front of a woman with a cocker spaniel on a leash. "I'm sorry — it's an emergency." I look at the receptionist. "I'm Denilyn Rossi. My mother brought my dog —"

"Yes, Ms. Rossi. Follow me, please." The receptionist is up and around the reception desk before I've finished my sentence.

"Is he okay? What happened?"

"I'm sorry, I don't know anything. You'll have to talk to Dr. Campbell."

She leads me to one of the examination rooms. When I enter, my mother is seated, Max is on the examination table, and Dr. Campbell is leaning over him, listening to his heart. One of the veterinary aides is holding Max in place.

The space is tight, so I go and stand where I can see Max but not be in the way. He's conscious, which offers me some re-assurance. "Is he okay?"

When Max hears my voice, he lifts his head, looks at me, and wags his tail. Dr. Campbell pulls the stethoscope from his ears, steps back, and motions for me to move forward so I can see my dog. I step up and rest my hand on his head. "Hey buddy," I whisper. I turn and look back at my mom and then at Dr. Campbell. "What happened?"

"He's a very fortunate dog. Your mother took action immediately and probably saved his life. I think he'll be fine. We'll administer an activated charcoal treatment, and then we'll want to keep him overnight to watch for signs of kidney failure, just in case."

"Kidney failure?"

Dr. Campbell steps forward again, "Let's get him off the table, then we'll leave you two to talk." It takes both Dr. Campbell and his aide to lift Max.

The aide attaches his leash to his collar again and hands it to me. "You can have a moment with him. I'll come back for him so we can treat him."

When they've left, my Mom puts her hand on my shoulder. I see something in her eyes that frightens me. "What . . . ?"

"Denilyn, he was poisoned. Someone . . ."

She begins to tremble, and I know that whatever happened is just hitting her. Adrenaline got her this far, but now . . . "Mom, here, sit back down." I lead her back to the bench along the wall of the examination room and help her sit. Max lies at her feet, obviously tired from whatever he's gone through.

I hand the leash to my mom, then go to the small sink in the room where there's a stack of paper cups. I fill one with water and take it back to her. I wait as she takes a few sips. "Are you okay?"

She nods. "Oh Deni, I was so afraid." She takes another sip of water, then hands the cup back to me. "I'd let Max outside, and you know how he is — he hates to be away from us at all. So when he didn't come back in a few minutes, I went to the door to look for him. He was near the back of the yard, and it looked like he was eating something, which was odd. So I went out to take a look." She rests her hand on her heart. "There was a dish — one of those aluminum dog dishes — with food in it. He'd just found it, I assume, because he hadn't eaten it all, and you know how fast he goes through a dish of food. Anyway, I shooed him away so I could take a look. I knew I hadn't put that dish there. I noticed a green-ish residue, like maybe something had been poured on the food. Then I noticed something had spilled on the concrete footing of the wall — a thick, neon-green liquid. It was antifreeze. I just knew it was antifreeze. You know that's toxic for dogs and cats." Her words come in a rushed jumble. "I picked up that dish and made my way back to the house as fast as I could, making sure Max was following me. I called the vet as soon as I got inside. The gal I spoke with told me to give Max hydrogen peroxide to make him vomit — she told me exactly how much to give him based on his weight. I added it to a little water in his dish, then added some beef broth, just like she'd suggested. He lapped it right up, and I took him back outside where he did just as she told me he'd do — he vomited, more than once. Thank, God. Then I got him into the car . . ." She grabs my hand and holds it tight. "If I hadn't found him when I did — if I hadn't seen what he'd eaten — I'd never have known. He would have died. Suffered, mind you, and then, almost certainly, he'd have . . ." Her eyes are damp and she sniffs. She reaches in the pocket of her sweater and pulls out a tissue and wipes her eyes and nose. "I am so angry!" She spits out at last. "Between what's happened to you, and now this, I am just so angry!"

There's a tap on the door, and the aide comes back into the room. "I'll take him back now. We'll give you a call this evening to let you know how he's doing. He should be fine. This is just a precaution, really. We're open until noon tomorrow, then gone the rest of the weekend. If he needs further care, we'll have you take him to the emergency pet hospital we partner with."

I nod, too stunned by what my mother's

told me to speak. I take the leash from my mom's hand and give it a gentle tug. Max gets to his feet, and I bend down and wrap my arms around his neck and bury my face in his fur. "You'll be okay, buddy," I whisper. Then I stand back up and hand the leash to the aide, who leads Max away.

Emotions roil within me — anger, gratitude, fear, grief, and . . . Anger. Like my mother, I am so angry. I completely understand the rage I saw on my mother's face. I turn back to her. "How could anyone do that to a dog? Who would do something so heinous to an innocent —"

"Deni . . ." She gets up from the bench. "There's more."

"More? There can't be more."

She reaches for her purse on the bench, opens it, and pulls out an envelope. She begins to hand it to me but then hesitates. "This was taped to the wall just above where the dish of food was." She holds it to her chest now as though she's decided not to give it to me.

"What . . . what is it?"

She stares at me a moment, then finally hands me the envelope. "Darling, I am so sorry," she whispers.

I open the envelope and pull out a single sheaf of paper with one line printed in the middle. A single question.

Who dies next?

I shake my head. "No. No!" I hiss through clenched teeth. "No! No! No!"

After spending several hours with detectives and others from the sheriff's department at the house, where they searched for evidence and peppered both my mother and myself with questions we didn't have answers for, we both feel drained.

"Excuse me . . ." Sonia Alejandro comes into the kitchen, where I'm making another pot of coffee. "We're about to wrap up here. You can probably hold off on the coffee unless you want it for yourselves. Most everyone's already gone."

I pour the water out of the pot I'd just filled and set it on the counter.

"So I guess that dog of yours isn't much of a watchdog?"

I look at my mom then back to the detective. I shrug, unsure of what to say. None of this makes sense.

"So, listen. I'd advise you to stay elsewhere for a few days. Whoever's threatening you means business. He's already, presumably, made one attempt on your life, Ms. Rossi, when he ran you off the road. Now he's attempted to kill your dog and left a note that tells you his intent. He knows where you live, and he didn't have any problem making himself at home on your property. We viewed the footage from your security cameras and didn't find anything. So he also knows the areas the cameras cover or don't cover. That far corner of your backyard is one of the few areas that isn't covered. I suggest you add an additional camera. I also suggest you hire a security company — I'd have a couple of security guards on the property at all times once you're back here to stay.

I'm happy to stay while you get some things together, and then I'll follow you someplace safe. Is there somewhere you can go until you can get another camera installed?"

"Yes, we'd planned on staying with friends."

"If you'll text me the address of where you're staying, I'd appreciate it." She hands me her card, which includes both her office and cell phone numbers.

"We've already packed a few things, so we're ready whenever you are."

"Great. I'll let you set your alarm, and then we'll be on our way."

March 4, 2017

After a fitful night, when I hear sounds of life in Jay and Gabe's kitchen long before dawn, I slip into my bathrobe and slip out of the guest bedroom. I make my way down the hallway, enticed by the scent of brewing coffee. I pass the room where I hope my mom is sleeping better than I did, careful not to make a sound.

"Morning," Gabe says quietly when he sees me. "Couldn't sleep?"

"Not really."

"Not too surprising based on all you've got going on. Coffee?" He holds up a full pot.

"Please."

Gabe fills a mug and hands it to me. I wrap my hands around it and breathe deeply — the rich scent comforting.

Gabe leans against the counter, takes a sip of his coffee, then gestures to the long farm table and chairs in their kitchen. "Have a seat if you'd like."

"I don't want to keep you."

"Nah, I have a few minutes. I'm heading out to the gym, then work. I need the workout, but I'm in no rush to get it. Know what I mean?"

I take a seat at the table, and Gabe sits down across from me. "Our people treat you okay yesterday?"

"Yes, they were great. I just wish they'd come up with something concrete."

"Yeah, me too. The only evidence we have so far is from the vehicle who hit you. I can tell you what type of tires were on the truck, the color of its paint, and can give you a good idea of the year and make based on your description of the headlights and front grill. But finding it without a license plate number, or even a couple of the numbers? That's a needle in a haystack scenario. Same with what happened yesterday. They found a few footprints and can tell you what size and style shoe the guy was wearing, but at this point, that's not going to get us too far."

He looks down at his mug, then back to me. "How'd your mom handle yesterday?"

"You mean besides saving Max's life?"

He smiles. "Yeah, besides that."

"She's amazing. Thank you for letting us stay here."

"You're welcome for as long as you need to be here. All of you. You know that."

"Max too? I'm supposed to pick him up later this morning if all is well."

"My man Maxwell can move in permanently as far as I'm concerned. Now Jay? She may have her own thoughts on that." He chuckles. "Nah, she won't mind. Don't let her fool you. She loves that dog."

"I know she does."

"Speaking of Max . . . What happened yesterday? He's a well-trained animal. He knows not to let anyone on that property."

"I'm glad to hear you say that. I spent a lot of the night thinking about that. He loves his food, but he knows when to leave it. When he's on alert, he wouldn't be swayed by food, at least I didn't think so. Something doesn't make sense."

Gabe stares at his coffee. "May make more sense than you think."

"What do you mean?"

He looks back at me. "Could've been someone he knows. Someone he's used to seeing out there."

"That's a short list."

Gabe shrugs. "Something to consider. You mention that to the officers last night?"

"No. Detective Alejandro said something about Max not being much of a watchdog, but I was so baffled . . ."

"Why don't you make a list of everyone who frequents your property. Pool guy, yard service, exterminator" — he hesitates —

"friends and family. Anyone Max would know."

"They've already asked me to do that. But that scares me."

"We aren't trying to scare you, Deni. We're trying to help you."

CHAPTER TWENTY-EIGHT

Denilyn
March 4, 2017

After Gabe leaves, I pull my coat on over my pajamas and venture outside to the patio. I drop onto a lounge chair, still thinking about the people who have access to my home and property. Gabe and Jay, Ryan, and besides the handful of service providers, just one other person: Keith.

I go through a short list of those who know where the cameras are located on the property and the area they cover. It comes down to those who installed the cameras, monitoring system, and alarm. At least those are the only people besides myself and my mother who I think have that information.

Is it really possible that while still incarcerated Mathison could have hired someone who knows my property? It doesn't seem feasible.

But I can't come up with any other explanation.

Fear, that ever-present intruder, wraps its tendrils around my soul. If my home isn't safe — I stare into the ink of predawn — then no place is safe.

There's nowhere I can go.

No way to protect those I love.

I swallow the ache in my throat. I can't live like this.

I can't.

As darkness releases its hold on day, the gray of dawn is broken by brilliance. The eastward sky is sheathed in orange with swirling shades of peach and fuchsia, like a mixture of oils on an artist's palette. Shafts of light, watercolor clear, layer the deep tones until an orb of light crests the horizon.

Steam rises from my second cup of coffee sitting on the table next to the lounge I'm lying on. I shiver but decide to welcome the sun's presence. I watch, rapt, as it ascends in all its glory, remembering it seems, after a long gray season, the power it holds.

I sit with that thought for several minutes as something new, or perhaps something remembered, forms within me . . .

Fear has exhausted me. Drained me. The circumstances of the last several weeks — or more accurately stated, the last almost eight years — have taken everything I have, both physically and emotionally. But more than that, they've robbed me of my own power — the power of who I am. They've robbed me of *myself.* There is no shame in the realization. The fear is not unfounded. If only it were.

But how long will I allow those who've staged these attacks to rule me?

Do I not still hold the power to choose?

Isn't it my choice how I *live* in the face of death?

He, or they, cannot take that choice from me.

I will no longer let them take that choice from me.

As the brilliant colors of the new day fade, I know this time has marked me in ways not yet fully revealed. But somehow the significance is undeniable.

"Sometimes in stillness, when we've quieted our minds, we hear from God."

"Thank You," I whisper.

It is the first time in nearly a decade I've offered my gratitude to God, at least for my own life or circumstances.

Perhaps that is the most important revelation of all.

"Hey, mind if I join you?"

I look over my shoulder. "Of course not."

"Lemme grab some java. Wait, on second thought, you comin' in anytime soon? It's cold out here."

"Yes, I think my feet and hands have gone numb. I'll come in and join you." I pick up my cup, get up from the lounge, and follow Jay into the warmth of the house. I settle back at the table where Gabe left me.

"More coffee?"

"Just enough to warm what I have." Jay comes to the table, coffeepot in hand, and refills my cup, then fills a mug for herself.

Once she's doctored her coffee, she joins me at the table.

I look across at her. "Your turn. Worst?"

"My turn? With all you have goin' on?"

I nod. "It's definitely your turn."

"Okay, worst? Gettin' up at this hour on a Saturday. You know you're gettin' old when your body won't sleep past sunup. Second worst, having Gabe work the weekend. But he's on a case that . . ." She shakes her head, and I read the sorrow in her eyes. "On second thought, that case is the worst. I've said it before, but it's unimaginable what people do to each other. Although, I know you don't have to imagine it. How you holding up? Really?"

I shake my head. "Nope, it's still your

turn. "Best?"

The warmth returns to her eyes with her smile. "Sitting across from you, here."

"Thank you." I know she means it. "In spite of everything, I'm grateful for this gift."

"So answer my question. How you doin'?"

"I'm exhausted. Worn out. Between that truck running me off the road, that series of texts, and then what happened to Max yesterday, I feel like I'm right back where I was when I went through this the first time. I'm at the end of my rope. But sometimes we need to reach the end of ourselves, don't we?"

She nods.

"I had a breakthrough of sorts, or at least the beginning of one, out there on your patio this morning."

"Oh yeah? Talk to me . . ."

"I'm tired of living in fear. I'm tired of looking over my shoulder wherever I go. I'm tired of the nightmares and flashbacks and panic attacks and . . . All of it. I'm sick of all of it. Jay, I've been living like that for almost eight years. Well, not quite that long . . ." Jay knows what I'm about to say — I can see it in her eyes. "Remember right after the attack?" She nods. "I was so . . . sure. So confident. Mathison had been arrested, and I thought I'd lived through the worst and survived. Remember what I did? And my faith?" I run my hand through my hair, my fingers landing on the scar from that night. "What happened to that woman?"

She waits for me to answer my own question.

"Fear is what happened. I've let him win . . . let fear rule."

She leans forward, just slightly, and her eyes narrow. "This is leading somewhere . . ."

"Jay, I've given up too much. I've hidden too long. You know what I've done to protect not only myself but everyone I love. I don't even talk about the most important things in my life, not with anyone except my mom, you, Gabe, and Ryan. No one at work even knows . . . I haven't even told Jon . . ." I wave the rest of the sentence away. She knows. Tears prick my eyes. "I can't do this anymore. I won't do this anymore. I can't live every day afraid of what the next minute will bring."

"That's because you're tryin' to do it on your own — in your own strength."

"I know."

"So?"

I consider what I'm about to say. Once the words are out of my mouth, there's no going back. "I'm done trying to handle it on my own. I can't control everything. If that *terrorist* got into my yard and almost killed my dog, after all I've done to try and keep my home and family safe . . ." I shake my head. "I can't do it anymore. I can't make it all work."

"Sister, all I've got to say is it's about time. No judgment. You know that. I'm just sayin' something's shifting, and it's time for something new."

"It is definitely time for something new. My circumstances may not change, but the way I react to them is going to change."

"I heard you say it, so you know I'm gonna be watchin'."

"I'm counting on it." I look down at the table, then take a deep breath and look back at Jay. "You know how sometimes an idea presents itself and it's so absurd, seems so ludicrous, you know you didn't come up with it on your own?"

"I've had one or two of those experiences."

"If anxiety is the body's reaction to a perceived threat, and fear is the reaction in the face of those circumstances playing out, then I want to create a situation where I face fear full-on."

"Keep talkin' . . ."

I lean forward. "I can't, nor would I want to, live through any of what I've gone through again. Nor do I want, in any way, to recreate those events or the myriad of horrific possibilities that run through my mind a hundred times a day. Instead, I considered something else that's always scared me. Terrified me, actually."

"I'm almost afraid to ask . . ."

With her dark eyes trained on me, I waver. "Maybe it's too absurd. It is. It's crazy."

"Oh no you don't. Don't you do that. If this wasn't your idea, and you're tellin' me it was inspired, then don't you dare back down from it. You hear me?"

I know she's right. "Okay, I'm going to . . . jump out of an airplane. Skydive."

Her eyebrows raise and her eyes look like saucers. But then her head bobs. "Yep. Okay. I can see that happenin' — I wouldn't ever recommend it to anyone, but I can see where you're going with this."

"Really?"

"I'm not sayin' I condone it, I'm just sayin' . . . Actually, I don't know what I'm sayin'. You know how rare that is?" She laughs, then grows serious. "Tell me what you're thinking again, because you know, testing God isn't wise."

"No, I'm not testing Him. In fact, it's just

333

the opposite. I'm testing myself, in a way. Putting my life in His hands intentionally. Or, more accurately, acknowledging that my life is in His hands — has always been in His hands.

"I've run from death — terrified of someone taking my life. I haven't *lived* because I've feared dying. Not only have I allowed this guy to already take my life, but I've allowed him, them, whoever, to rob those I love of who I am. Does that make sense?"

Jay's eyes shine, and she nods. "It makes more sense than you know, sister."

"But . . . what about . . ." I try to find words for the one hesitation holding me back, but emotion wells. "What about . . ."

"What about the people in your life who depend on you? If something happens to you? That it?"

Tears fill my eyes as I nod.

She reaches across the table and takes my hand in hers. "I love you. And I hate to break it to you, but you aren't God, not even in the lives of your family and friends. Either you trust Him or you don't. There's no in between."

"Okay," I whisper.

"So when do you jump?"

"Soon. Very soon."

CHAPTER TWENTY-NINE

Adelia
May 11, 2017

A noise, mosquito-like in its buzzing, disturbs. I will it to stop, but it continues. Again and again. Eyes still closed, I roll toward the sound, but the movement, so painful, wakes me fully. I open my eyes, then squint at the light filtering in through the open shutters. The river wails outside the window.

The buzzing, or vibrating, sounds again. I turn and look at the nightstand where my phone dances. I reach for it, look at the screen, and then answer. "H . . . hello," I croak.

By the time I dropped into bed following our run down the river, moonlight was giving way to daylight.

"You're alive? You didn't call."

"Uh" — I clear my throat — "I would have . . . eventually. What time is it?"

"10:25 a.m. You ready? You going to be able to handle this?"

I push myself up, and the muscles in my arms and abdomen scream. I collapse against a pillow, my entire body aching. "No . . . problem. But that's not really your concern, is it?"

"I'm just asking because this morning you sound like you're feeling your age."

I try to smile, but even my face hurts. "Maybe."

"Well, it's time to get up and get going. He's here."

I sit back up, fully alert now. "He's here?"

"That's what I said. You baited him, and he took the bait."

I am the bait, and he hasn't taken me yet. I close my eyes, head pounding.

"Now, reel him in."

CHAPTER THIRTY

Denilyn
March 19, 2017

I pull off the road into the parking lot, gravel crunching under my tires. My GPS alerts me that I "have arrived at my destination." A handful of other cars are parked in front of a hangar, and a sign that says OFFICE points to a walkway on one side of the hangar.

What am I doing? Mouth dry, I reach for the tumbler in the cup holder and take a few sips of water.

Both Jaylan and my mother offered to come with me, but I need to do this alone.

Though, not alone at all.

That's part of the point, isn't it? Acknowledging that I'm not alone, nor am I in control. This is an exercise in releasing control and letting go of the fear my attempted control, or lack thereof, has exacerbated.

I stare at the hangar, then turn the ignition off and set the parking brake.

It's now or never.

I get out of the car and head to the office, where, when I called, I was told I'd check in. A cool breeze rustles my hair. I've chosen a perfect day for this adventure — clear skies and warm temperatures for March. "Thank You," I whisper. Then I reach into my pocket, pull out a band, and gather my hair and pull it into a ponytail.

As I walk into the small office, I'm reminded so much of Ride the Kaweah and Mick that it puts me, if not at ease, at least into what feels like familiar terrain — a place where those who seek adventure or an adrenaline rush gather. Or maybe those like me who've come for their own reasons.

But rather than the safety talk I gave over and over at Mick's, here I'm asked to have a seat on a dilapidated vinyl sofa, where a brief instructional video offers the most basic information: I'll jump attached to an instructor — a tandem jump — and we'll jump from twelve thousand feet, and drop at a rate of approximately 120 miles per hour. The video then goes on to explain the basics of free-fall body positioning.

The entire instruction takes less than five minutes.

Once I've signed the necessary release forms, the young woman behind the counter, about the age I was when I started working for Mick, comes around, looks me up and down, then goes to a rack and chooses a jumpsuit, which she then hands to me.

I pull the suit on over the shorts and T-shirt I'm wearing. The young woman helps me into a harness and tightens it. Then she hands me a pair of goggles. Again, I'm reminded of Mick's, only I've traded a dry suit for a jumpsuit, a flotation device for a harness, and a helmet for goggles.

"You're ready," she says. "Head out that door and wait on the tarmac for your instructor. You're going up with a group of pros. You'll see them out there."

"Okay." As I make my way toward the door, I turn back. "Thanks." Once outside, I head for the group of guys. When I reach them, I pass them and stand alone.

I take in the azure expanse, watercolor clear. It seems to beckon in the same way the Kaweah once called my name. I breathe deeply, hoping to still what feels like the wings of hummingbirds fluttering within me. I adjust the harness on my shoulders and thighs, then shield my eyes and look at the sky again. This time a shiver trembles through me despite the warmth rising from the asphalt.

Anticipation or fear? I wrap my arms around myself.

As I wait, a young man, lanky, a chute packed on his back, breaks from the group of pros and saunters my way. "Ready to ride the currents?"

Currents? I'm very familiar with currents. But air currents? "Absolutely." I attempt a smile as I bend the truth, more for my sake than his.

He studies me for a moment, and then the fair skin around his eyes crinkles and he laughs. He turns and heads back to the group, tossing advice over his shoulder as he goes. "Stay loose and enjoy the ride. There's nothing like it."

I wipe my damp palms on the jumpsuit.

An engine throttles in the distance, and soon sunlight glints off the silver wings of a small plane taxiing our way. The plane rattles as it approaches. Loose nuts and bolts? The sound is unsettling.

"Betty!" one of the pros yells.

"Come to Daddy!" shouts another. Laughter and catcalls welcome the plane, *Betty Boop,* with her pouting red lips painted on its tail.

I hear the squeak of the office door swing

open and turn to see a man walking my way — he's older than I expected.

When he reaches me he sticks out his hand. "I'm Mike. You're jumping with me. This marks my thousandth jump, let's make it memorable. Deal?" His thick white hair lifts then falls with the breeze.

I wipe my hand again then take his and shake it. My voice is lost to me, so I only nod.

"Once those bozos jump" — he gestures to the others — "I'll connect you to my harness, you in front of me, then we'll go to the door. When I say 'go,' we jump. If you don't jump, I will, and you're going with me. Better if you take the lead." He chuckles. "Ready?"

I nod again.

"Good. Remember what you learned — arms stretched out, wrists straight, palms flat." He demonstrates. "Got it?"

Before I can respond, he strides toward the plane that's pulled up in front of us. I follow behind him.

As I wait to board, I take the young man's advice and work to loosen up. I shake my arms and hands, from shoulders to fingertips, then do a shimmy as though I can shake off the spiders of fear skittering up my spine. But then that's the point, isn't it?

To shake off fear, once and for all. That's what I've come to do. To prove to myself that the phantom known as Fear no longer holds me in its grip.

I straighten, square my shoulders, and take a deep breath. Then I follow Mike and climb aboard the plane. There are no seats, the other divers are piled close to one another on the floor. Mike points to an open space near him, where I lower myself, sit, pull my knees to my chest, and then look out the oval window next to me.

My breath catches and I lean in, cup my hands on the glass to cut the glare, and peer out.

It can't be . . .

Mouth dry, I try to swallow. Then I look away.

My heart batters my chest and my pulse roars in my ears, nearly drowning out the clamor of the plane's propellers. It isn't him. I'm imagining things. I turn back to the window and take another look, then stare at the man near the hangar. As I watch, he leans against the outside wall and pulls something from his shirt pocket and sticks it in his mouth. A cigarette? He lights it. It isn't him. He doesn't smoke. Or does he? It doesn't matter. It isn't him — it's impossible. I know where he is, and it isn't here.

I steady myself as the plane shoots down the runway then lifts. As memories flash, perspiration trickles down my back. I inhale then exhale. It wasn't him. Let it go.

Fear will not win. Not this time. Not ever again.

Within what feels like mere moments, the group of professional skydivers have all jumped, and I stand, back pressed against Mike, hooked to his harness. We brace ourselves against the pummeling force of wind as we wait near the gaping opening in the side of the plane. I pull the goggles from the top of my head down over my eyes.

My breaths are now shallow and my pulse races.

"Step to the edge," Mike yells. When I don't move, he yells again, this time his breath hot against my ear. I hesitate a moment more, then step forward, Mike stepping in sync with me. There's nothing to see but the vast expanse.

"Go!" Mike shouts.

Heart hammering my rib cage, I lean forward, eyes squeezed shut, and fall more than jump into nothingness, arms stretched wide. I anticipate the sensation of falling — stomach lifting to throat — but the sensation isn't evident. Nor is the velocity at which I know we're falling. When I dare to open my eyes, I'm only aware of the force of air pushing my cheeks back to my ears, which makes me laugh.

The free fall is like nothing I've ever experienced. I laugh again, the sound carried heavenward on the drafts, I imagine. Too soon I'm jerked, hard, and the harness cuts into my thighs as I'm pulled upward with what seems like exceeding force.

But then we're floating. Soaring. "Oh," I whisper. I want to take it all in, remember every exhilarating moment. I could ride these currents forever. The tension I'd felt is replaced by peace, pervasive peace.

Quietude. Silence. Wonder.

"That was a hard pull." Mike's shouted words behind me threaten to break the spell, but I assume the pull — the parachute opening and catching air — was harder than usual but fine. We're fine.

As we float, my eyes are trained on the ground below. The earth is a patchwork of tones. A river — the Sacramento River — is but a thread stitched across the quilt of colors. I search for familiar landmarks as my sense of confidence soars. I've done it. Faced fear, terror even, and —

Suddenly we're plummeting.

Tumbling.

Head first. Arms and legs akimbo.

Land and sky spin as they interchange. My lungs deflate. Pressure. The currents, tumultuous, pull me under and then spit me out. I can't breathe. Why can't I breathe? I gasp. I'm drowning. Help! Someone, help! But no . . . There's no water. Instead, I'm above, where there's nothing. Just . . .

Nothing.

Nothing to reach for. Nothing to grab. No way to save myself.

A scream sounds in my mind. Rings in my ears. Scathes my throat.

My scream?

Awareness hits. I'm going to die. It's my only thought.

I am going to die.

God is going to let me die.

Then . . .

Everything goes black.

"Hey!" Something shakes me — my shoulder. "Hey!" The voice, louder this time, is still faint, like I'm in a wind tunnel. I strain to listen. "You okay?"

Am I . . . okay? Eyelids weighted, I struggle to open them, then I . . . scream. I reach out to grab something, but there's nothing. I'm falling . . . falling . . .

Then I remember. It all comes rushing back. I jumped, we were falling, plummeting, upside down.

Now we're floating again. I jerk my head up and see the parachute, brilliant against the blue sky. Did I pass out? Hyperventilate?

"Congratulations!" he yells.

Who yells? Mike — his name is Mike.

"Your reserve chute worked!"

Reserve chute?

"The primary chute was bowed, tangled. I had to let it go."

I look down. This time there's no sense of wonder, no desire to pick out familiar landmarks. The closer we come to the ground, the faster it rushes to meet us. I just want to land, to have my feet on the ground.

Then the thought returns. The only thought I had time for. I was going to die. God was going to let me die.

Only, He didn't.

I'm alive.

But . . . what happened?

The image of the man standing near the hangar returns. The inky shadow of his beard, the way he leaned against the building as we took off . . .

As we near the ground, Mike yells again, "Pull your legs up. We're going down hard."

I recall the brief instruction in the video. For a tandem jump, you'll pull your legs up so you land on your back end. I do as Mike has instructed and pull my legs up.

As the ground rushes up at us, we crash into it. My back end hits first, then we roll several times and finally come to a stop.

"You okay?" Mike asks. Then he laughs and lets out a whoop. "That was memorable, all right." He unhooks his harness from mine, stands, then offers me his hand and helps me stumble to my feet. My tailbone throbs, and I suspect I'll have a few bruises from the landing, but physically I'm fine.

"What . . . what happened up there?"

"Like I said, the main chute was tangled. I knew it wouldn't land us, or at least not in any way we'd want to land."

"But . . . why? Why did it tangle?"

"They say odds are that one in every thousand chutes will fail. Could have been packed wrong. Who knows?"

"Packed wrong? Could someone have intentionally done that?"

"Intentionally? You paranoid?" He chuckles. "One in a thousand. It was just my turn. Count your lucky stars, little lady. You're in one piece." He pats my shoulder, then begins pulling in the parachute that's stretched out behind us.

I watch him for a moment as I process what he's said. Paranoid? No. Lucky? Absolutely not. Had I chosen this on my own, depended on my own strength this time, maybe I'd feel lucky. Instead, I know God has spared me.

I turn and walk away from Mike and head for the hangar where I saw *him*.

Bradley Mathison.

It was him. There's no doubt in my mind now. What I don't know is how. How he got out. How he knew to come here. As I cross the field where we landed, more puzzle pieces fall into place and the picture becomes clear. I'm sure of it.

He's out.

He's followed me.

And it was him who ran me off the road. It was him who tried to kill Max. And regardless of what Mike said, somehow it was him who tried to kill me today. And take Mike with me. I look back over my shoulder to where he's standing, parachute around his feet now, laughing with someone. He has no idea.

Paranoid? If he only knew.

Something roars to life deep within as I bear down on the tarmac, searching for him. Anger thunders to the surface. I will find him, and I will end this once and for all. My feet pound the asphalt as I go to the hangar where I saw him. When I don't see him there, I go out to the parking lot, but he isn't there either. I turn back and then barge into the office and sputter to the young woman who'd helped me. "Where is he? There was a man . . ." I turn and look around the office. But he isn't there. "Where is he?"

"I'm sorry, who are you looking for?"

But as I'm about to demand he be found, to tell her what he attempted to do, a small voice echoes in my soul and stops me as sure as though a hand were slapped across my mouth. *No.*

I hesitate.

No.

While the rage I feel is new, and my actions seem new, awareness dawns. I'm taking control again. Doing this on my own. If I found him, what would I do? Am I going to do what he's tried to do to me? Would I harm him? Kill him even? Would I become what he's become?

"I'm . . . I'm sorry." I shake my head. "Sorry." I take off the harness, unzip the jumpsuit, and step out of it, and then pull the goggles now dangling around my neck over my head. I put everything on the counter. "I'm . . . Nothing." I turn to go. "Thank you."

As I walk toward my car, that same, quiet

voice within whispers again.

Not yet.

CHAPTER THIRTY-ONE

Denilyn
March 19, 2017

After having a few more security cameras installed on the property, and taking Detective Alejandro's advice and hiring a security company to guard the property, I hoped to feel more secure at home. I couldn't expect Jay and Gabe to house us indefinitely. Nor could I just walk away from our lives at home.

But after today and the realization that Bradley Mathison is no longer in prison, home isn't the refuge it once was. Actually, it hasn't felt like much of a refuge since the attempt to poison Max and the note asking who would die next.

The two armed guards at the gates to the property make it more a prison than a refuge. But they are both an expense and necessity I can't *not* afford.

As I leave the small airport and merge

onto the eastbound interstate toward home, the earlier rage I felt lingers as I place a call to Sonia Alejandro, the lead detective on my case this time. *This time?* This has to end. As her line rings, I wait not only for her voice mail but also for the voice within — will it stop me again?

"Sonia Alejandro."

I'm surprised both when Detective Alejandro answers and when I sense nothing holding me back.

"Why wasn't I notified?"

"Excuse me?"

"Why wasn't I notified? He's out! He was there today. Why didn't I receive notification?"

"Slow down. Who is this?"

I take the next turnoff and pull off the interstate and into a parking lot as I talk. The emotion of the day — seeing Mathison, one more near-death experience, and the anger, the all-consuming, ravaging anger — boils over. All of it.

"Denilyn. Denilyn Rossi." My jaw aches with unreleased tension.

"Denilyn. Okay. Take it slow. Tell me what happened."

I take a moment, then start again, my tone measured this time.

"Bradley Mathison. He's out of prison. I

wasn't notified. I saw him today. He tried to kill me . . . today."

I relay the details of what occurred during my skydive and who I saw at the airport.

"You're certain it was him?" I hear the doubt in her tone.

"As certain as I am that I'm speaking with you. Unless he has a twin, it was him."

She's silent for a moment as though thinking. "That may explain a few things. Let me do some checking and get back to you. And oh Denilyn, I am glad you're okay. Pay attention and don't hesitate to call. I'll check again with the Department of Corrections, and I'll follow up with the skydiving company. You'll hear from me soon."

When I end the call, it isn't Bradley Mathison or the case I'm thinking about. Instead, I ponder Sonia Alejandro's words, *"Pay attention."* How often have others encouraged me to do the same through the years? But this time I understand the message to mean more than looking over my shoulder.

"I am paying attention. Finally," I whisper. "I'm listening . . ."

And I am listening, but the silence hasn't distilled the rage.

■ ■ ■ ■

March 20, 2017

On Monday morning, I arrive on campus early, knowing that I have several hours of reading and grading papers ahead of me. But as I sit at my desk, my mind spins with both the exhilaration of my skydiving experience yesterday and the horror of it. I struggle to process the contrasts. I also struggle to focus on the assignments that filled my email inbox over the weekend.

Anger, like a river, rushes still — its thundering drowns everything else.

Rather than tackling the assignments, I open my calendar app and go to the month of June. I stare at the first of the month and the note I've read so many times:

Eligible for parole.

If I needed a reminder that I can't control what happens, this is it. He isn't even eligible for parole, but he's out. What happened? I close my eyes and see him again as he was yesterday. The same shadow of beard beneath his fair skin and the way he leaned against the building, his shoulder and hip pressed against the metal siding of the hangar. He was leaner perhaps, and his hair a little longer, but I have no doubt that it was him.

If only he'd received a life sentence, but there wasn't enough proof to convict him of attempted murder. Not even the scar on my head proved he'd tried to kill me. The final charm was never linked to him. The charm that constituted a threat.

While he was placed at my mother's house the night of the attack, he swore he hadn't hit me, that someone else had been in the garage. He claimed he'd seen the shadow of a man, a baseball bat raised above my head, but it was dark and he couldn't offer any identifying evidence. He told authorities the man hit me, dropped the bat, then turned and ran out the open garage door. A convenient explanation. There were no identifiable prints on the bat.

He was the only one there. He'd stalked me, threatened me with the charms, whether the last charm was linked to him or not, and then attacked me in my mother's garage. I raise my hand to my neck as though his arm is still wrapped tightly around me, cutting off my airway.

Neighbors testified that they'd seen a car, later identified as Mathison's, parked a few houses down from my mother's that night. But they'd noticed no one else, no other unknown vehicles or people in the neighborhood.

It was Mathison. And Mathison alone.

Thoughts of that night, the memories, both of the attack and the aftermath, assault me with overpowering force.

I woke sometime in the predawn hours the morning following the attack with a bright light shining in my eyes. I jerked back and screamed, but like a nightmare, when I opened my mouth, the alarm succumbed to fear and refused to sound. I was powerless. Sure he was still shining that flashlight in my eyes and I could do nothing to help myself.

"Shh . . . It's okay. You're okay." An unfamiliar voice soothed.

I tried to open my eyes, but my lids were too heavy. And my head . . . I reached my hand up —

"Denilyn . . ." Someone gently pushed my hand back down. "You've been injured. You're in the hospital. Keep your arm down — you have an IV. Can you hear me?"

I couldn't nod — it hurt too much. I opened my eyes, then closed them abruptly against the light in the room. My head throbbed, the pain blinding.

"We're going to give you something for the pain. Just rest now." Then, as if she was speaking to someone else, she quietly asked, "Allergies to medications?"

"No." My mother's voice.

I wanted to reach for her, call her to come to me, but the effort was too much. My head pounded. "Head . . . hurts," I mumbled.

A hand rested on my shoulder. My mother's hand?

"Any chance she's pregnant?"

"I don't think so. I . . . don't know." I heard the question in my mom's tone. "Maybe . . ."

"We'll need to catheterize her. I'll take a urine sample to test for pregnancy — faster than a blood test . . ." Her voice, the doctor or nurse, whoever she was, faded or cut out. My memories after that, for days after, play like an old black-and-white movie — the film broken and spliced so that entire scenes are lost.

Due to swelling of my brain, I was told later, I was put into a medically induced state of coma — that deep sleep that left me unaware of both my surroundings and all that took place, yet at times oddly present.

My cell phone, sitting on my desk, rings, and I jump, startled from my reverie. It rings a second time before I pick it up. "This is Denilyn Rossi."

"Denilyn, this Sonia Alejandro. Is there a time today we can meet? I'd like to share some information with you and ask you a few questions. I can come to you."

"Oh . . . Well, I have a break this afternoon. If you don't mind coming here, that would be helpful. You could come to my office if that works."

"Yes, that's fine."

We set a time to meet, and I give her directions to find my office. But before she hangs up, I have to ask, "Did you find him? Why wasn't I notified?"

"We'll talk when I see you. I'll have more information then."

I'm tempted to press her but sense it won't do any good. I'll have to wait, though each minute feels like an eternity — as if the finish line is close but just beyond my reach.

Sonia, as she's asked me to call her, sits across from me, my desk between us. She sets a leather folio on my desk, opens it, and reveals a pad with scribbled notes. She glances at the notes, then looks at me. "If you voted in November, you may recall that Proposition 47 provided for the early release of prisoners whose felonies would be reduced to misdemeanors in order to address the overcrowding of California's prisons. The proposition passed, and they've released close to three thousand prisoners since January."

"Yes, I remember. But what does that have to do with Mathison? My understanding of the proposition was that it provided the reduced offense for those who'd committed property and drug crimes — not violent crimes."

"Right. But due to an error, Mathison was released as well. Something to do with the software used by the Department of Corrections. You weren't notified of his release because according to their records, he was still incarcerated. In fact, had you not seen him, you'd have likely never received any sort of notification. When I contacted them, insisting he was out, they did a little digging."

With jaw clenched, I lean forward. "When? When was he released?"

"March 13th."

"But" — I shake my head — "the accident, the texts, Max . . . That all occurred before the 13th. Are you sure of the date?"

"That's the date I was given, and I have to believe it's accurate."

"Okay, but he was at the airport. He's responsible for what happened there. He had to be the one who —"

"Hold on. I believe you saw him. But after a lengthy conversation with the owner of the skydiving operation, I'm convinced, as is he, that there was no way Mathison could have impacted your dive — the parachute you used. The instructors pack their own chutes, and then they pack one another's reserve chutes. They never have the same person pack both the primary and reserve chute. Even if Bradley Mathison knew how to pack a parachute, he'd have had no way of accessing the parachutes or of knowing which pack your instructor was going to use. It just isn't possible. What happened was an accident. I was told that approximately one in one thousand chutes fail. It happens. Will we pick up Mathison for questioning? Of course. But . . ." She shrugs.

"No. No, that doesn't make sense. If he was released by error, why aren't they looking for him? Why won't he be returned to custody?"

"He'd earned enough credit for good behavior that his actual release date fell just a few weeks before the date he'd have been eligible for release. It's done, Denilyn. Now" — she refers to her notes — "per Penal Code section 3003(f), as a direct victim you can request he not be allowed to live within thirty-five miles —"

"No! That doesn't help me. He was out less than a week and already found me, followed me. What good does thirty-five miles do? He's doing what he did before. Why can't you charge him?"

"If I can place him at the airport —"

"I placed him there. I saw him."

"As I said, as soon as we find him, we'll bring him in. I just don't know that I have anything that'll stick at this point. But I'm working on it. Okay? I'm working on it. I'm on your side."

I drop my gaze to my lap, unable to believe what I've heard.

"Denilyn, look at me."

I lift my head and stare at her. "What?"

She leans forward, her gaze intent. "I spent much of yesterday and most of last night reviewing your case. I went over reports, interviews, looked at evidence . . ." The shake of her head is imperceptible. Almost. "There are things that don't add up. Not for me. The equation doesn't quite work."

As I listen, something long submerged bobs to the surface of my consciousness, where it settles uncomfortably. I hesitate before asking, "Such as?"

"Well, for starters, that third charm. It was

sent from Seattle. The other two were hand-delivered. There was nothing found to place Mathison in Seattle, nor did they link him to anyone there. I'm not saying he didn't have someone send it. It's just a loose end — one I'd like to see sewn up. As far as I can tell, information about the bracelet and charms was never released publicly. So the charm came either from Mathison or from someone who knew about the bracelet and the first two charms."

"It had to be Mathison. There were less than a handful of people who knew about the charms — all of them very close to me. It had to have come from him."

"Well, I'd like proof of that."

"What else?"

"The accident, the texts, your dog, the note, for starters. If it wasn't Mathison, who was it?"

"It had to be him. There is no one else. He . . . somehow, he hired someone or he . . . I don't know. It had to be him."

"I'm not disagreeing with you, but we need proof."

She looks down at her notes. Then she stares at me for a moment before continuing. "Does the name Adelia Sanchez mean anything to you?"

"Adelia?"

She nods.

"Yes, she . . . Why?"

"Did you know she'd filed a restraining order against Bradley Mathison?"

I stare at Sonia, then shake my head. "No . . . I didn't . . ." I look away from her as I attempt to make sense of what she's said. "Before she . . ." I take a deep breath. "Before she died, he . . . hung around, but . . . She would have told us. That doesn't . . . That doesn't make sense. She would have told me."

"Her death was deemed accidental, is that correct?"

"Yes."

"But her body was never found?"

"No," I whisper. "The river . . . She fell . . ."

"Were you there? When she fell?"

"No."

"I see."

"What do you see?"

"Another loose end."

CHAPTER THIRTY-TWO

Denilyn
March 26, 2017

I pull the mail from the box, including a padded manila envelope. I flip through the pile of bills and advertisements as I walk back down the long drive to the house. When I come to the manila envelope with my name and address handwritten across the front and the familiar return address in the corner, I slow. Whatever is inside is from Adelia's mother. I continue my walk to the house, carrying both the mail and memories of the friend I lost.

But it's more than the envelope and whatever it holds — the memories began following my last meeting with Sonia Alejandro.

It's almost as if Adelia herself is whispering to my mind and soul.

When I reach the house, I go inside and drop the mail on my desk. Then I sit down, reach into the drawer for the letter opener, and slit the top of the manila envelope.

Inside is an array of items, but a small pink envelope stands out, so I pull it out first and open it, taking out the notecard inside.

Dear Denilyn,

As we approach the anniversary of Adelia's death, you've come to mind often. It's hard to believe she's been gone almost ten years. I still grieve her loss every day, though I now more often recall the joy she brought me rather than the agony of her loss.

I hope you also are remembering all that you enjoyed as friends.

Recently I came across the envelope of items you'd gathered from the cottage the two of you shared — items I'd missed when I moved her things. There was nothing of value, but I've included what you sent to me at the time. I thought you might appreciate the reminders of Adelia and the friendship you shared.

Love,
Maria Sanchez

I set the card aside and then dump the

contents of the larger envelope onto my desktop. I pick up a photo and gaze at the four of us, younger, leaner. We all wear shorts, and either a tank top or T-shirt. Ryan, Adelia and myself are burnished by the sun — our skin tanned. Jay wears a straw cowboy hat, her face nearly hidden in the shadow of its rim. Ryan's arm is draped around Adelia's shoulders, but he's looking around her to me. We're all smiling, laughing at something. The photo was taken on the Ride the Kaweah lot, yellow rafts piled behind us. I don't recall who took the photo or what made us laugh. It was unusual for Jay to be at Mick's, and I can't recall the occasion.

I pick up another photo, this one of myself and Adelia sitting at a table on the deck at Annie's Emporium, sandwiches and bags of chips in front of us. We'd just finished a run down the river. We both have our hair pulled back and are looking at the camera. Ryan took the photo, I remember.

I look at a few more photos, and then I pick up Adelia's driver's license, which had expired while we were in Three Rivers. Her mother had mailed Adelia her new license when it had been delivered to their home address. I'd found her expired license in the junk drawer in our kitchen, along with an expired credit card, which I pick up next. Memories rush in as I run my index finger over the raised letters of her name.

The day she'd fallen, Adelia and Ryan had taken the day off and gone into the park to hike. We were all supposed to meet for dinner at The Gateway later that evening, but neither Ryan or Adelia showed up. Jaylan and I waited for twenty minutes or so before getting a table. After another half hour, we went ahead and ordered. We didn't think too much about their absence. Sometimes traffic out of the park moved at a crawl. Or maybe they'd changed their plans. Cell service in Three Rivers was spotty, so they likely couldn't reach us.

It was later that night — around ten thirty or so, when there was a knock on the door of the cottage Adelia and I shared. Jay had come back with me after dinner, and we were watching a movie. I got up from the sofa, thinking Adelia must have forgotten her key. I went to the door, looked through the peephole, and saw that it was Ryan. Even in that brief glance, I knew something was wrong. I opened the door, and he walked past me into the living room, where he paced the small space.

I trailed behind him. "What's wrong? Where's Adelia?"

He said nothing, just paced back and forth.

"You gonna talk to us or not?" Jay's patience with Ryan was short, as usual.

He stopped and looked at Jay. "She fell." Then he looked at me. "She just" — he ran his hand through his hair — "fell. Slipped, or stumbled. I don't know. One minute she was there, the next she was . . . gone."

"Gone where?" I whispered, afraid to hear his response.

"The river. We were just going to sit on a rock, hang our feet over into the spray from the rapids. We'd taken our shoes off and were just going to sit. I turned my back for a second to set my shoes down. I heard her scream, and when I turned back, she was . . . gone."

"Gone?" I said again. I couldn't take in what he was telling us. Couldn't, wouldn't believe it was true.

"Where on the river?" Jay asked.

"Just below Hospital Rock. We were heading out of the park. We were hot, and there's that trail just off the road, at the scenic overlook. We pulled off there and hiked down. I . . . I tried to find her after . . . But you know what the water's like there. I couldn't see anything. So I climbed back up and flagged down a ranger . . ." He dropped onto the sofa next to Jay. "He called Search and Rescue. They searched until dark, but . . ." Elbows on his knees, he put his head in his hands.

"Oh God, no. Lord, no, no, no." Not seeming to know what to do with herself, Jay stood, looking down at Ryan. "No, this did not happen. Tell us this did not happen. That *trail* isn't a trail. That warning sign posted there is there for a purpose. Tell me you did not go down that trail."

He glanced up at her, then closed his eyes and shook his head. The anguish on his face said it all. "At this point, she's presumed . . . dead." He leaned back and closed his eyes. "They'll continue to look for her body."

"Dead?" I said. "No . . . she can't be. She can't be." I still couldn't process what he'd said. I couldn't process the possibility that she wasn't going to walk through the door at any moment. Adelia was a strong swimmer trained in white-water rescue. All three of us were. Jay was the only one who wasn't a guide, who didn't share our love of challenging the white water. How could someone as young, as strong, as well-trained as Adelia . . . "It . . . it doesn't make sense," I said.

"What doesn't make sense?" Ryan shot up from the sofa, the vein in his neck pulsing. "How does it not make sense? The number one cause of death in the park is drowning. You're the last person I have to tell that to — you tell rafters that stat every day." His face was red now, and he loomed over me as he spoke. "It makes perfect sense!"

I stepped back from him. I knew his anger wasn't directed at me, but it was still disconcerting. Startling in its intensity.

"Deni?"

I look up from the small pile of items on my desk to where my mother stands in the doorway of the office.

"You okay?"

I nod, then gesture to the photos and things. "I was just remembering. Maria Sanchez sent me some of Adelia's things." I look back at the photos, Adelia smiling up at me.

My mom comes into the office and around my desk. She stands behind me and looks over my shoulder, then reaches for one of the photos. "She was so beautiful. So young. I could never imagine what her parents went through. Still go through. Such a tragedy." She gives my shoulder a quick squeeze. "If you'll be here for a while, I thought I'd go into town to run some errands."

"Of course."

"I'll be back before dinner."

"Take your time."

After she goes, I gather up the items on my desk and slip them back into the envelope. I know the timing of their arrival is neither an accident nor a coincidence.

I needed to remember . . .

I cross the backyard, where spring is revealing itself in tinges of bright green. When I reach the gate, solid and nearly invisible in the wall, I turn and look back at the house and the natural drought-resistant landscape of the spacious grounds.

After the divorce, I could no longer fathom living in the house Keith and I had purchased together when our hope was high and our expectation was that we'd spend the rest of our lives together. If Keith couldn't deal with the stalking and the issues it presented, he was in no way prepared to deal with my injuries, recovery, and an impending trial. He came to see me just once when I was hospitalized. He admitted his faults, his immaturity, and confessed that in the fray that was our marriage at that point, he'd also become, if not involved with someone else, at least involved with the idea of someone else. A young woman on his sales team.

The tears he shed were genuine, I had no doubt, and it was clear he cried for more than what had died between us. He also cried for what he was choosing to walk away from — the hope of, the birth of, something new.

The house was too painful a reminder of all we'd lost.

Nor did I want to live in the home of my childhood with my mother. I wanted, needed, a project — something away from the city where water sang and stars shone bright.

A place where new life would bloom.

My father had left me a large sum of money, placed in a trust, not available to me until I turned thirty years old. It was money I hadn't touched. But after talking it over with my mother and asking her to consider selling her home and coming to live with us, I found exactly what I wanted and needed, and it seemed appropriate that my father would provide the means to fulfill my need.

The lot, just over an acre, sat above the north fork of the American River and included a set of steep, rickety stairs that traversed the bank down to the river's edge. The house, a dilapidated mid-century modern, offered both the space, style, and possibilities I desired. Its boulder strewn, overgrown lot, and the repairs the house necessitated, made the price right.

We moved in as soon as escrow closed, and I spent the next two years working with a contractor and landscape architect to create what I'd envisioned. When I accepted the position at PCU, my mother took over the daily tasks at home, including keeping the remodel on track.

The landscape architect came up with the design for the wall that now surrounds the property — something both secure, contemporary in style, and constructed with materials that fit with the natural landscape.

I turn back to the gate, push it open, nod to the man who stands on the other side, a handgun visible in a holster at his hip. I hand him a bottle of cold water. "I'm going down to the river for a while."

I descend the stairs, now reinforced and sturdy, the sound of the swollen river hastening to greet me. I stop and zip the light jacket I'm wearing, the temperature having dropped a full ten degrees since this time last week.

This time last week when I was jumping out of an airplane.

It seems so long ago now — so much has transpired in just seven days.

I need time alone, moments of silence — time to remember, to listen, and to discern what's next.

As I reach the last step of the stairs, I sit down, careful not to bump my still tender tailbone, and then I look out at the swiftly moving water. The river will swell more as the snowpack melts, causing the river to run, churn, and froth.

"I'd love to see you in action, on a river . . ."

"The American River has some great white water. We just need to take the time . . ."

The one thing Keith and I didn't have was time. We didn't take it when we could, and then it was too late. We are still partners in a sense, but no longer husband and wife. A loss, I realize again, I may always grieve.

That grief stirs the still new bubbling cauldron of anger within.

So much loss . . .

"But you didn't get me. You haven't taken me!" My proclamation of life goes unheard, except to my own ears.

God has spared me, but . . . why?

Why? I look skyward, where the daylight canvas is neither blue nor gray but rather faded like dingy cotton, a hazy cover of clouds. I wait, but no answer comes. Instead, an onslaught of memories taunt and the soundtrack plays.

"Please, Denilyn, please. I don't want to hurt you."

"Open your eyes, Denilyn. Open your pretty eyes."

But this time, instead of turning away, instead of drowning his words, instead of doing *anything* but hear them again, I let the memories play.

"So pretty . . ."

"I won't hurt you. I don't want to hurt you."

But then the soundtrack is interrupted . . .

"Did you know she'd filed a restraining order against Bradley Mathison?"

"She's presumed dead." Anguish slashed Ryan's features as he told Jay and me the news he'd received about Adelia.

The babble of the river is discordant now and annoys. I stand and step off the last step onto the rocky bank. The river runs just a stone's throw away.

"But her body was never found?" What was Sonia after?

I close my eyes, and the jumble of words sound in my mind over and over, the dissonance of the river as their background. He's hurt too many people, I want to scream. Too many. It wasn't just me but Adelia before me. How had I not known? How? Rage boils within. He has to be stopped.

This has to stop! I cry out to God from somewhere within myself. *It has to stop. Please, make it stop.*

When I open my eyes, my cheeks are damp and I wipe the tears I've shed. As I stare out at the river, the seed of an idea begins to root itself.

An unfathomable idea, and again, one I know is not my own.

I turn and go back to the last step and sit again and allow the idea to bud. I consider it from every angle. I weigh the implications, the risks, and come up short. I sit on the step until the sun is low in the sky and the chill of late afternoon has seeped into not only my bones but also my soul, where the idea has bloomed into a plan.

Then I ask a ridiculous question. *Are You sure?* The only response I receive is the assurance that settles within.

"When?" I whisper.

Soon.

The river babbles over boulders, around bends — its song alluring once again. But it isn't the American River that lures me.

It is another river.

Get ready . . .

I get to my feet and climb to the top of the stairs — I'm winded when I reach the top. I stand on the landing at the top, heart beating faster than I prefer. With all that's gone on in the last few weeks, I've let my daily workouts go. I turn around and walk back down the stairs. At the bottom, I turn and climb again, faster this time. Then faster still until I reach the top again. I turn and run back down, my hand hovering just above the rail. I count the steps as I go — "seventy-seven, seventy-eight, seventy-nine." When my foot touches the last stair, I turn and run back up, tailbone aching, the bruises on my legs throbbing, and my lungs burning. I run and I run, and when I reach the top step, I bend at the waist, hands on my knees, and gasp for air.

I have a lot to do to get ready.

A lot of work ahead of me.

CHAPTER THIRTY-THREE

Denilyn
May 5, 2017

The hour is early, dawn still just a hope, the house quiet. I stand in front of the mirror in my bathroom, the door closed. I barely recognize the reflection staring back at me. My shoulders are broader than they were a month ago, and my biceps defined. I've always exercised, taken care of my body, built my strength, but now that strength is visible beneath the skin.

But it isn't just the physical conditioning that's changed my appearance, made me unrecognizable to myself. It's the internal changes — the fire I see in my own eyes.

The pendulum has swung.

I rest my hands on the cool marble countertop and look down at the sink as I tick off a mental list. I've done everything I needed to do. I've taken care of everything and everyone. Jay, Gabe, and Ryan are aware of the trip ahead of me, though I've kept many of the details to myself. The last call I made was to Ryan.

"I'm taking some time away. I'm leaving in the morning."

"Where are you headed?"

"Three Rivers."

"Why now? You've never wanted to go back. What's the point?"

"I need to work through some things — things I've left undone emotionally."

"Where are you staying?"

"I have a place."

"That's it — that's all you're going to say? You're going to work through things. You have a place."

"Yes, that's all I'm going to say."

Ryan has stayed at my side through so much. It was Ryan who helped me through the stalking when Keith wasn't able or willing. It was Ryan who was at the hospital daily after the attack. When Keith made it clear the marriage was over, Ryan offered his support, both emotionally and physically — he was there to help with anything I needed. And later it was Ryan who recommended me for the position at PCU.

Ryan has watched out for me and watched over me.

But what I've allowed, the closeness we've

shared, hasn't really been fair to him. I'll never have more to offer him. I'll never offer what I know he wants.

It's time to loosen the bonds that have held us together, and I am the only one who can untie those knots, or at least begin to — and now, as I go away, it's a good time to begin that process.

There is one last item to take care of, to check off that mental list I've added and subtracted from over the last month. Something I will do for myself, and myself alone. I do, however, have another motive beyond what will serve me well.

I open the top drawer in the bank of drawers beneath the counter and reach for the items I need. I place them on the countertop and then look into the mirror again. I stare at my reflection for a moment, then I pick up the pair of scissors. With my other hand, I pull a clump of my hair taut. I lift the scissors and cut the hair as near to my scalp as possible. The long strands fall to the floor. I grab another clump and cut. And another. When I'm finished, I clip the hair closer to my scalp yet.

The reflection in the mirror is changing, but the transformation isn't complete.

I turn on the faucet and let the water run until it's hot. I cup my hands under the water, then bend and splash the water onto what's left of my hair. I add a dab of shampoo and lather it.

Then I reach for the razor and lift it to my head.

I am careful as I shave around the scar on the side of my head, gently maneuvering the razor over the ridge of it. As the last of the hair falls away, I turn my head so I can see the permanent image inked over the scar.

I trace the image of the sword, droplets of blood on its tip, a few landing on the open book beneath the sword. The Word of God — the Sword of the Spirit.

A permanent reminder of the power I hold within.

Not my own power.

But the Spirit's power.

How did I wander so far from that truth? How did I forget that power? I was so certain, so filled with faith after Mathison's arrest. God had protected me, fought for me. I'd wanted a permanent reminder of what He'd done. After the stitches were removed from the almost five-inch laceration on my scalp, and once it had fully healed, I'd had the design tattooed there. Jay had gone with me and occasionally held my hand through the painful process.

How did I wander so far from that truth? It doesn't matter now. There is no condemnation.

I finish the job I began, bend again, and rinse the soap from my smooth head. I reach for a towel and pat my head and face dry. Then I stare again at my reflected image, no longer seeing myself but the One alive inside me, the Power I hold.

After I've swept my hair from the floor, I leave the bathroom. In the bedroom, Max is still curled on my bed. He lifts his head, looks at me, and then sits up. "C'mon," I whisper. He jumps to the floor and follows me to the door, then across the hallway. I've already said my goodbyes, but I must see him one more time. Gently, I turn the knob of his bedroom door. As I open the door, his scent, all boy, wafts to meet me.

I listen for his breathing, as I have nearly every night since his birth just over seven years ago. The rhythm of his breaths are as familiar as my own. When I'm sure he's still asleep, I go to his bed and look down at him, my son. I reach for the shock of hair that's fallen across his forehead. I brush it aside, then bend and kiss the soft skin there.

"I love you, Nicky," I whisper.

Nicky — Nicolo Giovanni Rossi — named after my father, rather than his own father.

He stirs but doesn't wake. "I'm doing this for you . . ." I wish I could help him understand. But I barely understand myself. I only know it is time to set him free from the prison of protection I've created. It is time I allow him to come out of hiding, to grow into the person God intended. I meant only to keep him safe, but my fear has kept him a prisoner.

I do not speak of him to others beyond those closest to me — my mom, Jay and Gabe, and Ryan. I don't brag of his accomplishments. I keep no pictures of him on my desk. I haven't even spoken of him to Jon, someone who, I realize now, I could care for, deeply even. I haven't allowed myself to trust him with my truth.

I am also imprisoned.

My mother has helped care for Nicky since his birth and has homeschooled him for the last two years. We have held him close, nurtured him, disciplined him, loved him. But beyond all, I have protected him.

If not for his father, he'd have almost no life outside the circle of my protection.

But it is time to let go. To entrust him to the care of his heavenly Father.

It is a choice I make for his sake.

It is the lesson of trust I learned from diving out of a plane. My life is in God's hands.

I acknowledge His sovereign control. And now, much more difficult than letting go of my own life, I let go of my son's life. I acknowledge that he is in God's hands. Hands so much more capable than my own.

Whether I live or die in the month ahead, Nicky is set free.

It is not my child *he* wants.

It is me he's after.

If the plan succeeds, I live. If it fails, I most likely die. It's all or nothing.

But either way, it will finally end.

It will all finally end.

I look down at Max who sits next to me. "Watch over him while I'm gone." I bend and scratch behind Max's ear, then I kiss Nicky again.

I turn to go.

But I do not go alone.

■ ■ ■ ■

PART THREE

■ ■ ■ ■

Under my window it hurls itself, with the force of myth, over river stones, down rapids, riddled with fish. All day the voice of water roars. . . . Downstream, a trace of my blood feeds the sound.

LUCI SHAW

CHAPTER THIRTY-FOUR

Adelia
May 11, 2017

After the call that pulled me from the stupor of sleep with the information I've waited for, I dragged myself out of bed. I went to the kitchen, where I scooped extra beans into the coffee grinder, then set a pot of coffee to brew.

Now I sit on the deck, the sun already punishing, and sip the strong, black coffee, hoping it will revive me. Sunlight glistens on the river like diamonds sparkling on its surface. But the beauty is deceptive. While the Kaweah may be my ally, it is also a murderer, or at least a stealer of life. I learned that after Adelia's death, then again personally in the wee hours this morning as it reached for me and pulled me under. Only when I submitted to its pull did it let me go.

I set the mug down and pick up my wallet

from the table next to me, the worn leather smooth in my hand. I dug the wallet out of my purse before I came outside. I open it now and stare at the photo of Adelia, as she was so long ago, on the expired driver's license I tucked into the first flap of my wallet the day I received it from her mother.

Before submitting to the Kaweah's pull, as I fought its power, one question surfaced: is this terror what Adelia felt — is this how she died? Even now the thought causes my lungs to ache and my head to spin as though denied oxygen.

I can only hope that as she fell, she hit her head and was knocked out. *Please God, please have extended her that mercy.*

The photo on her driver's license is startling in the essence it conveys of her spirit. The joy of life that emanated from her. Jaylan asked me a question before I left for Three Rivers. *"Had something extinguished the light that shone from Adelia near the end? Or am I imagining that?"*

Hindsight offers fertile ground for imagination, but as I look back now, I do believe there were signs that perhaps answer Jay's questions. Adelia was as steady as a plank emotionally. Her mood was constant: upbeat, positive, and fun. She rarely, if ever, showed signs of discouragement or even the moodiness induced by hormones that most of my female friends, and myself, exhibited from time to time.

But those last two weeks it seemed she'd grown quieter. And one afternoon, from a distance, I witnessed a conversation she had with Mick, its intensity evident in their body language. Although I couldn't overhear what was said, I do remember thinking I'd never seen Adelia engaged in that manner. What was it Mick said that evoked that type of reaction? Or was it something Adelia said to him, a topic that produced an uncommon fervor in her?

I don't know. I may never know.

But I am here to find out as much as I can.

It is here, in Three Rivers, where my story will converge with Adelia's story once more. Adelia possessed a trifold strength, a braid of physical, emotional, and spiritual power. It is that power I hope to carry with me, that I pray I will embody as I assume her name.

Adelia's identity is all her own, but while I'm here, I leave behind the old Denilyn and the fear that plagued her. The fear that angers me now. That fear has no place here. While I am here, I am born anew, inspired by the friend now lost to me. And if I return home — *when* I return home — a part of Adelia will return with me. I hope to carry her spirit with me from now on. For we are indelibly linked, as Sonia Alejandro informed me.

There is one other reason I've taken her name. For reasons still unclear, we both attracted the same man.

And now I've lured him here again.

Simply by being here.

Here, where he can't touch those I love.

May 12, 2017

As I lock up the last storage unit, the late afternoon sun bakes my head and shoulders despite the sunscreen I reapplied earlier. I wipe the beads of sweat from my forehead and then make my way to the office, where a swamp cooler offers only a slight reprieve. Mick sits behind the counter, feet propped on the countertop.

"Bet that water felt good today." A toothpick hangs from one corner of his mouth.

"Oh, you're speaking to me today?"

He pulls his feet off the counter and straightens on the stool. "Now, don't be like that."

"I'm just never sure which mood I'll meet when I walk in here these days."

"Yeah, well, it's taken some adjustment.

You know Addie was special to me, like a daughter, really. Having you here, using her name, that's not the easiest thing."

I walk over to the small refrigerator Mick keeps behind the counter for employees and pull out a cold bottle of water. I unscrew the cap and then look at him. "I'm sorry. I know it isn't easy. But you know my reasons."

He shrugs. "May know them, but that doesn't mean I agree with them. Anyway, you're barking up the wrong tree."

"What do you mean?"

He squints at me, the leathered skin around his eyes wrinkling. "Nothing." He shrugs one brown, spotted shoulder.

"Mick? Is there something you haven't told me? Something I need to know? Are you ready to tell me what you and Addie were talking about that afternoon?"

"You take your bottle of water and get on out of here. When I have something to say, I'll say it."

I stare at him a moment, then turn to go.

"And cover that thing on your head with a hat. I shouldn't have to look at that."

"Whatever you say. You're the boss." I toss the comment over my shoulder as I walk out the door.

"Yeah, and don't forget it," he yells after me.

When I reach the Jeep, my dad's old Wrangler, I pull a beach towel off the driver's seat, meant to keep the seat cool, though it didn't do its job today. I left the luxury of air-conditioning behind when I decided to bring the Jeep rather than the new SUV I had to purchase when the auto body shop finally declared my old one a total loss. But the old Wrangler fits here and it makes me feel like a piece of my father is with me — a measure of comfort I welcome.

I make the five-minute drive back to the house, hot wind blasting through the open cab. I'm grateful I didn't forgo air-conditioning when looking for a house to rent. I knew better. As I drive, I wonder what Mick is keeping from me. Maybe it's nothing. But today he alluded to knowing something, didn't he? He's either not ready to share what he knows, or not willing.

In what way am I *"barking up the wrong tree"*?

And why won't he tell me about the conversation with Adelia? The first time I brought it up, he wrote it off. *"You know how many conversations I had with that girl? I don't know what you're talking about."*

But something in his eyes told me he knew

exactly the conversation I was referring to. Again, why would he keep what he knows from me?

Only Mick knows the answers to my questions.

After a cool shower, I make myself a salad — dinner, such as it is — and take it out to the deck. But after I've eaten, I'm restless. Evenings grow long here with little to do and no one to spend time with, unless I count a near deadly trip down the river with the young guides. I lift my arms above my head and stretch my still sore muscles. Then I pick up my dishes and take them back into the kitchen, where I load them into the dishwasher.

I go to the family room, park on the sofa, and reach for the remote. I turn on the TV and slowly flip through channels. Television is not part of my usual routine either at home or here, and nothing piques my interest. I watch a little of the evening news detailing world events. But I find the news intrusive, an irritant, although I can't pinpoint exactly why. I finally turn off the TV and relish the silence, or what has to pass for silence in this place where the river doesn't quiet until late in the season.

I get up from the sofa and wander through

the house, where everything from the decor to the books on the shelf were chosen by and belong to someone else. It's all become familiar, part of my daily backdrop, but none of it reflects who I am.

But then, neither do I reflect myself at the moment.

For the first time since arriving here, the sharp focus I've maintained wavers.

What am I doing here? What made me think I could do this?

Somewhere in this small, tight valley, Bradley Mathison waits. He will, I'm certain, try again to take me as his own, to take my life for himself. He will have me, one way or another. Nearly seven years in prison and just after his release, a release made possible only by an error, he was already here, watching, waiting, hoping I will die.

The thought chills me.

As I wander the rooms of this house that is not my home, my mind wanders too. I must not let it meander. I need something to occupy the open space. I go to the bedroom, where my laptop, untouched since I arrived here, is still in my briefcase. I pull it out and carry it to the table in the kitchen, where I turn it on and wait as it loads.

I've not checked my email since I've been

here, and tonight is as good a time as any to see what awaits my attention. I click the mail app and scroll through the contents of my inbox, deleting what is mostly junk. Both my university email and personal email come to this inbox, so there are a few general emails from PCU, event announcements and a couple of faculty updates. Then I see an email from Willow's address sent to my personal email address. Did I give her that address?

I open the email and quickly scan it.

Hi Deni,
    I know you're traveling or away somewhere, but I was wondering if we could talk. I've been . . .

I look away from the screen. The same sense of irritation I felt when watching the news nags now, but this time understanding accompanies the annoyance.

Like a sliver under the skin, both the news and now the email are foreign objects that have invaded a place not meant for them.

I have to focus on my purpose here. I can't go back, not even mentally. Not yet.

I close the lid of the laptop.

Focus. I have to focus.

I get up from the table and go out to the

deck, where the river reminds me why I'm here. I keep my eye on the constant current, moving forward at all times. Never ceasing. The same current that carried Adelia to her final resting place, presumably at the bottom of the reservoir, the reservoir appropriately named Terminus.

The same current that will carry me as well, either to join Adelia or to another place where peace will finally reign.

That is why I am here.

This is who I am for now.

CHAPTER THIRTY-FIVE

Adelia
May 13, 2017

When I get to Mick's property on Saturday, he's beat me there. The gate is already unlocked, and he's opening the storage units.

"You're early." I put the keys to the locks back into my pocket.

"Couldn't sleep. Too hot." He opens the last unit, then looks down and kicks at the dirt. A small cloud of dust rises. "Gonna be a short season if this keeps up."

"You think so? There's still a lot of snow."

"At this rate, it'll all melt at once. All or nothing."

"Cooler weather is forecasted for next week." My attempt to encourage him seems to fail.

"We'll see . . ." He turns toward the office. "I'll let you finish up here."

I begin pulling rafts and gear out of the

units, grateful I'll spend most of today on the water. Mick had me ride along in rafts guided by others the first few days I was back here. I just observed. The next couple of days I acted as guide, observed one day by Chase, the next day by Daphne.

This week I've had my own raft. The morning safety talk has offered a sense of familiarity — I'm accustomed to teaching others. Having my own raft provides another role I'm used to, one of authority.

It's a role I need to remember while I'm here.

Mathison has no authority over me.

As I pull the last raft out of the first unit, I'm aware of a vehicle pulling into the lot. Our first rafter of the day, I assume. When I turn and look over my shoulder, a battered pickup truck, circa 1980s, I'd guess, has parked under one of the trees overhanging the fence around the property. A guy gets out then looks around. As his gaze lands on me, I turn away. When I hear the door of the truck slam shut, I glance back and watch as he heads toward the office, my heartbeat racing.

It's him.

He didn't recognize me. He didn't. At least that's what I tell myself. That's part of the point of having shaved my head. Not only to expose the reminder of the Power that resides within me, but also to give me time . . .

I look back at the storage unit, head down.

I move to the next unit, where I pull the door of it open just enough that I can slip behind it and let it shield me. It makes unloading the gear awkward, but I'm not ready for him to see me.

He's followed me again, just as I knew he would. He's tracked me down. He's still watching me.

Always watching me.

Well, now it's my turn to watch him.

What is it they say? Turnabout is fair play?

When I told Sonia Alejandro of my plan, she balked. *"You will not go there. You will not use yourself as bait. I cannot and will not support your involvement in this . . . scheme. We will find him. But if you lead him away from this area, there's nothing we can do."*

By the end of that conversation, she'd agreed to coordinate with law enforcement in Three Rivers. Her last words play on my mind now. *"If you're going to do this, you must do it under the letter of the law. Do you understand? There can be no illegal activity. You are not above the law, Denilyn."*

I have heeded Sonia's warning. I will continue to heed her warning, though it may prove more difficult moving forward.

I will not stalk Mathison the way he's stalked me. Nor will I threaten him. Rather, I've ensured he is watched, both for my own protection and to facilitate the plan I'm here to carry out. Before my arrival, I retained a private investigator. Phil and his people are tracking Mathison. Watching. Waiting.

Just as Bradley Mathison has done himself for so long.

Phil's daily calls keep me informed.

Once he'd told me Mathison was here, I knew I had him.

It won't take long, I'm confident, to enact what I'm here to do. I am familiar, all too familiar, with Bradley Mathison's pattern. His presence in Three Rivers now, while I'm here, assures me I'm right.

A few minutes later, I hear voices coming from the direction of the office. I glance over my shoulder again, this time as Mathison and Mick walk out of the office together. I move back behind the door of the storage unit, where I can still see them, but I'm less visible.

They're coming my way. What is Mick doing? My fists ball at my sides.

They stop in front of a pile of rafts and kayaks, just short of the unit I'm unloading. I back up against the wall of the unit, making sure I won't be seen, my breaths coming in short bursts now. I wait until I hear their voices trailing off in the other direction. Then I step out of the shadow and watch.

Mick is helping Mathison carry a kayak to his truck. When they reach the truck, they load it onto the rack on the bed. Then Mick slaps Mathison on the back, as if they're . . . old friends? Then Mick heads back to the office.

I recall Ryan telling me that Mathison used to rent kayaks from Mick. But when I mentioned him to Mick that afternoon we met at The Gateway, he didn't act as if he knew Bradley Mathison. Although, he didn't act as if he didn't know him either.

Something about Mick's action, that slap on the back, strikes me as odd. More than odd. What is Mick hiding? What is his relationship with Bradley Mathison?

For reasons not clear to me, I never questioned whether I could trust Mick. I just assumed. Why?

As Mathison drives off, I head Mick's way, my feet pounding the dirt of the lot.

But he turns, looks at me, then shakes his head, the anger I read in his eyes as intense as my own. "Not now, *Addie.* Not now!" Then he walks away.

■ ■ ■ ■

May 19, 2017

It's been almost a week since Mathison showed up at Mick's and almost a week since I've spoken with Mick, who has successfully avoided me. What's Mathison up to? As I pull out of the Ride the Kaweah property following another exhausting day on the river and reach the stop sign at 193, rather than turn right to head back to the rental, I turn left onto the highway. I can't abide the thought of the empty house and the long evening that stretches ahead, the Kaweah my only companion.

Though I make the drive through the valley almost daily, it's always with others as we head to the put-in. This afternoon I'll make the drive alone, the wind filtering through the open Jeep, the river running alongside the road.

The restlessness that's plagued me for the last several days is insistent now. Maybe I'll go into the park for a quick hike, or maybe I'll stop before I reach the park's entrance and grab an early dinner somewhere. I have to do something. Anything other than what I've done almost every evening since my arrival here.

As I drive, the dense foliage along the roadway and the steep hillsides that loom on either side of the river close in. The sense of claustrophobia is nearly suffocating. There is nowhere to go. No escape.

But there is no need to escape. I'm meant to be here, I remind myself.

I mentally tick off the days I've been here and those still to come. Time is both standing still and running ahead of me. I spent so long hiding, first from Bradley Mathison, then from the memory of him and all that transpired. Now, as I'm waiting for him, it seems he's the one hiding.

Or if not hiding, at least he's no longer following me or even searching for me, it seems.

Before he showed up here, Sonia let me know they had picked him up and questioned him, but there was no evidence that he was involved in the accident that sent me into the wall of the canyon, the threatening texts I received — those three little letters — or Max's poisoning. While he confessed he did know where I live, there's no proof that he ever breeched the wall of the property. He denied any knowledge of my security system or cameras. Of course, his denial means nothing, but I can't figure out how he'd have known that one corner of the yard where Max was poisoned wasn't covered by a camera.

In the same way I had a hard time believing he could have, or maybe would have, hired someone, while he was still incarcerated, to run me off the road, I have a difficult time imagining him connecting with someone from the security company that installed the cameras on my property and manipulating information from them. It's the only way he could have known where he could enter the yard unobserved.

The person who could manipulate those types of actions would need to possess both cunning and savvy I can't quite attribute to Bradley Mathison.

But that thought leads nowhere but to the road of doubt. And I can't afford to doubt what I'm doing here.

I was led here.

Wasn't I?

I wait for some type of assurance, a settling of peace or something. But it doesn't come, so I reassure myself. Bradley Mathison is the only suspect, and he certainly terrorized me and attacked me. Whether the equation adds up or not, as Sonia Alejandro suggested, Mathison is the primary factor.

I was sure he'd followed me here, that I was his reason for returning to Three Rivers. Now I wonder if he even knows I'm here. If turnabout is fair play, maybe he's playing me, rather than the other way around.

Confusion, like the wind, swirls.

When I spoke with Phil this morning, he said Mathison is staying with his dad and picked up a job at a convenience store outside the park. He's gone between home and the job but almost nowhere else since his one trip to Ride the Kaweah. In Phil's words, Mathison is "squeaky clean." He also said he appears to be a loner and doesn't seem to have friends here. He kayaked alone after leaving Mick's last week.

I wonder again about his relationship with Mick. It looked friendly at least. I *will* pin Mick down on what he knows about Mathison, eventually.

As I round a bend in the road, the canopy of trees clears and Moro Rock, that towering monolith, becomes visible. I pull into a turnout where I can look at the rock.

I may not understand what's happening, or even exactly why I'm here. But I do know I didn't make this trip or set this plan into motion on my own. I did none of this of my own accord.

Whether God chooses to offer His assurance again or not, I will continue to act in faith. Whether I sense His presence or not, I will keep my eye on the rock and trust He is here, leading.

With those decisions made, the confusion, if not clears, at least dissipates for the moment.

CHAPTER THIRTY-SIX

Adelia
May 22, 2017

When I wake, sun filtering in through the open shutters, I stretch, grateful for one of the few restful nights I've had while here. I roll over and reach for my phone sitting on the nightstand. When I see I have a message, I'm surprised I slept through the ringing of the phone, then I realize the phone is set to vibrate rather than ring. I must have knocked it sometime last evening and accidentally changed the setting.

I open my voice mail and see the message is from Jaylan — the message came in last night. Odd. She knew not to call me here unless necessary. Is something wrong? I quickly press PLAY and lift the phone to my ear.

"Hey, sorry to bother you. Just got a quick question. You looking at your email? I need you to read your email. Something important came your way several days ago. It's from your friend Willow. You referred her to me. She signed a release so we can talk. Listen, you need to read her email and give her a call, please, regardless of what else is goin' on there. I mean it."

I can tell from Jay's tone that she meant what she said without her telling me so. Willow . . . I sit up in the bed and rub my hand over my head, then I climb out, pad across the room, and pull my laptop out of my briefcase.

I climb back in bed with the laptop, and once it's loaded, I go to my inbox and scroll through until I find the email from Willow. I read it, didn't I?

Hi Deni,

I know you're traveling or away some-where, but I was wondering if we could talk? I've been seeing your friend Jaylan, and she suggested I email you and tell you I need to talk to you. She said to tell you it's important and has something to do with whatever you're doing.

Before signing off, Willow included her phone number. What could Willow possibly have to tell me that has something to do with what I'm doing here? Did she misunderstand Jaylan? Why didn't I read her email? What is wrong with me? Then I remember why . . . The email felt intrusive. It pulled my focus elsewhere and . . . I set the laptop aside and pick up my phone again. I glance back at the number Willow gave me and key it into my phone. Wait, what time is it? I glance at the corner of the screen. Almost 9:00 a.m.? When have I ever slept that late? I press Send and pray that Willow will answer.

"Hey, it's me. Leave a message."

I sigh. "Willow, this is Deni. I just read your email. I'm so sorry. Give me a call. I'm available all day."

I end the call and toss the phone on the bed. As I begin to berate myself, a sense of peace settles me and quiets the condemning voice within. "All in Your time," I whisper. I trust God's perfect timing. I will hear whatever it is Willow needs to talk to me about when the time is right.

In the meantime, I need coffee. As I climb out of bed, my phone rings. I reach across the bed, grab it, and see the number I just called on the screen. I answer the call as I head for the kitchen. "Willow?"

"Yeah, hi. Sorry, I didn't recognize your number."

"No, that's fine. I'm sorry I didn't call

sooner. So, you're seeing Jaylan?"

"Yeah. Thanks for the referral."

"You're so welcome. I'm glad it's working out for you."

She's silent for a moment, then finally starts in. "Um, yeah. So I told her . . ." There's a tremor in her voice. "I . . . I mean . . ." She trails off again, as though nerves have swallowed her words.

"Willow, take a deep breath."

I hear her take a ragged breath.

"One more."

I hear her inhale then exhale, more easily this time. "Whatever you have to say, it's okay. I'm just here to listen."

"Okay. So I told Jaylan something . . . and she said it would be good to tell you too — that it was something you needed to know. I mean, I don't want to get anyone in trouble."

She stops and starts several times. Then she tells me what it is she shared with Jaylan. What Jaylan knew I needed to hear. I ask few questions, instead letting Willow fill in the blanks. She shares her own history, her pain, and how something that happened recently triggered what she'd gone through before. She unloads the burden she's carried and gives it to me. A burden Jay is also carrying now.

"I signed a release. Jaylan asked if I'd be willing, you know, to let you two talk."

"Thank you, Willow. What you've done, what you shared, was hard, I know." I can't process everything she's told me now. It will take time. Still, I know I must look at the pieces she's handed me and see where they fit. As much as I'd like to, I don't dare tuck them away. "Thank you," I say again.

I've stood in front of the coffeepot as I listened to Willow's story. Now I fill a mug and take it out to the deck. I drop into one of the chairs and set the mug on the table next to me. I stare out at the river as Willow's words replay in my mind. I couldn't let myself feel the impact of her story as I listened to her. I wanted to remain present for her.

But now . . .

A tornado of thoughts and emotions clouds my mind.

I can't process what she's told me. I don't want to process it. Yet I know I must.

What does it mean? The implications are . . . staggering.

Images flash.

How . . . ?

Memories play.

How did I not see?

On their own, the flashing images and

memories equate nothing. But added to the information Willow shared . . .

I come up with a disconcerting sum.

But the total, I sense, is larger than I see now. So much larger.

Despite the heat of the morning, I reach for a beach towel draped across the table and wrap it tightly around me. The warmth it offers is womb-like, protective. But it can't protect me from this . . . While it chases the chill from my body, it does little to thaw the cold, hard truth Willow offered.

"It's unimaginable what people do to each other . . ."

I get up and go back to the kitchen, where I left my phone. As I walk back outside, the towel draped around my shoulders, I open my contacts and call Jay.

Jay, who on some level has always known . . .

She answers and speaks for me. "You talked with Willow? She told you? Deni . . ."

"You knew, Jay. You knew."

"I did not know. I still don't know anything except that something is wrong. Something is very, very wrong."

"Jay," I whisper.

"I know, sister, I know. This is a hard pill to swallow."

"Do you think . . . ? Did Adelia . . . ?

"What? What are you asking? What are you sayin'?

"I . . . I don't know. I don't know. But there's more to this. So much more."

That buoy of discomfort that bobbed to the surface of my consciousness when Sonia asked about Adelia is now anchored and demanding attention.

Questions I pushed down, submerged, so long ago, will be ignored no longer.

"Talk to me, Deni. Talk to me."

Jay and I talked for hours. For the first time ever, I willingly let the reel of memories unspool, and I shared each one with Jay. Some fit a pattern we were beginning to see; others we couldn't make sense of. But like a movie on a screen, the story began to unfold.

The beach towel hangs across the arm of the chair on the deck where I still sit, discarded as the sun rose high overhead, blazing without mercy. My mug of coffee remains untouched.

As I consider all that was said between us, all the ground we covered in our conversation, and the ground we've walked together for so many years, I am more grateful than ever for the friendship woven through good times and bad. If only Adelia were still part of that tapestry.

Adelia . . .

I sensed our stories would converge in Three Rivers once again, perhaps on the Kaweah even. While I wanted to adopt her name while I was here, to embody her strength, there was another reason I took her name, but it was one I couldn't explain.

I still can't explain it.

But I trust understanding will come.

Now there's one more conversation I need to have. And it needs to happen today, the one day of the week Ride the Kaweah is closed.

I pick up my phone again and call Mick. He will talk to me this time. He has to.

I sit across from Mick on the deck of The Gateway, that place where our conversation, rather than reaching the ears of others, is lost to the thunder of the rapids.

"Listen, I know you're angry, but" — Mick takes the toothpick out of his mouth — "Brad isn't a bad guy. A little messed up maybe." He shrugs. "Yeah, okay, he's messed up, but he isn't violent."

"He isn't violent?"

"No."

I take a deep breath. "How can you say that? I've experienced his violence firsthand.

Have you forgotten that? He attacked me in my mother's garage. He waited for me around the side of the house, and when I pulled into the garage, he walked in through that open door and hid until I got out of the car. You can't tell me he wasn't violent!" A stray tear runs down my cheek, and I swipe it away. "I have the scar to prove it, Mick. Look!" I turn my head and point to the scar lingering under the tattoo. "He was there. I saw him, I heard him, I felt his hands around my neck!"

Mick leans forward. "He didn't mean to hurt you. He didn't. He got a little ahead of himself, that's all. I know him. I'm telling you, I know him. They never found his prints on that baseball bat, did they? And he swears he didn't mean to hurt you, and he certainly didn't hit you with a bat. He didn't. I don't know what did happen that night, but I know that. He didn't hit you with that bat."

I shake my head. "This is ridiculous."

"You see now why I didn't want to have this conversation? I knew you wouldn't listen to me."

I exhale and put my hands, palms down on the table. "I'm sorry. I will listen. It's just . . . I know what he did to me. I have the proof of it right here."

"What you think he did to you."

I raise my eyebrows. "Really?"

"Just hear me out."

I raise my hands in surrender and lean back.

"You remember what I did before I bought Ride the Kaweah?"

I search my mind. "No, I don't."

"I was a schoolteacher. That's right, 'ol Mick isn't as dumb as you think."

"I've never thought you were dumb, Mick."

"Well, whatever. I may not have as many degrees as you, but I got a master's in education, got a credential, and then taught for quite a few years right here in Three Rivers. Started with middle school — a tough age for kids."

I nod. "Yes, it is."

"Well, Brad was one of my students. He was scrawny for his age, and he got picked on a lot. Didn't have the best home life either. Lot of the kids who lived in these hills came from bad situations. You know that. Yeah, we've got our artists and business owners, but we've also got a lot of druggies. As far as I remember, Brad didn't have much of a family. No mom, and a dad who used. So when he got picked on, or what you doctor types call *bullied* today, he had no one to stand up for him.

"Sure, the school stepped in, but it didn't do much good. Kid finally got scared to say anything to me or any other teacher. Anytime we got involved, he'd get harassed, beat up, you name it. And when he got home from school, there was no one there to help him overcome. Know what I mean?"

I know all too well. Mick is describing the kids I've worked with, kids I've written case statements about, kids I've stood up for in every way I can. Kids whose stories not only broke my heart but also kindled my passion.

Kids whom I ultimately wrote a book for.

An image comes to me of Bradley Mathison at Kepler's Books the first day I noticed him. He stood behind an endcap watching me, my book in his hand. Then later he peered in through the window at me, my book clutched to his chest. Hadn't I wondered then if my book had meant something to him?

But putting Bradley Mathison into the same category as those to whom I offered not only sympathy but emotional help? I sigh. As a victim of the man we're talking about, I can't seem to separate what I know from what I've experienced.

"I kept in touch with Brad when he went

on to high school, and then afterward. He dropped out. A couple years later I tutored him — helped him get his GED. He finally ended up joining the army, but he washed out there too. He was a troubled young man, is still troubled, but I will tell you this: he wasn't violent. He didn't have it in him. Still doesn't. I'd stake my life on it. Don't get me wrong though. He's angry now. Angrier than I've ever seen him. Prison changed him, some for the better maybe. He got some help in there. But not all the change is good. He feels like you ruined his life — stole years from him. Maybe that's a healthy stance, I don't know. I know he stole a few years from you too. I get that. I do. But even as angry as he is right now, I really believe he won't hurt you." He shakes his head. "It just isn't in his DNA."

"What about Adelia? She filed a restraining order against Mathison. You don't do that kind of thing unless you're afraid of someone."

Mick leans forward and lowers his voice, and between clenched teeth, he says, "Deni, it wasn't Bradley Mathison Addie was afraid of."

I can barely hear what he's said over the pounding of the rapids, and it takes me a moment to make sense of his words. As I do, the things Willow said rush back at me, as does my conversation with Jay.

"What . . . what do you mean?" I don't need affirmation of what I already know, but I ask for it anyway. "She filed a restraining order against him. She must have been afraid of him." I repeat my statement more to myself than Mick.

"Addie knew he wasn't dangerous. She understood him, as much as anyone can understand what someone like that's gone through. She was pressured into filing for that order. It wasn't her idea."

Mouth dry, I reach for my water glass and take a sip, then set it back down. "Who . . . whose idea was it?"

He looks down at his drink on the table and shakes his head. When he looks back at me, I don't like what I read in his eyes. "You really need to ask that question?"

CHAPTER THIRTY-SEVEN

Adelia
May 23, 2017

I sit at the table in the kitchen, the cool air from the vent above rustling the pad of paper in front of me. I smooth the page where I've compiled a list, then add one more name. Before we left The Gateway last night, Mick advised me to take today to work through what he'd told me. He said he'd give my run to another guide. When I protested, he held up his hand. "You need the time. Take it."

This morning I'm grateful for his foresight. I slept little, if at all, last night. It's no longer a puzzle I'm collecting pieces to complete. Instead, it's the movie running in my mind. Memories play as reruns, but with them come previews of what's to come. As more of the story plays out, it includes twists I never could have predicted. Nor would I have wanted to predict them.

The story is more heinous than I could have imagined.

Yet I can't help chiding myself for not seeing it as it was happening.

How did I miss the signs?

Is it possible that we only see what we want to believe?

Bradley Mathison isn't without fault — that I know. But it seems he wasn't the only antagonist in the production.

The list blurs, and I rub my eyes. I am emotionally spent. Exhausted. But I have to carry on. Not only for my sake but for Adelia's as well. There is new purpose in my presence here.

I reach for my phone.

These calls won't be easy, but they are necessary.

Absolutely necessary.

The first call I make is to the president of Pacific Covenant University.

After what feels like hours on the phone explaining, imparting information, advising, asking questions, and mentally filing away details, I have just one call left to make. Though it's the most important call, I've saved it for last. Because it will take everything I have.

As the line rings, I know he'll answer,

because these days he almost always does.

"Hey, I'm surprised you're calling. How goes it in the legendary Three Rivers?"

I open my mouth, but nothing comes out. Where the other conversations were factual, this one dredges the depths of my emotional well.

"Deni?"

"Yes, sorry . . ." I swallow.

"You okay? You don't sound okay."

"I . . . know. I will be okay." While my emotional depths may be dredged, I don't have to hand all that comes up to Keith. Something I learned later. After. "How is he?"

"My buddy, Nicolo?" I hear the smile in his tone. "Little dude is great. Slaying a video game at the moment."

"A video . . ." I shake my head, then smile, though the effort is wearing. "I'm glad he's with you." And I am. I am always happy to share Nicky with his father. The time they have together offers Nicky the normalcy and fun — oh, so much fun — that I can't provide. "Can you talk for a few minutes?"

"Yep. He's already whipped me. I'll just let him keep racking up points. By the way, he is doing great, but he misses you. He asks about you every day."

I clear my throat. "I miss him too," I

whisper.

"So what's up?"

"I need to tell you something, and it's serious and it's going to require you to take some precautions. I'm sorry, but —"

"What's going on? Fill me in." His tone is serious now.

I close my eyes. How I longed to hear those words from him years ago, yet he couldn't offer them then. But he has grown. He's worked hard to grow. We are not the people we were when we married or when we divorced. We are healthier, stronger, wiser. Keith isn't just Nicky's father; he is the best father I can imagine for my son. Perhaps with the exception of my own father, there isn't a better role model I'd choose for Nicky.

Keith, on top of everything else we'd encountered that year, couldn't cope with the idea of fatherhood or the demands he supposed it would require. Those demands were not unrealistic. What he didn't factor in was the love he'd feel for that baby and the sacrifices he'd willingly make to care for him and provide for him, including doing his own emotional work.

"There are some new developments. They're complicated, and . . ." My voice catches. Not since my conversation with Jay have I let my emotions come through, unless it was the anger I initially felt with Mick. "Sorry. If you're not sitting down, you may want to . . ."

I go on to tell Keith what I've learned and what I suspect. I pour out the part of the story I know, and what I think I know. When I hear Nicky's voice in the background, "Dad . . . ," my heart clenches.

"Hey, hold on a minute, Deni."

I hear the murmur of their voices and then the joy of Nicky's laughter.

When Keith comes back on the line, we talk for a long time. I answer his questions, and he offers some feedback. Most of all, he assures me he'll take care of Nicky and take the necessary precautions.

When I end the call, I hold the phone, warm in my hand, for a long time, as I stare at nothing. Finally, I set down the phone and lay my head on the table. And for the first time since coming to Three Rivers, since assuming Adelia's name and wanting to embody her spirit and strength, I cry.

I let myself cry.

They aren't tears of weakness; they are tears of grief.

I cry for Adelia.

I cry for all that's lost.

And I cry for all I know is still to come.

Chapter Thirty-Eight

Adelia
May 27, 2017

I pull out of the garage of the rental, pause in the driveway, and then reach for my phone. The light streaming into the Jeep from the morning sun makes the screen difficult to read. I squint, check the time, and then quickly key in the text message I've planned: I'M IN THREE RIVERS. ADELIA IS ALIVE.

I press SEND, and then I turn off the phone.

I've cast the lure.

CHAPTER THIRTY-NINE

Adelia
May 27, 2017

I didn't want to be seen with Phil when I first arrived, didn't want others linking me to him, especially anyone who knew Mathison. Now it no longer matters. I sit across from the retired police officer on the deck of Annie's Emporium, each of us with a cup of coffee in hand.

He takes a sip of his coffee, eyeing me over the rim of the cup. Then he sets it back on the table. "Well, aren't you popular? Another guy? I can't wait to hear this . . ."

"I just need you to do your job."

"That's why I'm here, but I'll need the details."

I give Phil as much information as I think he needs, including what I know of the plan.

"Here's what has to happen, and no, I can't tell you how it's going to happen." I stare at him a moment. I need him to know

I'm serious. "I want — I need — a life sentence, to know I will never have to face him again, to know I'll never have to worry about him harming me or any member of my family or anyone I care about again."

"Just like the last guy?"

I nod.

"You framing this guy the same way?"

"I won't have to frame him. I just need him to be caught in the act."

"Murder."

"Attempted murder."

"Right."

"He *will* try to kill me. It won't be the first time, but it will be the last time. I need witnesses, including law enforcement. I need an arrest."

"Lady, you're nuts."

There is respect in his expression, despite his quip. I lean forward. "I'm not nuts. I have a son to protect." As I say those words, the gratitude that's overwhelmed me in recent days surges again. How many times was Nicky exposed, vulnerable? As hard as I worked to protect him, I missed the mark completely. In retrospect, the note left after Max was poisoned pointed to Nicky. He would have been next. I shudder despite the heat. "I'm just done. More than done. This has to end."

"Okay, let's get him. So how do you see this going down?"

"A lot of that is dependent on him. If he takes the bait, and he will, he could show up within the next four to five hours."

"You know, you sounded just as sure when you thought it was the other guy."

For just a second, my confidence wavers. But, no. "I wasn't entirely wrong, but I'm more certain now, okay?"

"You're the client."

"The first place he'll go, I suspect, is Ride the Kaweah. That's where he'll think to look for me. Can you have someone at the property within the next few hours?"

Phil looks at his watch then nods. "Got a description?"

"I do."

I give him the description and what to watch for, and tell him that Mick will also be watching. Then I wait as Phil makes a call to get someone posted on Mick's property.

"I need to know as soon as he's here. Just like last time."

"Got it."

"I'll be on the river today, so just text me. I may not get the text right away, but I will eventually. Once he's here, don't let him out of your sight."

We talk through a few more details, as many as I know at this point. Then I grab my coffee cup and stand. "I need to go. Whether he shows up today or not, I need to know."

He gets up from the table. "Be safe out there."

"Thanks. That's exactly what I intend to do. Oh, one more thing . . ." I look down at my phone, turn it on, and then wait for it to come to life. When it does, I have several messages and a slew of texts. I don't need to look to see who they're from. "I'm going to forward you texts and messages from him. I don't need to read them or hear them."

I don't want them to disrupt my focus. I won't allow him to do that to me. As I walk to the parking lot, I begin forwarding what's already come in.

These are not the first texts or messages I've received from him since leaving home. For the first time in all these years, I knew it was time to break away, to put some distance between us. I haven't responded to anything he's sent or the messages he's left, each more demanding than the last.

When I spoke with Jay, she said he'd done nothing short of hound her for information after I left.

By pulling away, I realize now, I usurped Ryan's control, or sense of control.

For one of the first times in our relationship, I now hold the reins.

And he doesn't like it.

Yet another memory plays on the screen of my mind as I climb into the Jeep. It was the first day of the spring semester, and Ryan offered to walk me to my car. I told him no. I was curt. Then as I walked to the parking lot, I was overwhelmed by the feeling, the fear, that someone was watching me, and a panic attack followed.

I now understand that there was nothing wrong with me — I wasn't crazy, regardless of what I felt. Instead, my body was alerting me to a threat. That biological component that warns me had gone into full alert.

Someone was watching me, stalking me, threatening me.

Ryan.

I am sure now that he stood at the window of his new office, with the view of the campus and parking lot.

The office he took without following protocol.

Did I forget a conversation about the office or paperwork I'd signed, as Ryan implied?

No. There was no conversation. No paper-work.

That was just one of his manipulations, just one of the ways he worked to undermine my confidence.

Day by day, more is coming into focus.

As I get off Mick's old blue bus at the put-in, I slip my phone into a waterproof case then zip it into the pocket of my splash jacket. I need to have it nearby today. Then I reach up and secure the bandanna around my head and put my helmet on over it. That done, I sidestep my way down the steep, rock-strewn embankment until I reach the spot where Chase and another guide have just put my raft into the water. "Thanks," I tell him as I step into the river and take ahold of the raft. Then I yell up the embankment. "Addie's crew, you're up!" I wait as six guys, all jocks, hotfoot it down to the raft.

The dread I expected to feel today is absent. Instead, I look at the crew climbing into the raft, and I'm glad I'm here. I look forward to taking on the Kaweah again. Today, I'd like to tell Phil, I do feel my age, and I'm proud of each of my forty-two years. I'm proud of what I can still do on this river.

The trip starts out fast and furious, all class IV rapids. There are few breaks on this section of the Kaweah, just short eddies in between the rapids. By the time we reach the Osterizer, the crew is working together, in sync, and taking on anything the Kaweah throws our way.

"Forward!" I yell.

They dig their oars into the water.

"Stop."

They lift their oars.

"Forward."

They dig in again.

The current rushes, carrying us into the rapid. Adrenaline, like an entity, crowds the raft.

"Back-paddle! Back-paddle!" I dig my own oar into the water at the back of the raft and push it against the force of the water, feeling the muscles in my shoulders and arms ripple. I dig in again, enjoying the power I've developed in my body. Power I've worked hard for. "Fifty yards. Good luck, guys!"

Osterizer bucks us like a bronco, lifting then dropping us and lifting again. We dip into a hole, and the river, like an ocean wave, tumbles over the raft, soaking us. Then we're lifted again, the left side of the raft riding high over a boulder, but rather than throwing us, tipping us, we glide over it before dropping again.

When we make it through the rapid, we paddle to an alcove of sorts between two large rocks and shift the raft so we can watch the raft behind us come through the rapid. As they're lifted over that same boulder that threatened to tip us, one of the rafters topples out of the raft. It happens so quickly.

"Swimmer!" one of our guys yells and then points to the person tossing in the water. Finally, she looks our way, flips over, and begins swimming toward our raft, her strokes strong and sure. The guy who'd spotted her leans over the side of the raft, then flips his oar around so the swimmer can grab the T-handle he holds out. With whoops and laughter, he and one of his buddies pull the young woman into our raft. Then they throw high fives all around.

The water is icy, the sun hot, and the entire trip exhilarating.

When we get off the river, rather than the exhaustion I've felt at the end of each day, I still have energy. Physically, I feel good. Great, even. Later, as I'm loading rafts into the storage units, I realize my muscles no longer ache.

I toss the last raft into the storage unit,

pull my keys from my pocket and lock the unit, then make my way to the office. As I go, I know for certain that I am ready.

I am ready for whatever is to come.

May 28, 2017

When I wake and roll over to check my phone, there are no texts and no messages. I'd expected more than nothing, a lot more. At 5:45 a.m., it's too early to call Phil, so I text him instead. WHERE IS HE? IS HE HERE?

Frustrated, I throw down the phone and lie back down. I stare at the ceiling. I was sure he'd come as soon as he'd received my text. Did Phil's guy miss him? Even if he had, the only place he'd go looking for me is Mick's, and Mick would have told me if he'd been there.

As I lie in bed and consider options, I realize what's happened.

I took control.

Now Ryan, through his silence, is wrestling back that control.

I will match his silence.

I will wait.

May 29, 2017

By Monday morning I begin to wonder if he'll come at all. Again doubt, that unwelcome intruder, niggles its way into my soul. I go about the morning routine I've established on the one day a week I'm not at Mick's. With Ride the Kaweah closed today, if he shows up, where will he go? Mick's house? Maybe.

I pour myself a cup of coffee then sit at the table in the kitchen. The pad of paper that's become the holder of the many details whirling through my mind sits on the table in front of me. I pick up a pen and write one word on the page.

psychopath

Is this what I'm up against?

Psychopathy is one of the more difficult disorders to spot or identify. Should I have seen signs of the disorder in Ryan? That's a question that doesn't serve me well now, so I have to let it go. Some of the characteristics are there, certainly, but they are also characteristics that can appear *normal.* Ryan's charm is certainly characteristic of psychopathy.

And if all I'm concluding about his actions are true, the telltale lack of empathy that psychopaths share is certainly evident, although he's covered it very well through the years. He also certainly displays a penchant for manipulation, but again, it's well covered.

But there are other characteristics that don't seem to fit.

I tap my pen on the paper then circle the term.

"Pay attention." The advice I've heard often comes back now.

Yes, I will pay attention. My life depends on it.

CHAPTER FORTY

Adelia
June 1, 2017

As dawn gives way to daylight, I stand on the deck, a light blanket wrapped around my shoulders, the morning cooler than yesterday. The tumult of the river is so constant, so familiar now, I barely notice its presence beyond the deck.

It's been almost a week since I sent the text to Ryan, since I cast the lure into deep, murky water.

The next full moon rises on June 9th.

Time is short.

Although doubt has intruded the last several days, I always swing back to a place of confidence. Not confidence in myself but rather in the plan given to me, even if it is still skeletal. It is not something I'd have come up with on my own, I remind myself again.

I was led here, I now realize, to discover

the truth.

But the truth doesn't negate the steps I was given, the steps I've already taken.

It's only the player, the primary factor, who changed.

When the moon is full . . .

These words settled in my soul the day I stood below my property looking at the American River. The day God planted the idea for this trip, this mission, in my mind and soul. One of the few clear senses I had was that whatever would take place would occur when the moon was full. The moon would be full only twice while I was here. One has passed; one is still to come.

When the moon is full . . .

What will occur on that early morning when the face of the moon blooms full again? I don't know. But I believe we'll meet at the river. There the veins of our individual stories will converge.

Ryan. Adelia. Denilyn.

And violence will mark the convergence of those forks.

Of this I'm certain.

As I pull off the highway and make the turn onto the small outlet where Mick's property sits, I look for Phil or one of his employees, but I see no one, though I'm confident someone is watching. Occasionally I've seen Phil, or seen a car I suspected belonged to whoever had taken the shift that day, but this morning I see nothing out of the ordinary.

As I pull up to the gate and then get out of the Jeep, it seems the landscape has changed. Dense cloud cover casts the property in neutral tones, and the air hangs heavy and damp. I unlock the gate, looking around again. Then I get back in the Jeep and pull onto the property. As I do, an SUV pulls off the highway and then stops at the gate. The frame around the license plate on the front of the SUV advertises a car rental company.

I glance at the driver, but even behind the cloud cover, the window reflects muted images obscuring my view. I look away, then pat the back pocket of the shorts I wear to assure my phone is still there.

I move to the first storage unit and unlock it, waiting for the SUV to either pull into the lot or move on. As I pull the door of the unit open, a truck pulls in behind the SUV. Mick. *Thank you.* After a moment, Mick taps his horn and the SUV continues down the road rather than turning into the property.

Though I couldn't see his face, I'm sure

the driver was Ryan.

Today is the day.

The fear I've come to know so well, the fear that's possessed me for so long, does not make an appearance. Instead, a prayer breezes through my mind as though it were the most natural action. *It's in Your hands . . .*

Mick parks his truck, gets out, and heads straight for the office. By the time he gets there, the SUV has turned around and is making another pass. The driver continues past the gate and then gets back on the highway.

He obviously saw me, but did he recognize me?

I have no idea what he's doing, but evidently he doesn't want to show himself yet.

I pull my phone out of my pocket and text Phil, alerting him to watch for a silver SUV. I give him the make and tell him the rental company named on the license frame. I also give him the first three letters from the license plate, I didn't have time to memorize the whole sequence.

I almost immediately receive a response to my text. I SAW IT. ON HIS TAIL NOW.

Although I expect the driver of the SUV to return, as the morning wears on and there's no sign of him, I wonder if my earlier sense was off. Maybe it was just another tourist checking out a white-water adventure company. Have I led Phil on a wild-goose chase?

But after I've given the safety spiel and we're loaded on the bus, pulling out of the property, the same SUV pulls off the highway and passes us as it turns onto the property. This time I have a clear view of the driver's profile, a profile I know very well.

Seeing him now, with all I know, fuels the fire within.

Less than five minutes later my cell phone vibrates and I find a text from Phil. HE'S HERE.

The timing of Ryan's arrival is calculated rather than accidental. He likely drove by this morning to check out the place, maybe to see if I was there. But he knows exactly when I'd leave the property for the put-in. He also knows when he'd find Mick, if not alone on the property, at least less involved with others.

Did he want me to know he's here?

Did he want me to see him?

I suspect that's the case.

I also suspect we've entered a game of cat and mouse.

But which one of us is the cat?

And which one is the mouse?

When I return to the property, I go through the usual routine until most of the rafters and guides have left the property. Then I head to the office, hoping to catch Mick alone.

"I've been waiting for you," he says as I walk in. He pulls a bottle of water from the refrigerator and hands it to me.

"Thanks." I hold the cold bottle of water to my forehead for a moment. "So, he was here?"

"Yep."

I wait for Mick to say more, but he doesn't. He just looks at me.

"So . . . ?"

"Nothing much to tell you." Mick takes off the baseball cap he wears, wipes his brow with the back of his hand, and then puts the cap back on. "He knows he's not welcome here."

"What do you mean?"

"He called several years back. Wanted to come back for a summer."

"I remember. He said you had all the guides you needed already, or something like that."

"That's what he told you, huh? You know

he's a masterful liar, right?"

"I'm learning . . ."

"Whether I needed a guide or not, I would have hired you or Addie back in a heartbeat, but that guy? No way. And I told him so. Told him I never wanted to see his face around here again. Not after what he did to Addie."

"The restraining order?"

"Yeah, that."

"You never told me exactly what happened. Was that the conversation I saw you and Adelia having that afternoon? When she seemed upset?"

He pulls the stool out from behind the counter. "Have a seat."

"Thanks." I settle on the stool as Mick leans against the counter.

"Ryan was the jealous type — that's probably not news to you. When Brad started hanging around, Ryan got heated. More than once."

"I saw one of those episodes at The Gateway, but I thought that was the end of it."

"Nope. He had a few other run-ins with Brad. Caught him following Addie around. He didn't mean any harm, but he shouldn't have followed her. The last time, Ryan threatened Brad, shoved him up against the outside of the post office, where he'd followed them. Pinned him there and told him that if he ever saw him near Addie again, he'd regret it. I don't know what all he said, but I got the gist of it from both Addie and Brad."

"Ryan never . . . told us that. But then, neither did Addie. Why?"

"I don't know for sure, but I do know that by that time she was afraid of Ryan. Much more afraid of him than Brad. Like I said, Brad was more of an annoyance, that's all. That afternoon you're talking about, she told me Ryan was insisting she file for a restraining order. Told her if she really cared about him, she'd prove it by getting rid of Brad. Accused her of all sorts of things. When I asked if he'd threatened her too, she clammed up. That pretty much told me all I needed to know." He looks at the floor and clears his throat, then looks back to me. "I told Addie I was going to the authorities. I didn't like what I was hearing. But she begged me not to. By the time I'd decided I didn't care if she wanted me to or not" — he shakes his head — "it was too late."

"Why did she stay with Ryan? Why did she go hiking with him that day?"

"I don't know. I don't understand the hold he had on her. Guess we'll never know."

Maybe Adelia wasn't as strong as she appeared. Or maybe Ryan was just stronger. Health and strength aren't always synonymous. Whatever the case, as I listen to Mick, waves of grief for Adelia wash over me. And for Mick. For all of us, really.

Except for Ryan.

My feelings for Ryan are tangled — strands of anger, betrayal, and astonishment are just the beginning of the knot forming within. Eventually grief will come. But not now.

I take a deep breath. "Mick, was Addie's death an . . . accident?"

"It was ruled accidental." He stares at me, his blue eyes watering. "But I never believed it. Told the sheriff that too. But . . ." He shrugs. "They checked Ryan out, even talked to Brad about him, but they couldn't prove anything. Without a body . . ." He looks back at the floor and seems to get lost in his own memories.

As do I.

Finally, I ask Mick, "What did Ryan say this morning?"

He sighs. "Not much. Came in like he owned the place. No surprise. Looked around and said, 'Things look good.' When I asked him what he was doing here, he said he was in the area and thought he'd stop when he passed by. I told him to get out and keep on going."

"That's it?"

"Mostly."

"Mick?"

"Yeah, okay. He asked about you. 'Denilyn around?' he says real casually. I told him no. Then I told him he'd best stay away from you, or he'd have me and the law to deal with."

"Mick . . ."

"I don't like whatever game you're playing, you know that." He looks down. When he looks back up, his eyes glisten with unshed tears. "I lost touch with Brad. I didn't hear what had happened to you or about his involvement until later. How that scuttlebutt passed me by in this town, I don't know. But the point is, I should have spoken up sooner. I should have pressed harder when I suspected things about *him*. Maybe I could've. Maybe Addie'd still be here. Maybe you wouldn't have that scar on your head. Maybe . . ." He shakes his head, then clears his throat. "I just . . . I didn't put it all together until it was too late."

"Mick, you did what you could at the time. We all did. We didn't know what we were up against. But we know now. I know you don't like this game, as you put it, but this has to end. It isn't just about me

446

anymore. It's about Addie, Mick. It's about one of my students, and it's about whoever comes after me. This has to end, and that's what I intend to do. End it. Permanently."

"I hear what you're saying, but I still don't like it. I . . . don't want to see you end up like . . . Addie." He turns and walks behind the counter, then faces me again. "By the way, he had one other question. He wanted to know if there was anything new on Adelia. 'Was her body ever found? Any remains ever turn up?' " Mick shakes his head. "About put me over the edge."

"What did you tell him?"

"I told him he'd have to talk to the authorities if he wanted that kind of information."

I nod. "Good. Good. Thank you."

While my intent was to leave the old Denilyn behind when I returned to Three Rivers, this evening, as I watch the colors of the sunset dance across the surface of the river, I'm reminded that there were, there are, valuable aspects of my life that I need to allow to infiltrate this space. My conversations with both Jaylan and Keith reminded me that while I have come here alone, God is with me, He often reveals Himself — His love and His strength — through those He's placed in our lives.

As the sun drops below the hills, I reach for my phone and call Jaylan.

"Hey you, glad to see your name on my screen. I've been thinking about you and prayin' too. Wasn't sure I'd hear from you again while you were there."

"Thanks, Jay."

"How're you doin'? You got a lot on your emotional plate, sister."

I ignore her question and get to the point. I know she won't mind. "Jay, what did you see in Ryan that Adelia and I missed?"

"Listen, I certainly didn't see all that was there, all that *is* there. If I had, maybe . . ."

"Regrets aren't going to get us anywhere. I've battled quite few of them this last week. I guess what I'm asking is what always rubbed you the wrong way about him? What . . . I don't even know what I'm asking. I'm just so . . ." I trail off, unsure how to convey what I feel.

"Shocked and angry and confused and . . . The list probably goes on. I get it. I'm feelin' all that too. Part of what I sensed more than saw with Ryan was a possessiveness, or maybe an entitlement. But it was always hard to pinpoint. But it was like he owned Adelia, and then you. But again, I could never really put my finger on any one thing.

448

Plus, he just plain irritates me, you know that."

I smile despite the severity of the circumstances. "Clearly the irritation is mutual."

"You got that right. So, I assume he's there?" I hear something unfamiliar in Jay's tone.

"Arrived today. Or at least showed up at Mick's today."

"Figured. He finally stopped houndin' me. Gabe intercepted his last text to me and told him to lay off."

"I bet that didn't go over too well."

"I don't care one iota how it went over. I'm done with him." She sighs. "You sure you know what you're doin'? 'Cause I've got to tell you, I'm concerned."

"Concerned or afraid?" It's the fear I hear in her voice.

"You know, a little fear is a healthy thing."

"I know." I hesitate. "I can't explain it, but I know I'm supposed to be here. I know God has led me here. And I know He's in control. When I jumped out of that airplane as a means of acknowledging God's sovereign hold on my life — whether I lived or died — I had no idea what was ahead and how important that experience would prove to be, you know?"

"I don't know, but I can imagine."

"Now I'm willing to risk myself . . . Or rather, maybe I'm just willing to relinquish my life to God, day by day, moment by moment. None of us knows what's ahead. We may think we do, but . . ."

"We don't."

"I don't want to make poor choices or act brashly. But when I sense God's lead, I want to follow wherever He takes me. You know what's weird?"

"What?"

"It just occurred to me . . . If my chute hadn't failed, if I hadn't had that near-death experience, the lesson wouldn't have had the impact it did."

"God causes all things to work together for good . . ."

I'm quiet a moment as I process what I've just said, and Jay's response. "Jay, maybe that wasn't God working something for good, maybe the chute failing was part of God's plan, or His allowance, or . . . something. Maybe there isn't a difference, but it seems different. Do you know what I mean?"

"I know what you're gettin' at, but what about Bradley Mathison?"

"Sonia Alejandro is convinced there's no way he could have gotten access to the chutes."

"How you feeling about that?"

"I'm not sure. When I told Mick what happened and that Mathison was there, he said he knew — Mathison had told him about it. He told Mick he'd followed me there, that he'd gone to say 'goodbye.' Mick said that when Mathison saw my chute come down without me, he'd figured it was the primary chute and that he knew I'd probably been terrified. He told Mick he had a good laugh over that. How am I supposed to believe any of that? I don't know what to think. I want all or nothing, you know? Clean lines, clear boundaries. Either it was all Mathison or it was all Ryan. How could it possibly be both? What is it about me —"

"Sister, this isn't about you; this is about each man and his illness. I also wouldn't put it past Ryan to use Mathison's fixation with you to suit his own needs. This is about them. Did you suffer? You bet. I don't need to tell you that, but you did not invite it. Not from either of them."

Jay's words, like a balm, soothe. "I guess I know that on some level."

"Embrace it."

"I will, eventually. You know, I was so angry after the incident with Max and then after that chute failed. So angry. But anger fueled so much. It's one of the reasons I'm here."

"Just sounds like some of that anger was misdirected. Now direct it and keep lettin' it push you forward. Got it?"

I look out at the current of the river, flowing swiftly forward, always forward. "Got it."

After talking with Jay, I sit for a long time and let her words replay, let her encouragement wash over me. Then, before it gets too late, I reach for my phone again. This time I call Keith and ask to speak to Nicky.

I listen to the lilt in his voice when he hears it's me. I listen as he goes on about a game I don't understand, a movie he saw with his dad, and the cake Grandma brought over for them before dinner. I smile through it all. I wipe away tears I'm glad he can't see. Then, finally, I tell him good night. I tell him I love him. And I make a promise I pray I can keep. "I'll be home soon, buddy. Soon."

CHAPTER FORTY-ONE

Adelia
June 5, 2017

I stand in the kitchen and stare at the coffee-maker. "Really? You're really going to do this?" I unplug it then plug it back in. Nothing. The panel is dead, as it seems is the entire machine. "Okay, I get it, I need to deal with the caffeine addiction. But not now. Not this week." I shove the machine, though not hard enough to do further damage. I don't want to have the price of a coffee-maker taken out of my deposit.

I begin opening cabinets and searching for another means, an old percolator, anything. I close each cabinet a little harder until I'm finally slamming the doors shut. When the upper cabinets offer nothing, I bend down and open a lower cabinet, one I realize I haven't opened since being here. There, front and center, is a French press.

"Thank You, God, and whoever owns this house."

I pull it out, grind fresh beans, and then boil water. Once the water is bubbling in the pan, I pour it over the grounds in the press and leave it to steep, or brew, or do whatever it does.

The waiting, the monotony, is getting to me. It's evident in my lack of patience this morning. Another day off looms ahead, and I have no desire to explore or hike or even see the river, though it's hard to miss it right off my back deck.

I just want this over.

I just want my life back.

I want, desperately, to go home.

I want to wrap my arms around Nicky and never let go. I want the weight of Max sitting on my feet. I want my mother's home-made lasagna.

I want to know I'll live to enjoy all of that again, to participate in my life again. I swallow the ache lodged in my throat, then reach for a mug, push the plunger on the coffee press, and fill the mug. When my phone rings, I roll my eyes. Like I'm twelve.

It's Phil. The morning check-in. I set the mug down and reach for the phone. Without looking at the screen, I answer it. "Give me your update, I'm listening."

"Phil?"

I still and listen. He says nothing, but he's there, silent, breathing.

"Hello . . ."

Ryan or Mathison? I pull the phone away from my ear and look at the screen. I don't recognize the number, but it's one of them. Mathison has stayed away, true to his word.

I take a deep breath. "When are you going to show yourself? When are you going to make your move? I'm tired of waiting." There is a steely tone to my voice.

I wait, but there's no response.

"If you want me, you're going to have to come and get me. But this time . . ." Rage roils within and my voice shakes. I take another deep breath. I don't want him to think it's fear that causes the tremor. "This time you face me. Have the courage to do whatever you're going to do, face-to-face. Do it!" I yell. "Do it! I am tired of waiting. Just do it!"

Hand shaking, I press End and toss the phone onto the countertop.

"Just get it over with!"

CHAPTER FORTY-TWO

Adelia
June 9, 2017

Each time my phone has rung since the morning Ryan called, or who I assumed was Ryan, I've wondered if it's him. Will he call again? I've watched my back more closely. Connected with Phil more often. His only report remains consistent: he's around, but he hasn't sought you out.

Phil said Ryan is spending a lot of evenings in the bar at The Gateway — he has a room in the lodge there. Does he remember Adelia as he sits at that bar? Does he think of Mathison and the accusations and threats he hurled his way?

Or has he so easily let all that go?

I lock the final storage unit then go to the office. Mick told me to come in before I left for the day. I walk into the swampy cool of the place, only a slight relief from the hot, dry afternoon.

Mick, who was finishing up a call as I walked in, hangs up the phone and looks at me. "So, you okay?"

"I am."

He comes around the counter and stands in front of me. "Clear skies and a full moon tonight."

I nod.

"You don't have to do this. You can get in that old Jeep of yours, hit the 5, and head north. Go home. It's as easy as that."

"Then what? He follows me?"

"You let the law handle him."

"They have nothing on him. Mick, we've gone over —"

"That student of yours could tell them what she knows."

"It isn't enough."

He looks down at the floor then back to me. He's quiet for a moment, but a storm brews in his eyes. "You be careful, okay? Just be careful."

"I will."

"Now, get out of here. And . . ." — he turns back toward the counter — "call me if you need anything."

"What did you say?"

He glances over his shoulder. "You heard me. Get out of here."

"Thank you, Mick. For everything."

As I cross the lot to where my Jeep is parked, the same questions I've asked all week pester again.

What's his plan?

What's he doing?

His behavior makes no sense to me. But then, I'm hoping to make sense of the non-sensical.

What now, Lord? What's next? Time is running out.

I climb into the Jeep, the towel covering the seat hot against my thighs. I sit there waiting for something, anything, but I still have no sense of direction, no idea what comes next. I turn the key in the ignition, pull out of the lot, and make the five-minute drive back to the rental. As I pull into the driveway, one word breezes through my mind.

Now.

With it comes the sense that it's time to act. I've waited long enough.

"Now?" I whisper. But what am I supposed to do now? I have no idea. I pull the Jeep into the garage and park. By the time I've walked into the house, an idea has begun to form.

I take my time. I pour myself a glass of iced tea. I make a salad and pick at it. I sit on the deck. Finally, I take a long, cool shower.

When I emerge from the shower, I wrap a towel around myself and go stand in front of the bathroom mirror. I turn my head so I can see the image inked there.

I am reminded of the power of God's Word.

Of the Spirit who resides within me.

I trail my fingers over the ridged scar.

If Mathison didn't hit me . . . I stare at my reflection in the mirror as Jay's comment comes back to me. *"I also wouldn't put it past Ryan to use Mathison's fixation with you to suit his own needs."*

Is that what happened?

Is it possible?

I think back to that night . . . Earlier in the evening, I'd left Gabe and Jay's, and gone to my car, parked in front of their house. Ryan followed behind me. He'd wanted to follow me home. As we stood there, he reached out and cupped my face with his hand, and I . . . pulled away. I rebuffed him. Again.

Was he angry?

Is it possible he did, unbeknownst to me, follow me home after all?

Could he have come into the garage while Mathison had ahold of me and used the opportunity to . . . Was Mathison's statement true? Had there been someone else in the garage? Was it Ryan?

I can't fathom it.

Or . . . can I?

The bat I was hit with belonged to my father. My blood was found on the barrel of the bat, but there were no prints or DNA evidence on the grip. Nothing. Either it had been wiped clean or whoever hit me had worn gloves.

Mathison didn't have time to put on gloves. But he could have wiped the grip, couldn't he? Though my memory of exactly what happened in those moments has always been fuzzy, it never seemed like Bradley Mathison would have had time to find and pick up that bat.

Whereas Ryan knew just where it was. He'd been in my mother's garage and even picked up and swung that bat a time or two.

Could he have had it in his hand when I ran, and hit me, then left without Mathison ever seeing him? It was dark, and Mathison wasn't expecting anyone else to be there. Could the lights from the neighbors' porches across the street have given Ryan enough light to hit his target? Hadn't Mathison said he saw a man's shadow? Impossible in the dark. A silhouette? Possibly.

Did the wrong man serve time for a crime

he didn't commit?

I look away from the mirror.

What about the charm? That third charm . . . Only four people knew about the bracelet and the charms I'd received. Gabe, Jaylan, Keith, and . . . Ryan. Ryan also knew Keith was in Seattle that weekend. How often did I say that only those closest to me knew about the bracelet, assuring whomever I was speaking to that none of them would have done anything to hurt me?

Ryan had both the means and the time to make a quick trip. Is it possible he flew to Seattle to purchase and send the charm from the very city where he knew Keith was working? But how would he have known the exact store, the exact charm?

Had he followed Mathison? Kept tabs on him? Did he know where he'd purchased the bracelet and charms?

Again, it doesn't make sense to me, but the thoughts and actions of a psychopath rarely fall within the parameters of sense.

I look down at the sink, turn on the faucet, and watch as water swirls then slips down the drain. I must let my swirling thoughts do the same — slip away. I take a deep breath. There are questions I may never have answers for. Answers aren't what I need, are they? Won't God reveal what's

461

necessary?

Has my faith grown enough in recent weeks to trust God even when I don't have answers?

I have no answers for what's to come tonight, or in the days ahead. I arrived here with a skeletal plan, certain God would reveal the steps as necessary. I prepared in the way I thought best, strengthening my body and my resolve — relinquishing doubt as it arose.

Tonight, more than any other time, without a clear plan, I must turn away from doubt.

I must believe.

I must choose to trust and follow Him, even in the dark. Especially in the dark.

It is not my strength nor my own plans that will get me through this. It is His power through me that will prevail.

Whatever is to come.

The only step I'm sure of is that under a full moon, I'm to put myself in harm's way to ensure this ends once and for all for myself and for those I love.

It seems a tenuous step at best.

Therefore, it's a step I don't dare attempt alone.

I walk away from the mirror and go to the closet, where I pull out a pair of slim-cut jeans and a cream-colored sleeveless blouse. When I've dressed, I go back to the mirror. My olive-toned skin is darker now, despite the sunscreen I've used faithfully. My shoulders are broad, the muscles in my arms defined. I'm slimmer and firmer, and look younger than I have in a long time. The fresh air, sunshine, and hard physical work have served me well.

My light green eyes flash in the mirror as I brush on a little blush then dab some gloss on my lips. I finish with a coat of mascara to enhance my eyes and then put on small gold stud earrings. I step back from the mirror, satisfied with my appearance.

I go back to the closet, where I slip into flat sandals — they are both stylish and something I can walk in or run in, should that become necessary.

Before I leave, I make one phone call. I let Phil know what I'm doing, where I'm going. He's been on alert all day, as have local law enforcement.

Then I tuck the phone into my purse, go out to the garage, and get into the Jeep.

It's almost nine thirty by the time I pull into a parking spot in front of The Gateway — a spot I had to wait for another car to vacate. Even from outside, I can hear the

463

music from the bar. Friday night in Three Rivers — The Gateway is the place to be. The only place open this late, for the most part.

I sit in the dark car for a moment, hands gripping the steering wheel. Slowly, I loosen my grip, take a deep breath, and then let go. "Your will, Your way," I whisper. I choose trust. Just as I did the day I jumped from that plane. "I trust You."

Then I get out of the Jeep and head for the bar, knowing full well this may be the last night of my life.

When I walk into the crowded bar, I stand still a moment, giving my eyes time to adjust to the dim lighting. Then I sweep the place with my gaze, looking for Ryan, who I assume is here.

He sits at the bar alone, one open seat next to him, which is a small miracle in itself on a Friday night. It's also the assurance I need. God is leading.

I cross the bar, walk up behind him, take a deep breath, and then pull out the barstool next to him. He turns and looks at me, and confusion clouds his features. When he recognizes me, he recoils. Leaning away from me, a look of disgust mars his face. "So it *was* you I saw at Mick's." He looks from my face to my bare scalp and the image inked there. "What are you trying to prove, Deni?"

I always knew there was one more reason I'd taken Adelia's name when I arrived here — a reason I didn't fully understand until this moment. If Ryan thought there was any chance Adelia was alive, if he'd come here hoping to find her, he might just possibly mistake me for her, especially in the dim light of the bar, so similar were our looks. Even without hair I could pass for Adelia now. Especially with the tattoo on my scalp and her penchant for ink.

But Ryan, more than anyone, knows Adelia is dead.

It wasn't Adelia who lured him back to Three Rivers.

He came for me.

I know that now with a certainty I didn't possess when I walked in the door just moments ago.

"I don't have anything to prove," I say casually.

He stares at me, then seems to relax. He leans closer. "I knew you'd come to me, eventually. You've always needed me."

"What?"

"I just had to make you see it."

"I don't understand."

He laughs and shakes his head. "You're not as smart as people think you are. Famous author, head of the department, Dr. Denilyn Rossi. You're weak, Deni. You've always been weak. You needed me. I was there every time you fell apart. Every single time."

I stare at him as understanding comes, then I lean close. "And you made sure I fell apart, didn't you? You made me doubt myself. You broke me so you could pick up the pieces. Is that what you did to Adelia too?"

"You don't know anything about my relationship with Adelia."

"Don't I?"

His eyes narrow, then, in a flash, he reaches for me and grabs my arm, his fingers digging into my flesh. "Get up!"

When I don't move, he leans over and puts his mouth to my ear. "I said get up!" He hisses, his breath hot. Then he stands and yanks me to my feet.

And I know, as I already knew, that tonight is the night. As the moon rises high over the Kaweah, he will try to kill me, just as he killed Adelia. I swallow, mouth dry, as he pulls me across the bar. As we near the dance floor, someone shoves him. "Go easy on her, dude."

I shake my arm from Ryan's grasp, then look at the guy whom I'm afraid may intervene. "I can handle him, but thanks." Then I turn back to Ryan, reach for his hand, and head for the door. I can't afford to have someone interrupt, intervene. As much as I want to avoid whatever Ryan intends, I must let this play out. This is what I've come here for.

As soon as we're outside, he grabs me from behind and pulls me against him. "How about a ride down the river? For old time's sake?"

There's no need to respond, he isn't asking my permission.

He pulls me tighter against him and holds me there, his breath hot on my neck. "This could have taken a different turn, you know. This all could have gone so differently. But no, you ignored me, rebuffed my advances. There was always someone else. First Keith. I thought you'd have learned your lesson with him. Then Mathison."

Mathison? He can't possibly think . . .

"Now there's Jon." He laughs, but there is no humor in the sound. "You and Adelia were just alike. One and the same. I should have known. But instead, I waited all these years. I kept waiting for you. But no more. He lets go of me and quickly grabs my

467

hand, his grip crushing. He pulls me across the street to the head of a narrow, steep trail, one I know well. It's on private property, and years ago, a lifetime ago now, we had permission from the owners to put in a raft here, just beneath the bridge. But it's a dangerous entry, the water still tumbling, racing out of Gateway Rapid.

My heart pounds against my rib cage and my breaths are shallow. Is Phil here somewhere? The sheriff's department? Is anyone here? I don't dare turn to look for them. When we're just under the bridge, Ryan stops and looks down at my feet. "Take off your shoes — you'll slip."

When I hesitate, he yells. "Take them off!" He has no concern others will hear him. His voice is drowned by the roar, the constant thunder of the rapids.

I bend and slip the sandals off my feet. When I loop them over one hand, he grabs them and tosses them down the trail, where they likely cartwheel into the river. Then he pushes me ahead of him and, still gripping my hand, nudges me down the embankment. As I traverse the narrow trail, sidestepping my way down, the loose dirt and rocks pressing into my bare feet, my phone shifts in the back pocket of my jeans, its presence reassuring, though it will do me little good now. As a sharp rock cuts into one of my feet, I wince, but I won't let Ryan see the pain it induces. I keep going.

There's nowhere else to go.

Nothing else to do.

When we reach the river's edge, a small raft bobs violently in the tumult, highlighted by the moon that's just barely crested the steep hills that loom over this canyon. The raft, it appears, is tied to a branch of a tree that's fallen into the water.

Did Ryan know I was coming? Or has he been waiting for me every night?

Not even Ryan would venture down this river without the light of a full moon, would he? It will be several hours before its light shines bright overhead. What is he thinking? I stand at the edge of the water and look into the raft. Even in the dark, I can see the neon bright PFD in the raft, buckled to one of the holds. The *one* PFD in the raft.

It's too soon to get into the raft and onto the river, and I'm definitely not getting in without a life vest. I need to engage Ryan, stall him. Without the light of the full moon overhead, I'll have no chance.

He starts to push me toward the raft, but I turn, then root myself. "Is this what you did to her? To Adelia? Is this how you killed her?" I shout.

He pushes me toward the raft, but I stand my ground. I'm stronger than he thinks.

"You don't know what you're talking about."

"I think I do."

"Get in the raft!"

I don't move.

He pushes me again, and this time I lose my balance but catch myself.

"Get in!" he roars.

When I don't move, he pulls something from his belt, something hidden under the loose shirt he wears. Then he grabs me and presses something against my neck. "I said get in," he seethes.

I lift my hand to my throat, to the cool, sharp blade pressed there. He bats my hand away then wraps his arms around me, holding my arms down. I struggle against him, using the strength I've built. In a burst, I raise my arms, pushing against his, but as I do, I lose my footing again and stumble forward as he falls back.

I fall to my knees and grasp for anything to stop myself from tumbling into the water. My hand lands in a bush, and I claw at a branch, not knowing if it will hold me or not. I wrap my fingers tightly around the branch and stop my fall. But before I can right myself, Ryan's back up and on me again, wielding the knife.

As I scream, Ryan claps his hand over my mouth, making breathing nearly impossible.

Where is Phil? Where are the officers he promised he'd alert? I have no chance once we're on the river. Either Ryan or the Kaweah will toss me out. I will drown. I will die tonight — I am sure of it.

Ryan presses the blade into my neck again, this time cutting the flesh. I gasp as a warm trickle of blood slides down my neck.

Finally, I still. I stop struggling lest he slit my throat. "You killed her, Ryan. You killed Adelia." I work to distract him.

"She fell," he yells.

"No!"

In one swift move, he pulls the knife away from my neck, releases me, and shoves me toward the raft. I tumble, my feet going out from under me, and then roll, missing the raft and landing in the turbulent river. The icy water is a shock on my bare arms and head. I reach out, grasping for anything, but come up empty. Somewhere above, bright lights shine, but then I'm yanked under and swept away.

I tumble, legs and arms akimbo, nothing to reach for, nothing to save me. I'm thrown then slammed against a boulder, water filling my nose and mouth, eyes and ears.

Water roars, my pulse throbs in my ears, darkness prevails.

I struggle against the pull of the river, but I am powerless in its grasp. Rather than the swirl of the hydraulic that pulled me in that night, now I'm at the mercy of a swiftly moving current that tosses me at will. I work to assume a defensive position, to roll to my back, but the water's force is too much.

I gasp, but as I do, I'm pulled under again, and instead of air, I inhale water, then the current spits me out and I cough, choke, gasp. My head spins, my lungs burn. Then I'm slammed again, thrown against something, and I land hard, on my back, pain splintering my body, and the last of my air is stolen from me.

My very last breath.

Somewhere above me voices murmur. I can't make out what they say. I can't decipher the words. Pain racks me. "Ooohhh . . ." I whimper. My body trembles. I try to wrap my arms around myself, but I can't. I can't . . .

"Denilyn!"

I turn my head toward the voice, the movement dizzying and painful.

"Stay with me!"

Every breath I take sears my lungs.

My head lolls the other way. Everything is dark. Black. My body shudders again. Shivers. I'm cold. So cold.

"Denilyn!"

I work to open my eyes, my lids heavy, but I try. I try. "I'm . . . here." My voice does not sound like my own. "I'm . . ." Finally, I'm able to lift my lids, open my eyes. "Where . . ."

"You're okay. We're going to get you out of here." His voice is distant, but his face is close. A bright light. Bright. I close my eyes against the light. But I can't cover my ears, can't block the sound. The river? The rapids? Yes, but there's something more.

"We're going to lift you."

Hands grip me, and I'm hefted from wherever I am, every inch of my body throbbing, then gently lain on something, or in something. I open my eyes again, and the bright light overhead illuminates the area, as though someone flipped a switch. Unfamiliar faces surround me. I start to lift my arm to shield my eyes from the light, but the effort proves too much. Instead, I turn away from the light, and just as I'm closing my eyes again, my mind registers another light. Less bright, a round orb. I squint and work to focus.

The moon.

It's the moon.
Under a full moon . . .
Yes.
The full moon.

Chapter Forty-Three

Denilyn
July 21, 2017

"Okay, just ten more. Nine more. You can do it, Mom, you can do it."

My arm is draped around Nicky's shoulders as he helps me down the stairs, but I bear my own weight.

He takes each slow step with me. "Eight more, seven, six . . ." When we reach the bottom step, the river is just a stone's throw away. Nicky, arms raised above his head, does a dance like a boxer who's won a championship. "You did it! You did it!"

I smile at him. "Now, who's going to help me get back up?"

He laughs. "Aw, Mom. You can do it."

I muss his hair. "Go play."

He dances off across the rocky shore until he reaches the edge of the river, where he searches for flat stones to skip across the surface of the water.

I lower myself to sit on the bottom step where I can watch my son relish the joy of play. The American River, just beyond him, lazy now, glistens in the afternoon light.

My son is free.

We are free.

This is what I fought for.

This is what God provided for. What He spared me to enjoy.

"Thank You. Thank You." I say again. And again. I've said little else since waking on that flat rock in the middle of the Kaweah, a helicopter hovering overhead, waiting to carry me out of that canyon, to carry me to safety.

"Whoa, Mom, did you see that one?" he yells.

I nod and smile.

I was battered and bruised, and sustained tears in the muscle fiber of my lower back, likely from the twisting and battering my body took as the Kaweah tossed me to and fro. But ultimately, that river, my ally, threw me up and out of its clutch. I landed on a large, flat boulder that jutted above the current.

That's where I was found.

I woke in a hospital in Visalia sometime a day or two later, a man standing by my bed.

When I opened my eyes, he smiled. "Mur-

476

der. You wanted attempted murder. You got attempted murder. Satisfied?"

I stared at him. "Phil?"

"Who else?"

"You . . . got him?"

"Well, not me personally, but they couldn't have done it without me."

"What took you so long?"

As he laughed, I closed my eyes and must have drifted off again, because that's all I remember of our conversation then. We've spoken since, of course. And yes, Ryan was arrested and charged.

Without Willow, I don't know where I'd be. It was her courage, her truth, that revealed what I'd missed for so long. After working as Ryan's TA for two weeks, she ran into him one evening outside her dorm. The next evening she looked out her window and saw a man standing in the shadow of a tree. When she left the dorm a while later, he was still there. He called her name. She hesitated, then turned and kept walking. He followed her, eventually reaching her and grabbing her by the arm.

"It was like . . . he owned me or something," she said as she told me the story. "Like he had a right to . . ." She'd trailed off, never finishing her sentence.

Another young woman may have ignored

him or reported him. But Willow ran and then hid. She dropped his class. Avoided him. Just as she'd done with the stepfather who'd watched her, followed her, and eventually raped her.

Ryan's actions touched shame so deep in Willow, all she knew to do was hide.

Jay recognized something in Willow's story — something she'd seen in Ryan herself, or sensed in Ryan. That possessiveness or entitlement she'd spoken of. Willow's story unlocked the truth and opened my eyes to a possibility I'd never considered.

Why Adelia? Why me? Why Willow? I'll never know.

Now, along with the anger that still accosts me from time to time, there is also grief. Grief for the man whose illness wounded so many. Grief, again, for all that was lost.

Including Adelia . . .

But now there is also joy.

And freedom.

Oh, sweet freedom.

August 20, 2017

After my first class, I cross the campus, where students sprawl on the grass, sit at outdoor tables, and crowd the bookstore. The warm scent of dry grass wafts, and beyond the campus the late summer river meanders. Soon the leaves will begin to turn.

I enter the English building, glance at my watch, and then find the classroom I'm looking for. I peek inside and see Jon connecting his laptop to the projector. It appears he's alone, just as I'd hoped.

As I come into the room, he looks up, stares at me a moment, then smiles. "Hi there. Wow, look at you." I see the appreciation in his eyes as I approach. "I love your hair." He raises his hand and looks at me, a question in his eyes. "Can I touch it?"

I laugh. "Go for it."

He gently pats the short spikes of hair on top of my head. "What prompted that? It's great, really, just . . . different."

I run my hand over my hair. "It's a long story."

"Ah . . ."

"But . . . it's one I'd like to tell you sometime."

"I'm always up for a long story. Just give me a call. Anytime."

I raise one eyebrow. "Anytime?"

The twinkle in his eyes assures me he's understood my meaning. "Well, almost anytime. Just don't call during the evening, at least not until after I've cleaned up the mac and cheese, made sure the girls are bathed, read them a rousing chapter or two of *Harriet the Spy,* and tucked them in for the night." He leans against the table where the projector sits. "Come to think of it, I go to bed myself after that routine. And don't call in the mornings, at least not until after I've dropped them off at school. I typically have ten minutes or so between my arrival in the parking lot here and the dash to my first class. You might catch me then."

I laugh. "Weekends?"

"Sure, in between soccer and ballet. Just give me a call. Anytime. Really. By the way, did you know I make a mean mac and cheese?"

"I bet you do."

He runs a hand through his thick hair.

"I'll tell you what — how about we come over some evening and you can share your recipe with me."

"We?" He looks puzzled.

Just a few months ago, I wouldn't have mentioned Nicky. Wouldn't have risked allowing someone into the prison I'd created for us. But now . . . "Yes, *we.* That's part of the story. I . . . have a son. He's seven. I'd love for you to meet him sometime."

He nods as he takes in what I've said. "Is he a mac and cheese eater?"

"A connoisseur, actually."

"Perfect." He smiles, then grows serious as though contemplating something. "You're different. Something's changed. And it's more than the hair, right?"

I nod. "Yes. I've changed. Everything's changed."

The door of the classroom swings open and students begin filtering in.

"Well, I'll let you go." I turn to leave.

"Deni . . ."

I turn back.

"I'll look forward to hearing that story. Soon, I hope."

I smile. "Yes, soon."

I sit at my desk, my chair swiveled toward the window. Haunting memories no longer play on the glass; images don't flash. The story Jon wants to hear, the one I will tell him, isn't over yet, I know. There is work to do. Wounds to heal. And not just my own.

But now it's a story I want to share.

I no longer want to hide in the shadows or look over my shoulder.

Fear will no longer rule me or my family.

I was made for more. We were made for more.

The sun filtering through the window shines bright, warming the office. I get up to close the blinds against the heat, but as I stand at the window, I change my mind.

The sun's power hidden for so long — it's time to let the sun shine . . .

God didn't give me a spirit of fear, but rather a spirit of love, and a spirit of power . . .

It's time to shine.

ACKNOWLEDGMENTS

Writing *Convergence* was a challenge to which I looked forward but one for which I learned I was unprepared. Writing suspense is unlike writing any other genre, and I had a lot to learn. I extend my gratitude to author Brandilyn Collins for her generosity in sharing her insight and knowledge with me. Thank you to Erin Ambrose, PhD, therapist and professor, for the time she spent with me and the many questions she answered related to this story. Thank you to David Qualls, former California Highway Patrol officer, for offering his expertise.

I am grateful for my critique partners who read as I wrote, right up to the last moments, and offered their insight and encouragement — Susan Basham, Brenda Bryant Anderson, and Laurie Breining — you're each a gift. Thank you to C.J. Darlington who stepped in at the ninth hour and saved me and this story by helping me do additional research. Thank you to Frank Root of Kaweah White Water Adventures in Three Rivers, California, for the time he spent answering C.J.'s questions. Frank's expertise was invaluable. I'm also so thankful for my son, Jared Yttrup, an employee of William Jessup University, who answered every text I sent. The information he provided related to a university setting made this story better.

As always, I am deeply grateful for the love and support of my family, Justin, Jared, and Stephanie, and my mom, Kathy, who understand when I "hibernate" toward the end of writing a book. My dear circle of friends offer the same grace and understanding as I disappear into the stories I write. Thank you.

Thank you to my editor, Annie Tipton, who suggested I give the suspense genre a try. I am grateful for Annie's encouragement and belief in my abilities. Thank you to JoAnne Simmons, copy editor extraordinaire, for making me look good. To the fiction team at Barbour Publishing — thank you!

Thank you to my agent, Steve Laube, who enthusiastically brainstormed this story with me as I wrote my sample chapters.

While my name may appear on the cover

of this book, writing a novel is a group endeavor. I could not have finished this story without the involvement of so many others.

And, as always, I am grateful to my wonderful readers who buy my books and spend their valuable time with my characters. Thank you for the words of encouragement offered through the reviews you post and the notes you send. You make this dream career a reality for me. Thank you!

ABOUT THE AUTHOR

Ginny Yttrup is the award-winning author of *Words, Lost and Found, Invisible, Flames,* and *Home.* She writes contemporary women's fiction and suspense. *Publishers Weekly* dubbed Ginny's work "as inspiring as it is entertaining." When not writing, Ginny coaches writers, critiques manuscripts, and makes vintage-style jewelry for her Etsy shop, Storied Jewelry (etsy.com/shop/ StoriedJewelry). She loves dining with friends, hanging out with her adult sons and daughter-in-law, and walking her rescue pup, Henry. Ginny lives in Northern California. To learn more about Ginny and her work, visit www.ginnyyttrup.com.

The employees of Thorndike Press hope you have enjoyed this Large Print book. All our Thorndike, Wheeler, and Kennebec Large Print titles are designed for easy reading, and all our books are made to last. Other Thorndike Press Large Print books are available at your library, through selected bookstores, or directly from us.

For information about titles, please call:
(800) 223-1244

or visit our website at:
gale.com/thorndike

To share your comments, please write:
Publisher
Thorndike Press
10 Water St., Suite 310
Waterville, ME 04901